Praise for the spectacular Playful Brides series by
VALERIE BOWMAN

THE RIGHT KIND OF ROGUE

"Anyone who adores engaging, meddlesome characters, a dashing hero, and an undaunted heroine will find that Bowman fulfills their dreams of the perfect romance."
—*RT Book Reviews*

"Poignant, entertaining . . . this was a fun book to read."
—*Romance Reviews Today*

NEVER TRUST A PIRATE

"Thrilling, delicious, and suspenseful."
—*Kirkus Reviews*

"Wonderful, sprightly repartee, a fast pace, and delightful characters blend together in another enthralling Bowman romance. Always smart and sassy, Bowman's heroines delight in piquing the hero; taunting and tempting. Together they heat up the pages and turn readers' thoughts to what original storyline she'll come up with next for their 'keeper' shelf."
—*RT Book Reviews* (Top Pick!)

"An engaging literary treat for all romance readers who don't take their historicals (or themselves) too seriously."
—*Booklist*

"Bowman blends a lighthearted romp through Regency London with a secret spy mission and, yes, action aboard a pirate ship for a perfectly lovely novel."

—*USA Today* bestselling author Maya Rodale

"A delicious mix of intrigue and red-hot romance. Bowman pens a fun, fast page-turner of a romance, filled with characters that communicate even as they struggle to trust each other. For readers who like a soupçon of suspense with their romance, this is a book to keep you guessing."

—*BookPage*

THE LEGENDARY LORD

"A sweet and fulfilling romance."   —*Publishers Weekly*

"Graceful writing enlivened with plenty of dry wit, a charming cast of secondary characters, and a breathtakingly sexy romance between a perfectly matched couple make Bowman's latest addition to her Regency-set Playful Brides series another winner."   —*Booklist*

"The words funny, smart, sensual, and joyous come to mind when readers pick up Bowman's romance."

—*RT Book Reviews*

"A deliciously witty, sexy historical romance that will keep readers turning the pages."   —*Romance Junkies*

"The story is filled with humor, a twisting plot, and vibrant characters that have become Bowman's hallmark. The chemistry is near-perfect, and the will-they-won't-they back-and-forth is exactly what romance readers want; the simultaneous tale of deceit, revenge, and espionage makes it all the more rewarding."

—Sarah MacLean, *The Washington Post*

THE UNLIKELY LADY

"Bowman keeps her prose and characters fresh and interesting; her book is an entertaining renewal of a classic plotline and well worth reading." —*Kirkus Reviews*

"Rich with fully developed characters and a plethora of witty banter." —*Publishers Weekly*

"A definite must-read!" —*San Francisco Book Review*

"Quick, lively entertainment at its best."

—*RT Book Reviews*

"A joyous romp in Regency England, filled with bright characters, scintillating conversations, and just plain fun." —*Romance Reviews Today*

THE ACCIDENTAL COUNTESS

"The references to Oscar Wilde's play are more of a tribute than a straight retelling, which keeps this hilarious and lively story from becoming too predictable. Bowman is one to watch."

—*Kirkus Reviews* (starred review)

"Readers will take the well-drawn, likable characters into their hearts, enjoying every moment of their charming love story as it unfolds in unexpected ways. Simply enjoy the humor and tenderness."

—*RT Book Reviews* (4½ stars)

"Merry, intelligent, and wholly satisfying. The plot is elaborate, and Bowman handles it with grace to spare."

—*USA Today*

THE UNEXPECTED DUCHESS

"Smart, witty, sassy, and utterly delightful!"

—*RT Book Reviews* (4½ stars, Top Pick!)

"Engaging characters, snappy banter, and judicious infusion of smoldering sensuality will have readers clamoring for the next installment in this smart and sexy series."

—*Booklist* (starred review)

"A fun, smart comedy of errors and a sexy, satisfying romance."

—*Kirkus Reviews* (starred review)

ALSO BY VALERIE BOWMAN

A Duke Like No Other

VALERIE BOWMAN

St. Martin's Paperbacks

This is a work of fiction. All of the characters, organizations, and events portrayed in this novel are either products of the author's imagination or are used fictitiously.

A DUKE LIKE NO OTHER

Copyright © 2018 by June Third Enterprises, LLC.

All rights reserved.

For information address St. Martin's Press, 175 Fifth Avenue, New York, NY 10010.

ISBN: 978-1-250-12173-8

Our books may be purchased in bulk for promotional, educational, or business use. Please contact your local bookseller or the Macmillan Corporate and Premium Sales Department at 1-800-221-7945, ext. 5442, or by e-mail at MacmillanSpecialMarkets@macmillan.com.

Printed in the United States of America

St. Martin's Paperbacks edition / May 2018

St. Martin's Paperbacks are published by St. Martin's Press, 175 Fifth Avenue, New York, NY 10010.

10 9 8 7 6 5 4 3 2 1

For my father, Minot Bowman Jr., with love.

My dad was the father to seven daughters.
He built us a little red playhouse in the
backyard with a real door and windows.
He drove us around in a blue Chevrolet station
wagon and let us use the CB radio.
He gamely installed an extra hot-water heater in
our house so we could all take showers.

He loved John Wayne movies, WWII Mosquitos,
and building things.
He was a captain in the Air Force and a pilot and
he left this world too soon on May 14, 1984.

I'd like to think he's still soaring among the
clouds, where I think he was the happiest.

CHAPTER ONE
London, July 1818

"You may have your promotion, Grim, on one condition, and I'm afraid it's a condition you're not going to like."

His booted foot propped over the opposite knee, General Mark Grimaldi sat across the desk from Lord Allen, the minister of the Home Office. The older, bald man was Mark's superior and one of the most influential politicians in the country.

Mark had been waiting for this day for what felt like his entire life. The adult part of his life, at any rate.

His breeches were smartly pressed. His shirt was perfectly starched. His cravat was expertly tied. His boots were shined to a glow, and he had a smile on his face. He was four-and-thirty years old. He'd worked his arse off, risked his life on numerous occasions, and given up nearly everything, all in the name of service to His Majesty. For the love of God. He'd nearly *died* for this promotion.

Condition? Who cared about a blasted condition? There was *nothing* the minister could say that would stop Mark. He would become the Home Secretary, the head of the Home Office, or die trying.

Mark tugged impatiently at his cuff. "Out with it. There's no condition I won't accept."

The minister stood. He folded his hands behind his back and walked slowly around to the other side of the desk where he towered over Mark, who remained seated. The minister cleared his throat. "Lord Tottenham doesn't want a secretary who is a bachelor. He wants someone settled."

Tottenham ran the Home Office. He was Lord Allen's superior. Tottenham would be the one who made the final decision as to who the new secretary would be.

Grimaldi narrowed his eyes on the minister. "What do you mean, *settled*?" But he already knew. The pit in his stomach told him.

"A family man," the minister intoned. "You must take a wife."

A *wife*? The word hit Mark like a bullet to the chest. He was entirely self-made. By choice. By highly calculated choice. Now he'd set his sights on becoming the Secretary of the Home Office. Failure wasn't possible. A wife wasn't about to keep him from it.

He clenched and unclenched his fist by his side. By God, the irony. The unmitigated irony. He'd given his life to his work. No ties. No regrets. He'd given up everything including a social life and now, now they were asking for him to take a *wife*? Politics could be both brutal and cruel. Today it was downright laughable.

"There is only one problem with my taking a wife," Mark intoned.

"What's that?" the minister asked, moving back around the desk to resume his seat.

This was it. The moment of truth. The time to admit to something he hadn't admitted to in years. A humorless smile twitched his lips. "I'm already married."

CHAPTER TWO
Somme, France, Late July 1818

Nicole raced across the lavender field atop her horse, Atalanta. Her head was down, the wind whipped her hair, and she had a smile of pure, exhilarated triumph on her face. There was nothing like racing a man and winning. The *Comte de Roussel* rode at her side. Or more correctly, he rode a few lengths behind her, trying to keep up. Henri was a kind man and a dear friend, but she had no hesitation whatsoever in beating him soundly at a race. Races were meant to be won, after all.

The fields were in full bloom and the fragrance of lavender filled the air. Nicole breathed in deeply, enjoying the sunshine on her face. It would probably cause more freckles, but so be it. She loved days like this. The sun high, the fields dry, the wind blowing her red hair. She never restrained the unruly locks when she rode. This was what freedom felt like.

Out of the corner of her eye, Nicole spied Rochard,

her servant, running across the field, flagging her down with his hat. "Madame, madame, you have a visitor," he called in country French as she neared him.

Nicole slowed Atalanta to a halt and shielded her eyes to look across the field. A visitor? She wasn't expecting a visitor today.

Then she spotted him. Her heart dropped into her boots. Her pulse stuttered, then raced. She would recognize that form anywhere. Tall, broad-shouldered, dark-haired, impeccably dressed. She didn't need to be close enough to see what he was wearing to know that. There was only one man who looked like that, who stood like that, who was even now watching her with a mixture of curiosity and ill-concealed distaste. Again, she didn't need to be close enough to know that.

Merde. Her husband was here.

The *comte* slowed his horse to a halt nearby. His gaze followed hers. "A visitor?" he asked in flawless aristocratic French.

"Oui." Then she swore under her breath.

"Who is it?" the *comte* continued. "An Englishman from the looks of him."

She curled her lip slightly. "Oh, he's English all right."

He was decidedly English and even more decidedly a complete ass. One she'd never thought she'd see again. At least not alive. It was so like Mark to arrive unannounced after all these years and expect not to be thrown off the premises. The element of surprise had likely been his tactic. If he'd informed her he'd be paying her a visit, she would have come up with some convenient excuse not to see him.

She sighed, pulled off one riding glove, and ran her

fingers through her tangled hair. She didn't question how he'd found her. The man was a master spy. Hunting her down had no doubt been easy for him. She straightened her spine and took a deep breath. Very well. Today was the day. The day she'd looked forward to and dreaded for the last ten years. Her day of reckoning with Mark Grimaldi.

She turned Atalanta, kicked her heels against the horse's sides, and raced to a stop at the gate near where Mark stood. Nicole dismounted, tossing her red locks over her shoulder, and strode purposefully toward him. She refused to take her eyes from him. He was not a man who responded well to any sign of weakness, which was why she'd gone straight to him instead of heading to the stables first.

Nicole removed her gloves as she approached. He would simply have to get over the fact that she was wearing riding breeches and a man's shirt. That was how she preferred to ride.

"Mark Grimaldi, to what do I owe the pleasure?" Her voice was carefully devoid of any emotion, save perhaps for the smallest bit of sarcastic emphasis, particularly on the word "pleasure."

Mark's dark gaze swept over her in that bold, possessive way of his, making her feel vulnerable, almost naked. He was the only man who'd ever seen her *in flagrante delicto*, after all. She was suddenly quite aware of how tight and revealing her riding breeches were. And how low cut the man's shirt was on her, the first button falling just above her breasts. It revealed a bit too much of her décolletage. Hmm. Too bad.

"Pleasure?" Mark intoned with the same sarcastic

emphasis. "That remains to be seen." His voice was just as deep and rough and *arrogant* as she remembered it.

"Came to torture me, did you?" She gave him a tight smile and put one fist on her hip. The other hand squeezed the soft leather riding gloves together so tightly her knuckles ached.

"Perhaps." He nodded toward the *comte*. "But first, aren't you going to introduce me to your friend?"

The *comte* had just pulled his horse to a halt behind her. Nicole bit the inside of her cheek to keep from saying something truly inappropriate and turned her head to the side while the *comte* dismounted. "Comte de Roussel, this is Mark Grimaldi." A note of dry contempt crept into her voice. "The last I knew, he was a corporal. Knowing him, he's probably the prime minister by now. Monsieur Grimaldi, this is the Comte de Roussel."

Henri, who didn't appear to have a blond hair out of place after his ride, nodded and bowed to Mark, tipping his hat.

"*General* Mark Grimaldi." Mark held out his hand for a proper shake.

Nicole's eyes flared slightly. She couldn't help a dig, though. "Not a field marshal?" More sarcastic emphasis.

Mark's obsidian gaze never left the *comte*. "I intend to skip that rank entirely. The wars are over now, or haven't you heard out here, rusticating in the country?" He waved his hand in a circle.

She didn't miss the snideness in his tone.

The *comte* glanced back and forth between the two of them, an apprehensive look on his face.

Mark tapped his boot on the ground impatiently. "I'm

also her husband, or weren't you going to tell your *friend* that, Madame Grimaldi?"

The *comte*'s eyes widened. He turned his head sharply toward Nicole. *"Mari?"*

"Yes, her *mari*." With the tip of one finger, Mark pushed his hat back on his head the slightest bit.

Damn him and his smug tone. "It's true," Nicole said, tossing her hair again. She reached up and stroked her horse's mane. "Come. I must get Atalanta to the stables for the groom to rub her down." She turned on her booted heel and began walking toward the stables, leading Atalanta by the reins.

Mark's deep laughter followed her. "Atalanta? Of course you would name your horse after a warrior woman who did nothing but cause her husband trouble."

Nicole's nostrils flared, but she didn't turn her head to look at him. Instead, she lifted her chin high in the air and continued her march toward the stables. "What trouble? She merely did what she liked and was scorned for it." Nicole quickened her pace, her stride purposeful. The two men followed her. Their boots crunched along the path behind her.

"Seems like Aphrodite would have been a more apt name. The steed of a woman who cuckolded her husband," came Mark's next taunt, sure and strong from behind her.

Nicole stopped and whirled around, her hair whipping over one shoulder. "Is your horse named Zeus, after a man who ruined the lives of most of the people around him?"

Mark's lips quirked. "No, I still have Jupiter. He's served me well all these years. And Zeus was a god, not a man." His lips spread open into an unrepentant grin. "Are you comparing me to a god?"

"We're speaking about your horse, not *you*," she replied before snapping shut her mouth. She might as well stop her barbs. He was clearly enjoying them, and she refused to let him march back into her life and make her angry so quickly. She'd spent too many years getting over him, and she intended to remain over him, no matter how he taunted her.

"Madame, would you like me to go?" the *comte* offered, clearing his throat.

"No, monsieur, please stay," she said, more to bother Mark than anything else. He clearly wanted Henri to leave. A momentary pang of guilt shot through her. It was wrong of her to put poor blameless Henri in the middle of her barb trading with Mark. Henri didn't deserve such treatment. She again resolved to stop responding to Mark's taunts.

The small party reached the stables and Nicole handed Atalanta's reins to one of the grooms. She turned to face the two men, her arms crossed over her chest, one knee jutted out, her boot tapping the ground in agitation.

"We'll go in the house and have refreshments, but first . . ." She forced her gaze to fix on Mark's hatefully handsome face. "Are you going to tell me why you came? I'm quite certain it's not for the tea."

"Of course I am, but I was hoping I could speak with you"—Mark eyed the *comte* up and down with obvious distaste—"privately."

Not half an hour later, the *comte* was on his way home and Nicole had twisted her hair into a bun and stuck it to the back of her head with some pins she'd fetched from her pocket. She refused to go upstairs and dress in a gown and pretend to be the perfect little quiet English wife Mark wanted. If he had something to say to her, he could say it to her breech-covered backside.

She did, however, have enough of a hostess in her that she led him to the front drawing room of the château and rang for tea.

"You look . . . well," Mark began, as she took a seat on the rose-colored settee in the center of the room.

She crossed her arms over her chest and arched a brow at him. "Spare me. We both know you need something from me or you wouldn't be here. You might as well save us both time. What do you want?"

CHAPTER THREE

Mark quirked his mouth into a half smile. Nicole had always been direct. It was one of the things that had first drawn him to her. She wasn't about to let him get away with arriving unannounced without admitting that he wanted something. Good, because he liked to be direct too. "You're right. I do want something from you."

"Say it." She crossed one leg over the other and for the life of him he couldn't stop staring at how those breeches hugged her long legs. Outside, he'd been slightly obsessed with how they hugged another part of her anatomy. And that shirt . . . the one that was exposing her chest in a way that made the back of his neck sweat. Leave it to Nicole to have her hair down and to be wearing breeches while riding around a French château on a horse named Atalanta. She'd been besting the *comte* in the race they'd been engaged in. That was also like her. She adored competition and hated to lose at anything. If he had any hope of her saying yes to his proposal, he needed to make certain he didn't become her adversary . . . again.

He glanced around the drawing room. Outfitted in rose and cream silks with the occasional hint of green, the room was tastefully decorated. The château itself was large and well appointed without being ostentatious. She had access to his money but had never spent a shilling of it. No, this was all a result of her own money or her family's.

He spread his arms wide along the back of the settee. "No reminiscing? No catching up? No discussing the good times?"

Her dark red eyebrow inched even higher. "Were there good times? I seem to recall those being few and far between."

"There were a few." In bed. He tugged at his collar.

She poked at the chignon on the back of her head. Only she could make a quickly put-together hair arrangement look effortlessly gorgeous. Several tendrils of the long red locks fell to frame her face, which wore a decidedly disgruntled look. "Out with it. I'm quite busy. I'm attending a dinner party this evening and I must dress."

Mark bit the inside of his cheek but ultimately he couldn't keep the comment that had sprung to his lips to himself. "A cleaner pair of breeches?" Damn, she looked good in those breeches. She looked good altogether. Better than good. The years had been kind to her. The fresh-faced plumpness of her cheeks had given way to a slenderness that made her cheekbones prominent. Her lips were still full and pink and inviting. Her hair luxurious, soft and smooth. Her eyes looked more world-weary, to be sure, but their sea-foam-green depths were still astute and intelligent. Her body was still trim and fit. Her thighs looked even fitter, probably from riding astride. Ahem. What he wouldn't give to see those thighs once more, to have them wrapped tightly around his—

"Despite my present appearance, I do own a gown or two." Her words snapped him out of his indecent line of thought. She gave him another tight smile.

He stood, crossed to the nearby sideboard, and poured himself a brandy. "Going to meet the *comte* again?"

"Careful," came her throaty voice from the settee. "It's nearly sounding as if you're jealous."

Still facing the sideboard, he cocked his head to the side. "Jealous? Whatever does that word mean?"

"The *comte* is a friend, nothing more." Her voice sounded dismissive. He didn't believe her, however.

Mark splashed more brandy into his glass. "I'm *certain* you'd tell me if he weren't."

"I'm *certain* you'd care."

Mark turned back toward her and took a healthy swig of his drink. "A man doesn't like to think of his wife in the bed of another."

She actually rolled her eyes at that comment. "Oh, *you've* been celibate all these years then?" she countered, her voice dripping with skepticism.

He had been, but he'd die a slow death back in the French prison camp before he told her that. However, he wasn't so unrealistic as to think Nicole would have remained untouched. They had agreed to part ways, hadn't seen each other in ten years. She was a beautiful woman in the prime of her life. Still, the notion of punching the *comte* dead in the face held a great deal of appeal at the moment. "I've never been one to kiss and tell, love."

She gave him a tight smile, which clearly indicated she didn't believe him, either. "You're a general now?" she asked abruptly, clearly ready to change the subject.

"I am." He moved to the window and looked out across the lavender fields, one arm held behind his ramrod-straight back as if he were surveying a battle-field. The stance was still comfortable for him even after all these years of working for the Home Office.

"I suppose congratulations are in order." The tea arrived and Nicole poured a cup for herself and splashed in a liberal amount of cream. He remembered that about her. She took her tea with no sugar, just cream.

"No congratulations needed," he intoned, taking another swig of brandy.

The silver spoon she used to stir her tea clinked against the delicate china teacup. "I must admit, I've often wondered when I'd get a missive that you'd been killed."

His chuckle was humorless. He turned to face her. "Such little faith in me? Or wishful thinking?"

"Neither," she replied, lifting the cup to her pink lips. "Just a profound knowledge of how reckless you are."

He inclined his head. "Used to be."

"Really?" She raised a brow. "Is that why you've come? To tell me you've changed?"

He chuckled. "I haven't changed *that* much."

"I'm not surprised." She set down her teacup and crossed her arms over her chest. "Tell me, Mark, why *have* you come?"

He saluted her with his glass, the amber-colored liquid shining in the afternoon sunlight. "You were right. I need a favor from you."

She didn't so much as bat an eyelash. "Of course you do. What's the favor?" She picked up her cup once more and took a sip.

He downed the final splash of brandy and met her gaze. "I need you to return to England with me for a few months and pretend to be my loving wife."

CHAPTER FOUR

Nicole nearly choked on her tea. The warm liquid slipped down her windpipe and she spent the next several moments battling a coughing fit. If Mark had just told her he wanted her to join him in a traveling side-show she couldn't have been more astonished.

Once the coughs subsided, she set aside her teacup and dabbed at her watery eyes with a handkerchief she'd produced from her pocket. Then she cupped a hand behind her ear. "You want me to *what*?"

Mark set his empty glass on the sideboard and strolled nonchalantly toward her. "I believe you heard me." His tone had lost its typical condescending note. "I'm being considered for another promotion. Quite a large promotion. To Secretary of the Home Office."

Nicole's brows shot up. "Secretary of the Home Office?" She gave a long, drawn-out whistle. She'd known he was ambitious. Known he would go far. But that lofty position was something she'd never even guessed he'd be eligible for. It was essentially the head of all the spies in England. He'd have the ear of the King. Mark would wield more power than she'd ever imagined. She lowered her gaze to her cloudy tea and did her best to keep her face blank. "So your political ambitions are finally being realized, but what does that have to do with me?"

Mark tilted his head to the side and studied her face. "Unfortunately it has a great deal to do with you. They want a family man to be the secretary."

She furrowed her brow. "Did you tell them about your family?"

"No." His snapped rejoinder nearly cut her off. "My family has nothing to do with this. They merely want a man who's settled instead of a bachelor."

Of course. She should have known better than to mention his family. Clearly, he was still as prickly about the subject as ever. "Ah, so you hope trotting me out after all these years will secure you the position?"

He cocked his head to the side and nodded. "Something like that."

She set her teacup on the silver salver that rested on the table at her knees and crossed her arms over her chest once more, regarding him down the length of her nose. He had a great deal of explaining to do. "Why don't you just hire some biddable little thing to *pretend* to be your wife?"

He sighed and rubbed his forehead. "There are people who know we're married, Nicole. Not many, but a few. If I'm caught in a lie I might sacrifice the position."

"So you *did* consider it?" She laughed and waved

away his reply. "No need to answer. I'm *certain* you considered it."

He cocked his head to the side again. "By the by, what does your family think of you living in France all these years?"

Her breath caught in her throat. Was he truly going to ask her about it so casually after all these years? Fine. Two could play at this game.

"I didn't give them much choice in the matter."

"You didn't give anyone much choice." Was it her imagination or was there an edge of anger in his voice?

She stood, pressing her hand to the strangely hollow place in her breast. "I write to Mother when I can. We keep in touch."

"And all of this?" He waved a hand in the air. "How do you manage it?"

How dare he ask about her resources? He had no right to. She hadn't taken so much as a tuppence from him in all these years. "You of all people should know that working for the War Office can be lucrative. I've also done some work for the authorities here in France."

"Ah, yes, your *career*. Start a branch of the Bow Street Runners in Paris, did you?"

Purposely ignoring that remark, she made her way to the sideboard where she poured herself a finger of brandy. She could not allow him to bait her like this. *Merde.* Why couldn't she bring herself to toss him out on his handsome head? "Care for some more?" she asked in her most gracious hostesslike voice. It was entirely fake.

"Yes," he replied simply.

Forcing herself to rein in her escalating emotions, she

poured two glasses of brandy, proud her hands didn't shake despite her pounding heart. She crossed the thick carpet to hand him his glass.

Mark raised the brandy in the air in a silent salute. "I see you're still unconventional."

"I see you're still preoccupied with your work." She turned on her heel to take a seat on the settee across from him again.

He took a seat next to her on the settee, then leaned down and braced his forearms on both knees, holding the glass between his legs. "Will you do it?" He searched her eyes, the slightest hint of vulnerability in his. His voice didn't contain a trace of wheedle, not a hint of coaxing. He didn't need it. The man radiated charm from his smallest finger, and God help him, he knew it.

Nicole narrowed her eyes on him. The damnable man was more handsome today than he had been ten years ago. He was still fit, muscled, and tall. He was still broad-shouldered and his dark hair and eyes still smoldered with arrogance and intelligence. His nose looked slightly different, however. It had been perfectly straight. Now it was a bit crooked, as if it had been broken a time or two. Unfortunately, that small imperfection made him even more handsome. Not only that, but his blasted lips were still firmly molded. A thought she'd had about exactly no other man's lips before or since. She shook her head, trying to clear it of thoughts of both his handsomeness and his lips.

Would she do it? *Merde*. He was an arrogant son of a bitch striding back into her life after all these years demanding that she play along for his sake. What in the hell did she owe him? Nothing. However, there *was* something she wanted in return. Something only he could give her. This seemed like the *perfect* opportunity to get it.

"I'll consider it," she said, undulating her fingers along the side of her glass, and arching one brow in his direction. "On one condition."

CHAPTER FIVE

Damn her. Nicole had refused to tell him what her condition was before she'd dismissed him to go upstairs and prepare for her blasted dinner party. Mark was still sitting in her drawing room with his half-full glass of brandy, contemplating their exchange. She was obviously enjoying this, his being at her mercy. He couldn't blame her. He'd enjoy it too if he was in her shoes. Or boots, as the case may be. Another vision of her striding to the sideboard in those skintight breeches shot through his brain, making his own breeches uncomfortably tight. Bloody hell. He hadn't come here to lust after the damnable woman. He'd come here to ask her for a favor. One he had every reason to believe she'd refuse.

She'd told him to come back tomorrow afternoon. She would tell him her condition then. She hadn't offered to allow him to stay here tonight. He would have refused at any rate. He'd rented a room in town at the inn, not having any idea what sort of welcome (if any) he'd get. He'd half expected to be nursing his wounds from her sharp tongue right now and perhaps even be on his way back to England empty-handed. The fact that she hadn't said no was already a small victory.

However, her one condition sounded ominous. He clenched his jaw. What could she possibly want from him? To stay away from her after he secured the position? He already had. She knew that wouldn't be an issue. To increase her allowance? The woman was richer than most women in England and France. She hadn't touched the money he'd provided for her. She was hardly hurting for income.

The only other thing he could think of was . . . divorce. It was something he'd never allowed himself to contemplate. Something that would bring shame and scandal upon both of them. Something he had assumed was unnecessary. They both went about their lives perfectly happily. A divorce seemed superfluous. Perhaps Nicole was in love. Perhaps she wanted to marry the *comte*. If that were the case, a divorce might well be what she was after. Mark's stomach gave a sickened jolt at the image of Nicole lying in bed with the *comte,* her glorious red hair splayed across the pillows, her gorgeous face tensed with pleasure . . . That was a damned uncomfortable thought.

Mark tightened his fist. Yes, he could well punch the bloody *comte* in the face. If nothing else, it would be interesting to see if he could still lay a man flat with one punch like he had in his youth.

Mark took another fortifying swig of brandy and concentrated on the matter at hand. Nicole must realize that if he needed a wife in order to become the Secretary of the Home Office, a divorce would only bring censure. He couldn't possibly hope to retain the position with that sort of scandal hanging over his head. Perhaps she meant to ask him for a divorce after he was established, and her condition would be his promise that he would grant it when the time came.

Mark scrubbed his free hand through his hair and groaned. It was no use guessing what she might want. Women rarely made sense to him and Nicole less so than all others. He would simply have to see what she said on the morrow.

But he wasn't about to wait around the inn all evening alone and stew on it.

A footman walked past the open drawing room door, and Mark called to the lad. Mark pulled open his coat and plucked a large French bill from his inside pocket. He waved it over his head between two fingers. "Do you know where Madame is off to tonight?" he asked in flawless French.

The footman shook his head. "I don't, *Monsieur,* but I can find out from Madame's maid."

Mark nodded. "Do that and be quick about it. There's something for the maid, too, if she can provide the correct directions."

The footman scurried off and Mark leaned back against his seat and crossed his booted feet at the ankles. He took another swig of brandy. It slid slowly down his throat, burning away his lingering concerns over a possible divorce.

He took a deep breath. It wouldn't be difficult to gain entrée to a dinner party or soiree or wherever Nicole was off to tonight. Since the wars had ended, the French loved to invite colorful Englishmen to their parties. Mark would have the perfect opportunity to watch Nicole and her *comte*.

CHAPTER SIX

That arrogant bastard was here. At the Duc de Frontenac's soiree. Nicole stood in a small, discreet circle of friends in a corner of the *duc*'s huge drawing room, while Mark boldly occupied the center of the room. He held court in a circle of French girls who were vying for his attention as if he were royalty. He wore dark black superfine and a white starched shirtfront and startlingly white cravat with a black coat and tight black breeches. He looked good too, blast him. Nicole had missed the simple elegance of the English attire. France was a lovely country and prided itself on its couture, but she'd begun to tire of the lacy sleeves and overly embroidered colorful coats the men here wore. Mark stood out like a black panther in a sea of peacocks. He always had.

She'd met him at her grandmother's house. Grandmama was throwing a ball. She'd invited a group of soldiers who were just back from the war in Spain. Nicole had been twenty years old, beginning to wilt on the shelf, having been out for two Seasons. Mother and Grandmama were both set on her finding a husband that Season. So she was freshly coiffed and begowned, and set out in Society like a prize pig at a fair. But she was bored. Endlessly, hopelessly bored. Balls and parties were not her sort of thing. She preferred active pursuits like riding her horse and racing her male cousins through the fields. She'd always had far too much energy for the activities encouraged of proper young ladies. Embroidery and playing the pianoforte? Dreadfully dull. Those pursuits required one to sit in one spot for *far* too long. Not to mention that she questioned precisely *why* anyone would want to do so. What purpose did such activities serve?

Nicole had always longed to do something *useful,* and she finally had found just the thing. She had a secret. One Mama and Grandmama knew nothing about. In fact, if either of those ladies learned what she'd been up to of late, they'd no doubt have a pair of conniptions. Nicole had recently secured a new, if unofficial, position with the Bow Street Runners.

She'd been planning it for weeks after surreptitiously reading the runners' advertisements in the paper. The elite group of lawmen operated out of a building connected to the magistrate's office on Bow Street and they used the London papers to spread word about the criminals they were looking for. Knowing that, as a woman, she would not be taken seriously unless she proved herself, Nicole had gone on a private mission to help the runners.

Dressed in breeches and a boy's shirt (purchased on the sly from one of the footmen), just last week she'd chased down two criminals known to rob ladies on Bond Street. If there was an area of town she was familiar with, it was Bond Street, the fashionable shopping district frequented by members of the *ton*. Honestly, the two thieves stuck out like sore thumbs in the crush on Bond Street. It hadn't been difficult to find them. They'd knocked over Miss Winnie Simmons and stolen her reticule, then run down the street to the arcade. Nicole knew of a shortcut to the large, covered shopping area. She ran behind the stores and mews and cut off the two, halting them at the end of a pistol she'd borrowed from her father's collection. She'd delivered the thieves and the stolen reticule to Bow Street with dirt on her breeches, a rip in her sleeve, and a huge smile on her face. She'd never been happier nor felt more useful.

That night at Grandmama's ball, she'd been hiding behind a potted palm, hoping to avoid dancing with the Marquess of Tinsley, whom both her mother and her grandmama were eyeing as her most prized potential suitor. The boredom finally broke her and Nicole wandered over to the refreshment table to see if she might be able to surreptitiously pour a bit of wine in the punch bowl, like she had last time. Wine always made punch taste better and it certainly made such dull evenings easier to withstand.

Out of the corner of her eye, she spotted one of the extra servants Grandmama had hired for the evening reach over and pull a large serving spoon right off the end of the table. He dropped it directly into his pocket, neat as you please. Nicole blinked. The servant had some nerve. When he slipped out of the room soon after, her instincts took over. Meting out justice was ever so much more interesting than pretending to be enjoying a party, after all.

Being careful to stay back several paces so the thief wouldn't be aware, she followed him out of the room and down the corridor to the stairway that led to the servants' hall. At the entrance to the stairs, he glanced over both shoulders. Nicole pressed her back against the wall, holding her breath. The culprit proceeded to rush down the stairs and Nicole counted to ten before following him. She hid in the shadows near the bottom of the staircase and watched him hastily gather his things from a cubbyhole in the empty servants' dining room. Then he made his way to another short set of stairs that led up and out onto the back stoop next to the gardens.

She counted ten again and followed him. By the time she reached the darkened gardens, the man was halfway across the yard, heading toward the wooden door under an archway that led to the mews. He was about to get away.

"Stop! Thief!" she called without thinking. She'd been much more dramatic and much less subtle back then.

Instead of stopping, the man took off running. Again without thought, she lifted her skirts and chased after him, her delicate satin slippers ripping against the gravel. Pausing to open the gate slowed him down and Nicole was only steps behind him as he raced across the alley toward the mews.

She was about to demand that he stop again when a shadow emerged from the darkness and tripped the servant easily.

Nicole stopped short and watched in awe as the shadow materialized into a man. A tall, broad-shouldered man. She took a step back and sucked in her breath.

The servant jumped up as if to continue his flight, but the man laid him flat with one solid punch to the head. The servant flew backward and remained prostrate on the gravel, snoring.

Nicole's heart hammered in her chest.

"What did he steal?" A deep voice accompanied the shadow's broad shoulders.

"A . . . a spoon," she replied, swallowing hard, finally realizing she should be concerned for her safety. The servant could have hurt her and now she was out in the dark alone with a complete stranger who obviously had no compunction in committing violence. She wished she had brought her father's pistol, only there had been no time to fetch it.

She eyed the shadow again. Her brain told her she should be frightened, but a thrill of excitement shot down her spine. This time she took a tentative step toward him, hoping to catch a glimpse of his face.

"A silver spoon," she clarified. Too bad. It was too dark to see his features.

"Ah, the aristocracy does love its silver," the deep voice said as the shadow bent down and rummaged through the servant's pockets. A spray of light from the room above the mews cast a glow upon him. All she could see at the moment was his back. He wore a soldier's uniform. That served to ease her nerves a bit. Surely a soldier wouldn't harm her. Would he?

He located the spoon, stood, and offered it to her. The

light played across his features then and Nicole sucked in her breath. Dark hair, darker eyes, a strong brow, perfectly straight nose, and the most heavenly firm lips anyone had ever been graced with. Good heavens. Since when did she look at men's lips? Hmm. Perhaps since she'd noted how large and wet and bulbous the Marquess of Tinsley's were. The marquess dabbed at them with his handkerchief often, never failing to make her shudder. *This* man's lips, however, were the opposite. They were . . . kissable.

"I believe this is yours?" the soldier said, startling her from her indecent thoughts.

Nicole glanced down, realizing he'd been holding the spoon out to her the entire time.

"Oh, yes, yes, of course." She reluctantly took the spoon from his hand. His fingers brushed over hers. They were both wearing gloves, but the contact still caused an unfamiliar and delightful pang in her middle.

"Looks as if someone will be in need of a new footman," the handsome stranger said, pulling his hand to his side.

"Yes," she answered inanely. She should thank him, turn, and rush back to the house as quickly as possible. She'd been reckless coming out here. She needed to change her shoes before her mother saw them and scolded her for ruining them. For some reason she couldn't make her feet move, couldn't turn away from this enigmatic man.

"What is your name?" she blurted, ignoring years of proper schooling on etiquette and decorum. One did not ask a man his name. One certainly did not ask a man his name while alone in the dark near the mews.

Surprisingly, the man laughed. She liked his laugh. It was deep and genuine. "What is yours?" he asked.

She smiled at him coyly. "Why won't you tell me yours?"

"Ah, sweetheart, you're clever. Always answer a question with a question when trying to find out something from another person. It gives you the upper hand."

She couldn't help but smile wider at that reply. He was cagey. He'd also called her "sweetheart" and she should slap him for that. Instead, it sent a funny little tingling sensation all the way down to her toes. No one had called her "sweetheart" before. No one she wanted to, at least.

"Aren't you going to tell me?" she prodded. She'd never been one to give up when she really wanted something, and tonight she really wanted to know this man's identity. He was obviously one of the soldiers who'd been invited, or so she guessed, but she wanted his *name*.

"Suffice to say I'm someone who enjoys a stroll in a darkened garden more than being cooped up at a ball meant to assuage the guilt of the aristocracy."

"Assuage the guilt?" She blinked. What in the world did he mean? "Grandmama invited several friends to this party as well as the soldiers."

"Grandmama?" His dark brows arched. "You live here?" He nodded toward the mansionlike town house.

"Yes, my mother does too." She shot the hulking edifice a quick glance. Her cheeks warmed. She'd never felt embarrassed to be wealthy before, not even when she'd been at the runners' office, but suddenly the house seemed ostentatious. Where must this soldier live? Had he ever seen such a grand home before?

"What about your father?" he asked.

"He died when I was a child." Why was she telling this complete stranger so many details about her life? The truth was, she'd barely known her father. Her uncle and her cousin Harry took care of her mother, her grandmother, and herself.

"I'm sorry to hear that, sweetheart. I lost my father too young as well." Genuine regret sounded in his deep voice.

"I'm sorry too," she murmured.

"Who did you say your mother is?" His handsome features moved in and out of the shadows as he cocked his head to consider her.

She fought her smile and lifted her chin. "You didn't tell me your name yet, why should I reveal mine?" This felt suspiciously like what flirting must feel like.

His smile returned, a white flash in the darkness. "Very good, sweetheart, eye on the prize."

"You're obviously a soldier." She wanted to kick herself for the foolishly obvious words as soon as they escaped her mouth.

"What gave me away?" He grinned at her and his teeth were perfectly even behind those arresting lips. He took a step toward her.

"Your hair arrangement, obviously." She grinned back and took a step forward as well. Did this soldier like to be teased? He was certainly much more interesting to speak with than the Marquess of Tinsley, a man who never encountered a jest he didn't misunderstand.

"Ah, it has a tendency to do that." The soldier removed his hat and ran his fingers through the slightly curly dark locks. His hair looked like black silk. Nicole longed to run her fingers through it too. She squeezed the spoon in her hand instead.

"I must get back," she finally announced, hoping the regret in her voice wasn't too obvious. "But before I go, I'll give you one last chance to tell me your name."

His grin was utterly captivating. "Why would a nice young lady like you want to know a mere soldier's name?"

"So I can follow your career?" The words flew from her mouth before she had a chance to stop them. "Besides, my uncle says there are many years of fighting ahead of us. How do I know you won't be a captain one day?"

His posture straightened and a spark of determination shone in his dark eyes. "I'm going to be a general. You can count on it." And then, "What's your father's name?"

She plunked her free hand on her hip. "That wasn't even a good attempt."

"You cannot blame me for it, can you, sweetheart?" His teeth flashed again in the darkness.

Every time he called her "sweetheart," her palms got sweaty and her heart raced a little. The endearment felt . . . illicit.

"I'll just go back in and ask Joseph, the footman, to call the watch to get this"—she glanced down at the still-unconscious thief—"ne'er-do-well out of here."

"No need. I'll take care of it," the handsome stranger replied.

Very well. There wouldn't be a bounty for a crime like this. Bow Street wouldn't be interested. She reluctantly returned to the house, stealing a glance at the soldier twice as she went. He tipped his hat to her, and her stomach did a little flip.

Oh, how she hoped she would see the handsome stranger again.

Loud laughter brought Nicole's attention back to the *Duc de Frontenac*'s dinner party. With Mark there, sucking up all the oxygen, she was suddenly aware of how stuffy and close it was in the crowded room. Her kid slippers pinched her feet, making her want to step out of them and flee, shoeless, onto the balcony for fresh air.

It was no surprise that Mark had come here tonight. The man was pure arrogance. No doubt he'd waltzed right into the party this evening and demanded entrée. She should have guessed he would. He wasn't one to sit around in a rented room crossing his fingers and contemplating things. He was a man of action. They'd had that in common when they met. No doubt he'd bribed a servant to tell him where she would be tonight. The man was a master spy; deducing her whereabouts was hardly a challenge. It had been her mistake to leave him unattended in her château. She'd have to speak to the servants.

The crowd in front of her thinned, allowing her a momentary uninterrupted view of Mark, head to toe. She hadn't been mistaken earlier at her house. He looked good. No wonder the French ladies hovered around him. She'd been shocked to see him today. Shocked and a bit elated. *Not* because she missed him. Never that. *Only* because she'd always expected that the next missive she received about her husband would be the news of his untimely demise.

He was smart, he was calculating, and he was an excellent spy. He was also reckless. He'd do anything to get his man, win his case, excel at anything. His own life was nothing in pursuit of his goal: to be the best damned spymaster London had ever known. She'd heard enough rumors about him over the years. He'd accomplished that goal and then some.

He'd managed to survive the wars. He'd managed to get himself promoted to the rank of general. And now he needed her? For another promotion. She sagged against the wall. Of course he did. His work was all he cared about. At the expense of all other things . . . including their marriage.

She hadn't told him what her one condition was. It may have been petty of her, but she wanted to make him wait, to make him squirm and wonder. For a man so used to being in control, waiting was torture. But, she also hadn't been ready to vocalize what it was she wanted. The moment he'd asked her for a favor, she'd known. She'd always known what she wanted from him. He wasn't going to like it. He might well say no, even if it cost him his promotion, and that was why she needed more time to come up with the perfect way to phrase it. She'd learned long ago that with Mark, presentation made a difference. He was too smart to be manipulated. She had to be careful, very careful.

She nodded politely at something one of the people surrounding her said and then asked the *comte* in a quiet whisper if he might fetch her a glass of champagne. Henri trotted off to do her bidding and her attention immediately reverted across the room to where Mark stood. He was clearly in the middle of a story because he was speaking with his hands while the ladies surrounding him all stared at him with wide eyes and rapt interest. Nicole had intended to come to this soiree tonight, enjoy the company of her friends, and hope that the right words to explain to Mark what she wanted would present themselves in the morning. A good night's sleep often helped with such dilemmas.

But she'd underestimated Mark. She'd forgotten for a moment how used to getting his way he was. He wasn't about to not follow her out tonight. He'd want to see what she was up to. See what company she kept. Try to guess at what her one condition might be so he would have the upper hand in tomorrow's negotiations.

Henri returned with a glass of champagne and presented it to her with a flourish. She couldn't help but think that Mark would never present anything with a flourish. The man was not a flourisher.

"Merci beaucoup," she replied, gracing the *comte* with her most flattering smile. Frenchmen so loved to be flattered. Mark didn't need to be flattered. His own arrogance outweighed anyone's flattery.

She took a long sip of champagne, trying not to let her gaze travel yet again to her husband in his arresting black evening attire, the pretty French girls in pastels hovering near him like beautiful butterflies.

She couldn't help herself. Within moments she was glancing across the room at him again. She narrowed her eyes. Yes, he was here for a reason. He wanted to guess her condition. Too bad for him it would be the absolute last thing he would ever guess.

CHAPTER SEVEN

Mark kept his most charming smile glued to his face. The smile he used when he was at a party surrounded by women lavishing him with attention. He smiled and nodded and even winked at one or two of them, the boldest ones. But he didn't enjoy their simpering company, and while to all appearances it looked as if he was paying attention to each of them and enjoying himself, his senses were fully attuned to what was happening across the room . . . with Nicole.

She'd traded the snug breeches for a dazzling ball gown of sapphire blue. The bodice hugged her generous bosom and fell in graceful folds down her long legs. She looked . . . magnificent. But then she always had. The two of them had had a score of problems, but attraction had never been one of them. He would be lying, however, if he didn't admit he preferred her in breeches.

The damned *comte* was hovering near her, his thin

hand sometimes darting out to touch her arm. Mark growled under his breath. He'd done his research on the *comte* this afternoon. The man came from a dull if reputable family. He owned a nearby estate that was mostly supported by the lavender trade. He was rich but not indecently so, and he'd been hanging after Nicole for the last two years.

Mark took another sip of his champagne (damn, he wished it was a brandy) and replied in fluent French to something one of the cheekier young ladies had said to him. The French were much bolder than the English. They said and did things that would be considered scandalous at *ton* events in London. It was one of the things he appreciated about this country. One of the few things.

Another covert glance showed her laughing at something the *comte* had said and lifting her graceful white-gloved hand to her forehead to expertly swipe away a red curl that had come loose from her coiffure. Mark narrowed his eyes on the couple. What he hadn't been able to discern in his research this afternoon was whether Nicole was infatuated with the *comte*. For that, there was only one way to tell and he was engaged in it at the moment . . . watching them together.

"Mesdemoiselles, you must scatter," came a musical voice from behind him. "You are behaving like a hive of bees. No doubt the general is afraid you may sting him."

Mark turned his head to see a lovely blond woman in her early thirties waving her hands at the young ladies surrounding him. The ladies lifted their colorful skirts, frowned, and gave him reluctant looks as they flew away to the four corners of the room, leaving him alone with the blond woman.

"May I refill your glass?" she asked him, still speaking in what was clearly her native language. She wore a flowing golden gown with rubies at her throat. Her sharp blue eyes seemed to miss nothing.

"I'd prefer something stronger if you have it?" He afforded her his infamous grin.

"*Oui*, but Nicole was right, you *are* charming," she said with a sly smile.

She snapped her fingers and a footman rushed over. She ordered Mark a brandy and turned back to him while the footman hurried off to fetch the drink.

"Nicole told you I'm charming?" he asked, somewhat surprised by the news, but grinning nevertheless. He'd never met a compliment he didn't like.

"*Oui, très charmant.*" She held out her hand to him. "I am the *Duchesse de Frontenac*. I believe you met my husband."

Ah, so she was his hostess. Yes, he had met her husband earlier tonight in the man's study. He'd asked for a few minutes of the *duc*'s time, which had resulted (as he'd hoped) in an invitation to tonight's party.

Mark took her hand and executed a deep bow over it. "My pleasure, entirely, *Madame la Duchesse*. Thank you for graciously inviting me into your home."

Her tinkling laughter followed. "You invited yourself according to my husband, but I must say I'm pleased. I've been eager to meet you for quite some time."

Mark hid his smile behind his champagne glass. The French were forthright. He appreciated that. No doubt that was why Nicole liked it here. He downed the rest of the contents of his glass just before the footman returned and replaced it with a filled brandy snifter.

"Quite some time?" he echoed belatedly, letting the words linger.

"But of course. Your wife has told me a great deal about you. Nicole and I have been friends for an age."

It surprised him to know Nicole had confided in someone. A Frenchwoman at that. Obviously the *duchesse* was someone who could be trusted. He still had issues of trust when it came to the French. "I'm certain her words were flattering," he replied with an edge of irony in his voice.

"*Some* of them were flattering," the *duchesse* replied, taking a dainty sip of her champagne.

"And the ones that weren't?" he ventured, arching a brow.

"Numerous," she said simply, with the barest hint of a shrug.

"I see." His smile widened to a full-out grin. "How long has Nicole lived here?"

The *duchesse* looked at him out of the corners of those perceptive eyes. "Something tells me you already know that, *monsieur*."

He did. Three years. She'd been in Paris before that, but he'd wanted to see if the *duchesse* would tell him the truth.

"Besides," the *duchesse* continued. "Does it not seem strange to you that a husband would fail to know the whereabouts of his own wife?"

"I assumed Nicole had told you that we're . . ." He cleared his throat. "Estranged."

"Yes, she's told me." The *duchesse* glanced over at Nicole and nodded. "We are quite close. I know many things about Nicole."

"Such as?" He couldn't help but ask.

The *duchesse* raised her glass to her lips and sighed. "She is clever, she is beautiful, and she is *très* . . . lonely."

"Lonely?" Mark nearly spit out his brandy. He struggled to keep his face blank. "She doesn't look lonely to me." In addition to the *comte,* there were at least three other men hovering near Nicole's skirts.

He focused on Nicole's features. It was true. Her face was devoid of animation, despite her engaging smile. Her eyes held a certain . . . sadness?

"Looks can be deceiving as I'm certain you know, *monsieur*?" the *duchesse* said.

He turned his attention back to the blonde. Had Nicole told the *duchesse* what he did for a living? That he was a spymaster? Something told him she knew. "Only too well," he replied cryptically. Yes, looks *could* be deceiving. And so could words.

It reminded him of the night he'd met Nicole. She'd seemed so special then. So different from other young woman. She'd seemed lonely then too.

Mark located an animal's water dish around the side of the mews and splashed it on the face of the man who'd stolen a silver spoon from the most intriguing young woman he'd ever laid eyes on. Too bad she was an aristocrat . . . and no doubt a debutante at that. The worst kind of aristocrat. Naïve, innocent, and heavily guarded . . . usually. It had been a surprise to see her outside, chasing down a thief. Not the usual sport for a gently reared girl.

She obviously didn't have much sense. She could have been killed or raped. If not by the chap who'd stolen the spoon, then by him. Of course he was no rapist or murderer, but she didn't know that. She'd been unwise to leave the party alone. Especially looking like that. Her hair was the deep red of fire. Her eyes were a curious green color. Her face looked as if it had been drawn by a master. High cheekbones, slight winged brows, petal-pink lips that pursed when she was amused. He'd been toying with her by not telling her his name, and he wasn't entirely certain why. He'd pretended he didn't know her either, but of course if her grandmother lived here, she was the granddaughter of the dowager Countess of Whitby. It would be simple enough to ask someone and discover the girl's name.

The thief sputtered and woke up. Her pushed himself up to his elbows uneasily and lifted a hand to rub the large knot forming on his forehead. "Wot in the 'ell is going on 'ere?" he growled.

Mark leaned down and braced a hand on his knee. "You have been caught stealing, my friend, and I suggest you hie yourself off before the good lady of this household calls the watch on you."

The man's eyes widened with panic. "It was ye wot 'it me?" The thief scrambled to his feet, his eyes filled with fear.

Mark straightened and then bowed. "Yes, it was me."

The man patted his pocket, obviously searching for the pilfered spoon.

"It's not there," Mark said calmly, leaning one shoulder against the side of the mews, lighting a cheroot, and regarding the chap down the length of his nose.

"Ye took it?" The man's face remained scrunched into a scowl.

Mark pulled the cheroot from his lips. "I gave it back to its rightful owner, who indicated that she might ask a footman to call the watch on you, as I said. I suggest you go."

The man took a tentative step backward, eyeing Mark with suspicion. "Ye're not gonna turn me in?"

Mark waved the cheroot in the air. "I have better things to do than incarcerate poor people who make bad decisions. I suggest you look for decent work and stop this type of thing. The army is always looking for good men, you know."

The man shook his head slowly. "I'm not a good man."

"No, you're not, but you could be. Think about it." Mark reached inside his coat and pulled his calling card from his pocket. He handed it to the man. "If you decide you'd like to change your life, get in touch. Otherwise, begone."

"Thank ye, thank ye, sir," the servant said. He stooped to gather his bundle from the ground and took off at a lumbering pace around the side of the mews.

Mark turned around and contemplated the town house. Then he tossed his cheroot to the ground and snuffed it under his boot. He sighed. He would make his way back into the ball. No doubt he'd regret his decision, but he wanted to see the redhead in full light. Would she be as beautiful as he imagined? There was only one way to find out.

Mark shook his head, bringing his thoughts back to the *Duchesse de Frontenac*'s ballroom and his gaze back to Nicole's familiar face. Memories were dangerous. They could make you want things that were impossible, like people to be different from who they were.

"Is she happy here?" he asked, turning his attention back to the *duchesse*. The words surprised him. He hadn't meant to ask them.

The *duchesse* glanced wistfully in Nicole's direction. "She spends her time at the local orphanage, tending to the children."

Mark furrowed his brow. An orphanage? *That* was surprising. Was that what Nicole wanted him to think she was doing? Had she asked the *duchesse* to tell him that? He narrowed his eyes on the *duchesse*. "And?" That wasn't all Nicole spent her time doing. He was certain of it.

The *duchesse* shrugged. "She occasionally assists the local police with solving a crime or two."

"The *gendarmerie*?" Mark's crack of laughter shot across the room. "*That* sounds more like her."

"Yes. The *gendarmerie* are quite thankful and extremely discreet."

"Does the *comte* know what she does?" Mark couldn't keep himself from asking, again imagining his hands around the *comte*'s slender throat.

"You'd have to ask the *comte*," the *duchesse* replied with a wry smile.

Mark stared across the room at the couple. "Are they lovers?" If he were going to ask a great many blunt questions this evening, he might as well ask the one he wanted to know the most.

The *duchesse* clucked her tongue. "Ah, my dear general, you'd have to ask your wife that question, for I am not one to tell such secrets."

"The French do love their secrets," he intoned, his hand tightening around the snifter.

"*Oui*," the *duchesse* replied, taking another dainty sip from her champagne flute.

Mark nodded toward Nicole and her band of admirers, staring down the *comte*. "He wants her, doesn't he?"

The hint of a smile touched the *duchesse*'s lips. "Of course. They all do, but her heart belongs to only one."

CHAPTER EIGHT

When the *comte* opened the doors to the balcony, a slight breeze brushed the hair away from Nicole's forehead. She stepped outside ahead of Henri while he held open the door. She strolled over to the balustrade, braced her hands on it, closed her eyes, and breathed in the heavy scent of lavender.

The *comte*'s boots tapped out the sound of his slow approach. "Enjoying yourself?" he asked.

"Immensely." She opened her eyes and turned to face him, a forced smile on her lips. "I simply needed a bit of fresh air."

The *comte* tipped his head back toward the brightly lit ballroom. "Is he bothering you? I can ask him to leave if—"

"That won't be necessary." Nicole didn't have the heart to tell Henri that "asking" Mark to leave would be an exercise in futility. The man did precisely what he wanted, precisely when he wanted to do it.

"Why has he come?" Henri asked, his light blue eyes probing, his white-blond hair slightly stirred by the breeze.

Nicole sighed. She opened her mouth to answer just as the doors to the balcony flew open and Mark came striding out, two glasses of brandy balanced perfectly in one hand. With a look on his face that was both smug and confident, he marched up to them and offered one of the glasses to Nicole. "I thought I'd replace that weak champagne with something you'd prefer."

She arched a brow at him. "Subtle as ever, I see."

Henri tugged on the lapels of his yellow embroidered silk coat and cleared his throat. "*Monsieur*, the lady and I were having a *private* conversation and—"

"And now the lady and *I* intend to have one." Mark plucked the champagne glass from Nicole's fingers, deposited it in the *comte*'s limp hand, and waved him away. "If you would be so kind as to return this to the kitchens, I'm certain Madame Grimaldi would be thankful."

Henri's nostrils flared. He was no doubt wondering precisely how rude an Englishman could be. Unfortunately for him, he had no clue how impolite and stubborn this *particular* Englishman could be. Nicole needed to intervene, to diffuse the situation. "It's fine, Henri. The general obviously has something he wants to say."

"Will you be all right?" Henri asked, searching her face solicitously.

"Oui," she replied simply, nodding, grateful for Henri's concern.

Behind Henri's back, Mark rolled his eyes. Nicole narrowed her eyes at Mark, but soon the Frenchman was on his way back to the ballroom with both glasses of champagne clutched in his fists, the tails of his long coat flapping behind him.

Nicole turned to face the darkened lavender fields again. She didn't want Mark to catch a glimpse of her smile, but she'd asked Henri to come out here precisely for this reason. To see if Mark would follow them.

She sensed him behind her, as though they stood no more than a pace apart.

"Thank you for this." She lifted the brandy glass to her lips.

"My pleasure," he intoned. The timbre of his voice thrummed through her center.

She shook away the feeling. He had followed her, of course, but it wasn't because he was jealous. If he was, it wasn't about her. He didn't care about *her.* He only cared that another man was sniffing around something he considered his. Mark was arrogant and competitive. If the *comte* had been out here with his cigar box, Mark would have arrived and demanded its return. In fact, if she didn't mistake her guess, he was probably itching for a fight. She should warn Henri to stay away from him.

She sighed and settled her shoulders into a straight line. "So, what did you want to speak with me about . . . alone? I told you I'd give you my condition *tomorrow.*" She hadn't realized how much she'd missed speaking her native language. Even though she'd learned French from tutors as a child, English with its crisp syllables and sharp consonants was her first language love.

Mark turned to face the fields, too. He leaned down and braced his forearms on the balustrade. He was so close their arms nearly touched. The scent of him, his subtle cologne, teased her nostrils.

"Were you going to allow the *comte* to kiss you out here?" he asked.

Her brows shot up of their own volition, but she hid her surprise behind her glass, thankful for the darkness on the balcony.

She shrugged one shoulder. "Were you going to kiss the butterflies?"

"Butterflies?" Mark's brow knitted into a frown.

"Yes. You had quite a group of young ladies surrounding you earlier."

Mark scratched at his jaw, a jaw Nicole couldn't help but notice hadn't been shaved since this morning and was slightly stubbled. She remembered how that stubble felt against her—she flipped open her fan and fluttered it in front of her face.

"Girls aren't my type. I prefer women." Confidence dripped from his voice.

"Do you?" She flipped the fan closed and took a small sip of brandy, trying not to think about the women he'd, ahem, *preferred,* since last they'd been together.

"Yes."

"Like?" She braced herself for the answer. How in the name of Hera had they got into this dangerous conversation?

"You."

For a split second her breath caught, but then she

forced the laughter through her tight throat. "Trying to flatter me, so I'll agree to your request."

He turned his face away from hers and stared out into the fields. "Is it working?"

"It depends." Another single shoulder shrug.

He turned back and studied her, his face surprisingly somber. "On what?"

"On whether you'll agree to my condition." She hadn't meant for her voice to sound quite so imperial.

"Which is?" His firmly molded lips quirked into a half smile, but he turned his face back to look at the fields again.

She blew out a deep breath. "Something I'm not prepared to tell you until tomorrow. I haven't changed my mind, but I admire your tenacity."

He watched her out of the corners of his eyes. "You knew I'd be here tonight, didn't you?"

She nodded and lifted her glass to her lips. "Of course."

"Is that why you came out here on the balcony with the *comte*? To make me jealous?"

She touched her fingertips to one diamond earbob. "*Are* you jealous?"

"Excessively so." He said it with enough of a hint of sarcasm that she wasn't certain he wasn't jesting.

She lifted her chin. "He wants to marry me."

He still wasn't looking at her, but out of the corner of her eye she saw his jaw tighten. "You're already married."

A strange thrill shot through her. She was taunting him, for once. It wasn't often that one had the upper hand with Mark Grimaldi. "A condition that can be rectified," she breathed.

CHAPTER NINE

Mark watched Nicole saunter back into the *duc*'s ballroom, her hips undulating as she went. He was hard. Blast. When was the last time he'd even looked at a woman with lust? Over the years, he'd taken himself in hand of course, but that had been a physical act, like eating or sleeping. It had been necessary and he'd always had a vision of red hair and petal-pink lips and green eyes the color of sea foam while he'd done it.

He turned his back on the ballroom and stared, unseeing, at the darkened fields, his free hand knotted into a fist. Now he knew for certain. Damn it. The *duchesse* had all but told him Nicole was in love with the *comte*. She was planning to ask Mark for a divorce. That was her condition. Very well. If that was what she wanted, his only option would be to negotiate for time.

Would she agree to remain married for one year? Two? A year would be the minimum he could agree to.

He needed time to establish himself in his new role. He needed time to work out the details of a divorce, politically. If he spoke to the right people, called upon the right friends, they might be able to accomplish it with little fanfare and hopefully minimal gossip. It would be extremely delicate, and one of them would have to plead to either impotence or insanity. Neither was palatable, but perhaps they could think of something to obtain a quiet divorce. His mind whirled with the possibilities.

Damn. He squeezed his eyes closed and let his head drop forward. How had he got into this situation? The irony was not lost on him. He had spent nearly two decades of his life in service to the Crown. The Crown had demanded everything from him, his loyalty, his time, his lifeblood. There had been no room for a relationship, much less a marriage. It had been nothing but fortuitous that he and Nicole had become estranged. Had they remained together, no doubt she would have left him for lack of attention.

And now, now that he'd sacrificed everything for his position, they wanted him to settle down and play the happily married man. It was ludicrous, but he'd known his day of reckoning with Nicole would someday come. He couldn't escape it forever.

She had expected a missive informing her he'd been killed. She'd nearly received precisely that. Five years ago. He'd been in a French prison camp. They'd tortured him unmercifully. He'd been on the verge of death. His good friend and fellow spy Rafe Cavendish had saved him. Rafe and some of the other spies had snuck into the camp in the middle of the night, overpowered the guards, and sneaked him out. He'd spent months recovering, a dozen bones broken in addition to his nose.

He lifted his head again. A humorless smile curled his lips. Yes, he'd sacrificed everything for this work, including all relationships. He couldn't even have friends. Not true ones. Rafe and his twin brother, Cade, were the closest he had to friends, but even they had to remain at arm's length. He was their superior. They reported to him. He couldn't risk getting too close. It was the price he paid for being in charge.

Nicole had no idea how right she'd nearly been. Every day in that bloody prison camp, he'd thought of the nights he'd spent with Nicole during their short-lived happiness. Those memories had got him through some of the darkest days of his life, but he'd return to the prison camp before he'd admit it to her. She would only throw it in his face.

He turned toward the ballroom. Leaving his snifter sitting atop the balustrade, he pulled a cheroot from his inside coat pocket and strolled to light it from one of the candles that rested on a nearby table. He sucked the sweet smoke into his lungs and blew it out in a perfectly formed O.

Nicole hadn't been who he thought she was when they'd married. He'd quickly learned she was a scheming liar. But in those dark, hellish days in the camp, he'd pretended she was the fresh-faced, intriguing girl he'd fallen in love with, innocent and free. The kind of girl who would run down a thief in the mews and charmingly flirt with a virtual nobody in the army.

Mark groaned. He supposed it was inevitable, them

ending this way, her asking for a divorce to marry the *comte*. The *duchesse* said she was lonely. Mark didn't believe it. There were obviously plenty of men eager for her attention and charms. Perhaps by lonely, the *duchesse* simply meant Nicole wished she could be free to be with the *comte*.

As much as he wanted to punch him, Mark couldn't blame the *comte*. Nicole was gorgeous, intelligent, and full of life. She would be a fine wife . . . to the right man.

Mark couldn't blame Nicole either. She shouldn't have to suffer through life alone for the sake of a marriage that never should have taken place.

He crossed back over to the balustrade and downed the rest of his brandy. Everything would be fine. He was confident they could come to some sort of an arrangement that would make them both happy on the morrow.

CHAPTER TEN

Nicole stared into her wardrobe, pressing her palm against her cheek. What did one wear to have what was certain to be an extremely uncomfortable discussion with one's husband, whom one hadn't seen in ten years? Not counting yesterday.

She finally settled on a simple pink morning gown with capped sleeves and lace along the bodice. It displayed her décolletage to prime advantage, which was what she liked best about it. Mark had glanced at her décolletage last night. It had been surreptitious, granted, but she'd noticed. And she'd been pleased by it. She wanted to have every advantage in this discussion and she was not above presenting a bit of cleavage to secure the upper hand.

Her maid helped her into the pink gown. Jacqueline arranged Nicole's hair into a loose chignon, pulling out a few strands to frame her face, the way she liked it. She placed her family's set of pearls around her neck and dabbed lavender perfume behind both ears. When they were finished, Nicole stared at herself in the large, wooden-framed looking glass in her bedchamber. Did she look as different to Mark as he did to her? Still himself, but infinitely more appealing with new muscles and a thinner face and tiny lines next to his eyes that heightened the air of authority he'd always possessed. And that crook in his nose that somehow made her want to trace it with her fingertip. Or did she just look aged to him? A former beauty (or so she'd been called) rusticating so long the bloom had worn off.

A slight knock at the door startled her back into the moment.

"*Monsieur le Général* is here, *Madame*," one of the housemaids reported.

Nicole glanced at the clock on the wall. Mark was right on time. Wasn't he always? His colleagues called him the stone man. Emotionless, calm, collected, always rigidly in charge. He had no friends. Friends could betray him. He had no family. At least none he would claim. He *was* like stone. Like a statue, not a human being. He would never allow himself such a flaw as to be late to anything. Very well. He was here and she'd promised him her terms. She might as well get it over with. The worst he could say was no, and she'd prepared herself for that.

She took a deep breath, sucking in her belly and exhaling slowly. There was only one way to face this pivotal moment. With courage. If she didn't ask for this now, she would never get it, as this was certain to be the only time her husband would appear on her doorstep, hat in hand, asking for a favor. She had to take advantage of the opportunity, but still, her nerves caused her legs to tremble as she slowly walked out of her bedchamber, down the corridor to the top of the staircase, and grasped the marble bannister.

She descended into the foyer, made her way to the front drawing room, and stood before the door, her heart beating like a hare's foot in her chest. She swallowed hard and pushed open the door with a sweating hand.

Mark stood near the mantelpiece, his arm braced atop it, one hand arrested halfway through his dark hair. He wore dark gray breeches, a sapphire waistcoat, and a white shirtfront. His black boots were shined to perfection, as always.

The moment the door opened, he dropped his hand and turned to face her. Why did the man have to be so dastardly handsome? Aside from the new crook in his nose, his face looked as if it had been carved from stone. His hair was always perfect, even after he'd been rubbing his fingers through it. It sprang right back into place, the slight curl and the shine of the dark locks falling expertly into step as if they were his soldiers, too frightened of him to not do his bidding.

Nicole's eyes met his and a spark of something that felt ever so much like lust shot through her core. Breathing heavily, she immediately dropped her gaze to the floor. Lust? Lust would not be helpful in this discussion. She needed to keep her wits about her. She was about to negotiate with a master.

She glided to the settee and gathered her skirts to take a seat. "Would you care for some tea?" she asked in a voice that was far too high and unsteady.

"No," he said, striding toward her. "All I want is to hear your condition."

She cleared her throat, hoping that would help with the high-voice issue and settled onto the edge of the settee. "Always direct to a fault."

"Did you expect any less of me?" He grinned.

"No, take a seat, Mark." That was a negotiating tactic. If he was sitting too, they would be equals.

A disgruntled look on his face, Mark reluctantly sat. He chose a chair at right angles to the settee and leaned toward her, forearms braced on his thighs, his powerful frame so close she could smell the scent of his lightly applied cologne. Spicy and reminiscent of the forest. She closed her eyes. More lust. Not helping.

"Look," he began. "I know what you're going to say."

"You do?" She furrowed her brow. She'd seen him speaking to Louisa, the *Duchesse de Frontenac*, last night. Surely her friend had not told him what she wanted, had desperately wanted for years.

"Yes," he replied. "I've been thinking about it all night. I'm certain there's a way we can determine how to make it work."

She forced herself to smother her laugh, pressing her lips together awkwardly. "Make it work? I thought perhaps you already knew how it worked."

He shrugged. "I do, of course, but there are complications. You must know that. It's far from simple."

She pressed her lips together harder this time. Unexpected laughter bubbled in her chest. "I've never considered it *simple*, but precisely what do you mean by . . . complications?"

"You know, the usual. Legalities, gossip, that sort of thing. And there is always the issue of timing."

She narrowed her eyes on him. What in heaven's name did he think she was asking of him? "Timing? Legalities?"

Mark straightened a bit. "Yes, with my new role, the timing of the thing will be of the utmost importance. Surely you can understand that. A divorce has the potential to cause a great deal of scandal for both of us as well as our families."

A wave of cold shock stiffened her spine and she gasped, pressing her fingertips to her throat. "A divorce!"

"Yes," he replied, squinting at her. He hesitated. "Isn't that what you want?"

Nicole sagged against the settee cushions, her heart thrumming madly with a mixture of exasperation and trepidation. "No, you dolt. I don't want a divorce. I want you to have sex with me!"

CHAPTER ELEVEN

Mark sat on the green-and-white-flowered Louis XIV chair in the middle of Nicole's well-appointed French drawing room, completely dumbfounded. His mouth opened and closed, his eyes blinked repeatedly, and his head cocked to the side as he tried to make sense of the words that had just emerged from his wife's lips. Surely, he had been wrong before a time or two in his life. When he was younger, a child, perhaps. It had been a long while, but incorrectness wasn't a *completely* foreign feeling to him.

He just couldn't precisely recall a time when he'd been wrong. He sure as hell couldn't recall a time when he'd been *this* bloody wrong. For the love of God, he'd been as wrong as Napoleon's timing at Waterloo. As wrong as wrong ever got.

It was an unexpected feeling. As a result, he was anything but his usual calm, collected self when he stared at Nicole and echoed in a stunned voice, "Have *sex* with you?"

She shot to her feet and strode to the mantel, crossed her arms over her chest, and whirled to face him, her eyes blazing green fire. "Yes, you idiot. I want a baby. What in Hera's name made you think I wanted a divorce?" There was a slight redness to her cheeks that made her all the more appealing. She was magnificent when she was angry.

"Last night you said the *comte* wanted to marry you," he retorted. Wait. What? She wanted a *baby*?

"He does want to marry me, but that doesn't mean I want to marry *him*."

Mark stood too. He followed her to the mantel and stopped not two paces from her, his arms crossed over his chest. He'd let the *baby* comment go for the moment. "Then why did you mention it?"

She hastily shrugged one shoulder. "You seemed preoccupied by his presence."

Mark pressed a fist to his forehead where a headache was beginning to form. How the hell had he misread this situation so damned badly? "The duchess led me to believe you have a bevy of admirers."

"Also true," Nicole clipped.

"Wait." He shook his head, still trying to come to terms with what she'd said. "Are you telling me you *don't* want a divorce?"

"No, I don't want a divorce," she snapped. "Are you mad? That would bring an avalanche of shame on both our families."

He narrowed his eyes on her. "Are you having an affair with the *comte*?"

She gave Mark a condemning glare. "That is none of your business, but if it makes you feel better, no. Any child I bear would be yours without doubt if you agree to my condition."

Mark paced away from her and scrubbed his hands through his hair again. He wanted to pull out his bloody hair. What she'd just said was so unexpected, he was having trouble comprehending, it, and he sure as hell didn't know how to respond, which was the antithesis of how he usually handled things. Normally, he knew precisely what his opponent was going to say. How had he not seen *this* coming of all bloody things? A baby? A baby meant they would have to make love. But she hadn't said that, had she? She had used the word "sex." Which was curious. What in the hell was going on?

He rubbed his eyes with the balls of both hands and faced her. "You want a *baby*?" The word felt oddly foreign.

"Yes." She nodded matter-of-factly. Her throat worked as she swallowed.

"From me?" It was an asinine thing to ask, but his surprise was making him asinine today.

She cocked her head and replied in a voice dripping with sarcasm, "You happen to be the only husband I have."

Jesus Christ. Mark pressed his fingers against his throbbing temples. "Why has this never come up before now?"

She actually rolled her eyes. Rolled them. "Because you've been avoiding me for ten years. Or didn't you recall that?"

"I have *not* been avoiding you for ten years. You've been in France for ten years."

Her eyebrows rose. "Oh? You've never visited France in the last ten years?"

He flared his nostrils. "You haven't visited England?"

"There's little use arguing about this." She slashed an arm through the air. "The fact is that you know my condition and it's up to you to say yes or no. The cards are in your hands. It's your play, General."

He paced away from her. Damn it all to hell. He'd thought about a divorce. He'd been prepared for a divorce. He'd been ready to *accept* a divorce. A baby? He had no bloody idea how he felt about a baby. He'd never considered one, had just accepted the fact that he would remain childless. Given the state of the rest of his family, it was probably best that way.

"Why?" he finally demanded, pacing back toward her.

"I want a baby. You happen to be the only means by which I can respectably get one."

"But *why* do you want a baby? There's no title to secure."

She clenched her fists against her sides, her arms straightened and shaking with what he could only assume was pent-up rage. "Oh, yes, of course, you would think that's the only reason I would want a baby."

"Tell me *why*," he demanded through clenched teeth.

"What does it matter?" She looked away, the stiffness draining from her arms. Was it his imagination or did he see a flash of vulnerability in her eyes before she glanced away? She swallowed and her throat worked.

"I'm curious," he replied, tempering his angry tone.

She turned her back to him, facing the doors. "Curiosity isn't part of this negotiation. Suffice it to say I want to be a mother. What do you care? You'll get an heir and I'll care for the baby entirely. You won't have to lift a finger."

He studied the graceful line of her slender neck, the little wisps of russet hair that had escaped her chignon. "You expect me to rut with you, produce a child, and never see the babe again?"

Nicole took a deep breath. Her shoulders lifted and settled back. "You may visit, if you choose. A child should know his father. I simply wouldn't *expect* it of you."

An odd mixture of hurt and outrage shot through Mark's chest. What kind of monster did she take him to be? He stalked in front of her to see her face, and force her to see his. "You think I'd leave my son in France of all places?"

She raised her chin to look him in the eye. Her cheeks were flushed. "I would be willing to stay in England until he's, say, ten years of age."

"And go where afterward?"

She splayed her hands wide and shrugged. "Back to France? Anywhere."

"What if the babe is female?" he added.

She nodded slowly. "So be it. I only require the one."

He narrowed his eyes on her. "What if I want an heir?"

One red eyebrow shot up. "I assumed you didn't give a toss or you'd have come looking for me before now."

That was so close to the truth he snapped his mouth

shut. They stood in charged silence broken only by the steady tick of the mantel clock.

Finally, Mark drew a deep breath and fixed his gaze on hers anew, searching for . . . what? He wasn't certain. "So that's it, one child? You don't care whether it's male or female. We . . . what? Make love until you find you're with child and then we stop, I assume."

"Precisely, but . . ." She bit her lip and glanced down at her slippers, the red in her cheeks deepening.

Oh, Christ, this couldn't be good. "But what?"

"It wouldn't be . . ." Her voice was nearly a whisper.

"Wouldn't be what?" He leaned closer to better hear her.

She lifted her head again, the color still riding high on her cheeks. "It wouldn't be 'making love' as you said. It would merely be sex for the purpose of procreating."

All the air rushed from Mark's lungs. What in the name of God was the woman talking about? He splayed his hands wide in a gesture of complete exasperation. "I don't even know what that means."

She delicately cleared her throat. "We don't need to . . . ahem . . . enjoy it. That's all I mean."

His head jerked back as if she'd struck him. "Sweetheart, I'm going to enjoy it one way or another."

Her mouth fell open, but she snapped it shut in a scowl. "Fine. I only mean it doesn't have to be anything more than . . . the act."

"The *act*?" He was truly affronted. "You may recall that our time together in bed wasn't our problem." His tone dropped, and for a moment, he let his gaze slide over her features. "We always enjoyed ourselves, Nicole. I did, and I know you did too. You never had to act."

Her eyes locked with his for an instant and darted away like a frightened bird. "Must you make this more difficult than it needs to be?"

He braced a forearm against the mantel and stared at her. "Yes, I think I must."

She balled her hands into fists at her sides. "You're infuriating. Just give me your answer. Yes or no."

Mark straightened, brushed his hands down his lapels, turned on his heel, and strode toward the door.

"Where are you going?" she called after him, her voice slightly panicked.

"Back to the inn. This time *I* need time to think about it."

CHAPTER TWELVE

Nicole spent the next few hours *trying* to reply to correspondence. Her cousins from England had written her. Her mother had written, too. As usual, Mother's letter was riddled with persistent questions about whether she and Mark had been in contact. Letters had also arrived from acquaintances in both England and France. Nicole had put off her correspondence for weeks, preferring to go for a ride or to do something active versus sitting at a stuffy table in a pristine room to write about things that had already happened.

She was more interested in what was going to happen and how she could participate in it. It was why she'd chosen the life she had. Why she'd come to France. The French were less judgmental than the English. They overlooked things like women wearing riding breeches and married women being husbandless for years. Few people had asked her questions about her husband in all these years. The *duchesse* had. She was a dear friend. But even Henri had only asked a few questions, nothing too prying. Nicole had left England and her family for more than one reason. But despite the friends she'd made and the life she'd created in France, she was still lonely.

She propped an elbow on the writing table and rested her chin on one palm, the quill balanced in her other hand. She tapped the writing instrument against the vellum. What was Mark going to say? He had to say yes, didn't he? He wanted his promotion more than he wanted anything else and she'd already made it clear that the babe would not be a burden to him. An image of his face, the way a muscle jumped in his jaw, darted through her memory. She'd angered him when she'd told him it would just be an act. It had wounded his pride.

The man took great pride in his performance in bed. She couldn't mock him for it. He had been magnificent. She fingered the lace at the edge of her bodice. The nights she'd spent with him had been unforgettable. She still woke up some nights, restless and drenched in sweat, remembering them. A small sigh slipped from her lips. She'd been rash. She should have waited for him to say yes before she told him it would just be an act. Her own pride had got in the way, as it was prone to. She had wanted to wound him. It was deuced uncomfortable, asking one's husband to take one to bed. He'd rejected her ten years ago. She didn't want him to think she actually looked *forward* to it.

Feeling restless, she tossed down the quill. *Was* she looking forward to it? Ever since he'd arrived with his demands, she'd tried not to think about how it would be to be in bed with him again. If they even used a bed. A reluctant smile tugged at her mouth. They didn't have to. He'd taught her that. Up against a wall could be quite enjoyable given the right partner, and blast it all, Mark had been the right partner. They'd only stayed together a few months after their marriage, and in those few months he'd learned every inch of her body, knew exactly where to touch her and how. He'd taught her his body too. She knew what he liked and how to—

Her cheeks flamed. She grabbed a delicate boned fan from her desktop, snapped it open, and fanned herself rapidly. *Merde.* In the one day Mark had been back, she'd blushed more than she had in the entire last ten years. How could he do that to her again? She was no longer a modest young girl. She was a woman full grown.

She'd considered it all last night, had been unable to sleep because of it. She and Mark would have to have relations in order to produce a child. That was a fact. But she couldn't give herself to him again. She couldn't open up all those old emotions that had scarred over in the last ten years. She could *not* allow that to happen, and the only way it wouldn't happen was if they didn't repeat the passionate nights they'd spent together when they'd been young and, she at least, had been in love. That would end in heartache and disaster. She'd barely survived it the first time. She couldn't live through it again. To make their bargain work she must have a condition on her condition: they would simply have sex. *Not* make love.

She wasn't naïve. She understood a man enjoyed the act regardless of whether a woman did, but Mark had never left her unsatisfied. In fact, he'd taken gratification in her pleasure, ensuring every time they made love that she had her release before he took his. The man was stubborn, unsympathetic, and dominating, but by God, he was a master in bed.

Even the simple act of having sex with him would be difficult for her. It would make her vulnerable. Expose her. Not just her body, but her mind and heart, too. A vague, strange thrill shot through her. This was a dangerous dance where her heart was concerned, and if he didn't agree to her second condition, the only outcome guaranteed was pleasure like she hadn't known in ten years. Her pulse raced at the thought. It was something she would have to accept to get her baby. It would be worth it. To have a child of her own. Someone who would love her unconditionally and never leave her, someone to devote herself to.

She shut the fan and laid it back atop the desk. A babe had been her dream for many years. Now that the wars were over, it was time. She'd never expected to have the opportunity. She would have died a slow, painful death before she would have contacted Mark and asked him for a baby, but when the opportunity appeared on her doorstep asking for a favor . . . A smile of satisfaction crept to her mouth. That was a different matter entirely. She would be a fool not to try to get what she wanted out of this.

Nicole stood and crossed to the window. She pulled back the silken drapery and looked out across the fields behind the château. She rubbed a hand up and down her suddenly chilly arm. She tried to picture a small child playing happily in the meadow below. Her chest filled with a tight yearning that felt supremely different, yet just as profound, as what she had once felt in Mark's presence.

He had asked her why she'd wanted a baby. She hadn't expected that. She'd die another painful death before she told him the real reason. Because she was . . . lonely, because she wanted at least one being in this world to love her forever. Her father had died when she was a child and her mother had never made it a secret that she disagreed with every one of Nicole's choices. It was one of the reasons moving to France hadn't been a difficult decision all those years ago. She'd been able to escape both her disastrous marriage and her mother's censure. The only person she'd truly missed (other than Mark) had been her grandmama. When word had arrived three years ago that Grandmama had died, Nicole had cried bitterly for weeks. She couldn't even return to England. The letter had arrived a fortnight after the funeral.

She traced a fingertip along the windowpane. She had an unhappy past with her own mother, but she would never allow such a relationship to form between herself and her own babe. A baby would be a chance to start the loving family she'd never known. A baby would be there every day and would need her. No more loneliness.

Mark would mock her if she told him that. He already believed she was a scheming liar. His past had made him a distrustful son of a bitch, even when it came to his own wife. He'd seemed so open and different, so unlike the Marquess of Tinsley and the other fops her mother and grandmama had wanted her to marry. She'd chosen Mark because he was so unlike the others . . .

because he didn't seem as if he wanted a wife to be a biddable puppet who did and said all the customary things.

Soon after their wedding he'd shown himself to be exactly like all other men. He hadn't valued her for her uniqueness. He'd rejected her for her differences. He'd accused her of lying to him, of being disingenuous before their marriage. He'd allowed their marriage to be destroyed over it.

She let the drapery drop across the window, a barrier between herself and the radiant sunlight, and returned to her desk, to the dutiful dullness of correspondence and the merciful escape it provided from the painful thoughts of the past. None of those thoughts mattered now. The only thing that mattered was the fact that she finally had her chance to get what she wanted.

All Mark had to do was say yes. They'd both get something out of this godforsaken marriage. If Mark agreed, however, the next few months would be excruciating. Her stomach clenched. She would have to return to England to play his loving wife. How he intended to tell everyone why he suddenly seemed madly in love with a woman he'd managed to forget about for the last ten years was something she'd leave to him to explain.

Regardless, she would have to be in his company for weeks, and in his bed, or somewhere, at night so he could fulfill his end of their bargain and get her with child. It would only take a few months at most, wouldn't it? He'd already asked her to stay for a few months. That implied three. Three months. The same amount of time they'd spent happily married. No doubt he'd decided that was the amount of time in which it would seem believable that they were a true couple. It would be excruciating.

Nicole forced herself to sit at the desk and spent an inordinate amount of time arranging her skirts. She still didn't relish the correspondence, distraction or no. Mark had mentioned perhaps wanting to be in the babe's life. She would allow that. She couldn't deny him. In the eyes of the law, she and her baby belonged to him, after all. She could happily stay in England, perhaps buy a small cottage in the country, allow her child visits with his father and travel to see her family and old friends. That part wouldn't be so bad, but could she survive the next few months in Mark's constant company? In Mark's bed?

There was only one way to find out.

The butler knocked on the open door, scattering Nicole's thoughts. He bowed when she turned to face him. He held a silver salver with a note on it. "*Madame*, this missive came for you just now," he said in French.

Nicole stood, crossed the thick blue rug, and tugged the missive from the salver. She recognized the wax seal. The Grimaldi *G* sat large and imposing in the middle of dark green. "*Merci*," she said to the butler, who immediately retreated from the room.

Nicole returned to her writing desk and used her silver letter opener to break the seal. She quickly scanned the words. In Mark's bold scroll it read, "*I have a condition to your condition. We'll discuss it over dinner tonight. I'll be there at eight.*"

CHAPTER THIRTEEN

The wine and the first course had barely been served when a clearly perturbed Nicole plonked down her glass atop the ridiculously long dining table, glared at Mark, who sat at the far end, and said loud enough for him to hear, "What's your condition to my condition?"

Mark flashed her his infamous grin. She looked resplendent tonight, and even more tempting when her temper matched the fiery tones of her hair.

He stood, gathered his plate, cutlery, and wineglass and marched down to the seat directly to her left.

"What are you doing?" She eyed him warily. She clearly couldn't stand the suspense. He intended to enjoy himself.

"Moving closer of course. Or would you prefer I shout about our marital intimacies across this insanely long table?"

"We don't have marital intimacies," she whispered, a near growl.

He leaned toward her and ensured his breath brushed the tender side of her neck when he spoke. "Not at the moment, but we're about to, sweetheart."

She snatched her glass from the table and took a long draught. "What's your blasted condition?"

Mark sat back in his chair and regarded her, taking a sip of the red wine in his glass. It burned a comforting trail of heat to his belly. "What do you think it is?"

She rolled her eyes and tilted her head to the side. "*Must* we play this game?"

"Just one guess," he prodded, still grinning.

"Very well. If the child is a son, you will want him with you more."

Mark's bark of laughter bounced incongruent merriment around the staid dining room. "You think I wouldn't care if I sire a daughter?"

Nicole shrugged, set aside her glass, and took a spoonful of her turtle soup. "I assume she wouldn't be as important to you."

This time he rolled his eyes. "Shows you how well you know me. I may well *prefer* a daughter."

"What?" She blinked, her brow wrinkled in a frown. "Why?"

"I understand you and your dynastic roots love male heirs, but my father was from Italy and girls are cherished there."

"Yes, but your family—"

"I prefer not to speak about the *rest* of my family." He clenched his jaw.

She gave him a tight smile. "Oh, yes. I know only too well how sore a subject the rest of your family is."

"Good then. We agree not to discuss it." He spent a few moments rearranging his silverware next to his plate.

"Very well. Is that your condition, that you spend time with your child? I've already told you that can be arranged. I have no objection."

Mark shook his head. This was a fraught subject for him. Family. Any family. All family. He'd loved and been loved by his mother and father, but he'd hardly been wrapped in a familial embrace by the rest of the clan. His mother had tried for years to convince her father to accept her husband and son. When that didn't work, after a final insult from his grandfather that Mark remembered all too well even though he'd been a lad of eight, his mother had given up. She and Mark's father had moved their little trio to a small town in Devon and lived a quiet, simple, happy life. His father worked as a shoemaker in a village. To Mark's knowledge, his mother never tried to contact her family again.

As for Mark's father's family, they had lovingly sent letters, but they lived in Rome, so far away they might as well have been on another planet. None of them ever visited, and Mark's father and mother never took him to Italy. He'd been an adult before he met his Italian relatives.

Because of his childhood spent with no siblings, Mark's thoughts about family mostly centered on the damage his mother's relatives had done. She'd been devastated by their rejection. That was not how family should act.

When Mark married Nicole, their courtship and marriage had been quick. He'd barely had a chance to think about their future before they'd become estranged. In the years since, he'd been so focused on his career and political ambitions he'd never considered the fact that being without Nicole meant he was giving up his only chance at siring an heir. He purposely hadn't allowed himself to think about it.

Now that possibility was sitting next to him enjoying turtle soup. Nicole's confronting him with something he'd pushed out of his mind made him uneasy. He wasn't prepared, but he sure as hell wasn't about to have a child of his be born into this world and not know him. He also found the notion of having emotionless sex in order to produce a child repellent. Children should be conceived from love and passion . . . and pleasure.

"I would like to spend time with my child, yes. But that's *not* my condition," he finally told her.

"Then what is?" Her eyes flashed green fire. She was clearly growing impatient.

He let his gaze linger on her face, then meander down to her décolletage. "I find the notion of merely copulating unacceptable. We have to make love or all bets are off."

CHAPTER FOURTEEN

Nicole's spoon hit her soup, splashing liquid onto the pristine linen table cover as she shot to her feet. "What? No. No. No!" The man had obviously gone mad.

Mark merely sat back and regarded her calmly, blinking his unfairly long eyelashes at her. "Why are you so upset about this?"

She braced her palms against the tabletop and glared at him. "No, absolutely not. Simply no. I can't. I won't." She could not explain to him why but she couldn't live through such a condition. Why was he making this so difficult?

"I fail to see what your objection is. If you recall, we had some remarkable times in bed." His grin was unrepentant. She wanted to slap it off his handsome face.

She recalled all right. She was doing her blasted best *not* to. "That has nothing to do with it."

He lifted his wineglass and slowly swished the liquid around. "It has everything to do with it. If we're going to create a child, we might as well enjoy ourselves."

"No. Absolutely not." Her heart was doing its best to pound straight through her bodice. He was being an ass on purpose. There was no other reason for him to make this demand. He wanted to see her squirm.

A footman came bustling into the dining room. When he saw that Mark had moved to the other end of the table, surprise registered on his face. The servant hurried to deliver Mark's bowl of soup to him.

Mark waited until the footman left before prodding Nicole again. He continued to swirl the wine in his glass slowly. "Are you refusing my condition?"

She narrowed her eyes. Two could play this game. He wanted his blasted promotion, didn't he? She'd do well to remember that. "Yes. I refuse." She raised her chin in the air and stared down the length of the table, declining to look at him.

"Fine." He set down his glass and crossed his arms over his chest. "Then I'll return to England and do my best to get my promotion without you, and you can remain childless."

Her lip curled. Damn him to hell. He was calling her bluff. "You'd give up your promotion over such a ridiculous demand?"

"I refuse to be used as a stud horse. I have a chance of getting promoted without you. You, however, have *no* chance of having a legitimate child without me."

Her fingers curled tightly around her wineglass while her heart continued to hammer in her chest. "You bastard," she ground out.

He grinned as he took a sip of his wine. "I assure you I'm no bastard. Although you must know that that is an option for you. You could have your *comte* impregnate you. I've been here for two days. No one would gainsay you if you turned up with a babe, say, nine months from now."

A growl roiled in her chest, threatening to break free. "You know I wouldn't do that."

"I don't know that at all." The humor in his features faded. "I don't know who you are anymore."

A sort of hopelessness fell over them, smothering the banter. "Did you ever?" she whispered, staring at her wineglass and not him.

They sat in a mournful silence for what felt like an eternity before Nicole slowly lifted her glass to her lips and drained it. She glanced at Mark. "Damn you. Why are you making this so difficult?"

He regarded her somberly, leaning back in his chair. "Seems you're the one making it difficult, sweetheart. If you want my child, a legitimate heir, you simply have to agree to enjoy yourself in bed with your husband. That doesn't seem like too much to ask. I fail to see why you're fighting it."

Nicole blew out a long breath. She had to think about this reasonably. Rationally. To take the emotion out of it. The man was right. Damn him straight to hell, he was right. She was being ridiculous. More importantly, he'd already staked his offer by saying he would return to England. She knew him well enough to know that once he made such a claim his damned pride would keep him from changing his mind.

If she wanted a baby, a legitimate baby, she would

have to agree to his terms. He'd got her. *Merde*. There was no way she would try to claim an illegitimate child as his. It wasn't in her nature. She was married, by God. Perhaps not happily, but she took her commitment seriously and she refused to cuckold her husband, no matter what he'd been doing all these years. She had never heard any gossip about his light-o'-loves, but then again, it was one of the reasons she lived so far away. Hearing about him would only hurt, and she'd forbidden her mother from mentioning news of him. It didn't keep Mother from asking about her marriage, but it did keep the woman from sharing any tidbits she might have heard about Mark from the London gossip mills.

Nicole stood and tossed her napkin onto the seat of the chair. "I've lost my appetite. I assume you've already arranged passage for us back to London?"

He inclined his head, that infuriating grin returning to his lips. "Naturally."

"Fine. I agree to your terms and I want to leave at sunrise on the morrow. The sooner we get this over with, the better." She turned on her heel and stalked from the room.

CHAPTER FIFTEEN

Mark arrived at Nicole's house just as the sun was emerging the next morning. Mist was still rising from the surrounding lavender fields, and deer frolicked by the side of the long winding dirt road that led up to the house. Mark rolled down the carriage's window shade and looked around. He sucked in two lungsful of crisp, early morning air, pungent with the scent of lavender. France would be a lovely country . . . if his enemies hadn't lived here.

In town, he'd hired a coach to drive them the entire way to Calais, where they would board a packet to Dover. The journey would take two days. After dinner last night, which he'd finished with a triumphant smile on his face, he'd spent the remainder of the evening searching for the best accommodations he could find on short notice. He'd managed to locate a reasonably comfortable conveyance with a reasonably sober driver. More importantly, the man was willing to drive them the entire way to Calais . . . after Mark had offered to pay him handsomely, of course.

Nicole was late. Wasn't she always? Mark waited in the foyer, his hands clasped behind him, rocking back and forth on his heels, while she and her maid scurried about upstairs. He'd consulted his gold pocket watch at least three times before Nicole finally emerged at the top of the staircase. He glanced up at her and his heart thumped faster. She carried herself regally in a gray traveling gown with a silver pelisse and matching bonnet. She was dressed for him, for a journey they were about to take together. He had the oddest sense that he was taking her home.

Two footmen preceded her, carrying one large trunk between them. A blue and white embroidered satchel rested in the crook of her arm and her gray silk reticule dangled from her opposite wrist. She gave Mark a smug look as she marched down the steps and past him out the front door toward the waiting coach.

"I hired a carriage large enough for your maid to ride with us," Mark said, jogging to catch up with her. He hadn't brought his valet on this trip but he fully expected Nicole's maid to return with them.

"That won't be necessary. Jacqueline won't be joining us. Her sister is due with child any day now and she prefers to remain here."

"You aren't bringing a maid?" Mark blinked.

Nicole sighed. "No. I will have to hire a temporary one when we arrive in England."

"That won't be a problem." Mark busied himself opening the door to the coach, but his mind raced. They would be riding together alone the entire way to Calais. For some reason that made him vaguely uncertain. He'd planned to be a charming and jovial travel companion to Nicole and her maid. But he and Nicole alone would be . . . God. How would it be?

The footmen loaded Nicole's large trunk in the back of the coach next to Mark's much smaller one. Mark helped her up into the interior of the vehicle. She did not look at him. He climbed the steps and settled in the seat across from her. Nicole had placed her satchel on the floor beside her feet and her reticule on the seat next to her.

Before Mark could speak, an older female servant came hurrying out of the front door carrying a large basket. She bustled up to the coach and pushed the hamper inside onto the floor. She spoke in French. "*Madame*, I prepared food for you and *monsieur*. For your journey."

"Thank you, *Madame* Duval," Nicole replied in French. "That is kind of you."

"When do you think you will return, *Madame*?" the woman asked next, tears filling her eyes.

Nicole glanced uneasily at Mark. "I don't yet know. I will write and tell you as soon as I have an idea."

"We will miss you, *Madame*," the cook said finally.

"I will miss you too, *Madame* Duval." Nicole's face filled with tenderness for the servant.

The cook gave Mark an accusatory glare before backing away from the conveyance. The footmen pushed up the steps and closed and secured the door. Mark rapped twice on the top of the coach to signal the driver they were ready to leave. The coach took off at a steady clip down the long drive toward the road.

"I assume you informed the *comte* you are leaving?" Mark couldn't help but ask.

"I wrote him a note this morning," Nicole replied, without taking her attention from the scenery beyond the window.

Mark watched her carefully from beneath hooded eyes. The jolt of the carriage gently swayed her body. The slender column of her neck strained as she stared out into the lush countryside. Her nostrils flared slightly. She was clearly angry. She didn't like having to agree to his condition. Excellent, he thought dryly. Sex with an angry wife was certain to be a pleasure. Had he pushed her too far? Had he demanded too much? Only time would tell. The bigger part of him had already decided he'd worry about that later. For now, he'd got her to agree to come back to London with him. A smile touched his lips. Victory.

"How is your family?" she asked, plucking at the folds of her skirts, still not looking at him. She was getting back at him for his mention of the *comte*.

"If you mean my father's family, they are well. I was in Rome not a year ago."

"And your *mother*'s family?" She opened her reticule and rummaged around inside, still not meeting his gaze.

"From what I hear, they're doing well," he bit out. "My cousin John recently became betrothed. Or so the papers say."

"You hear about your family through the papers?" she asked, finally meeting his gaze.

"Does that surprise you?" He slumped down, one elbow braced against the coach's seat.

"I suppose it shouldn't." She set her reticule to the

side and began unbuttoning her gloves, clearly settling in for the long ride. "Who is the fortunate young lady?"

"John's *fiancée*?" he asked. "Fortunate because she'll be a future duchess?" He continued to watch her intently while pretending not to. He was suddenly jealous of her gloves, their proximity to her delicate fingers, her milky skin. The slow, deliberate way she was removing them made him shift in his seat.

"No. That's not what I meant at all." Her voice was sharp. "I meant fortunate because your cousin is a good man."

"Of course you did," Mark replied, a hint of sarcasm in his voice. "I forgot you know him." He shook his head and averted his gaze out the window. Best not to watch her until she finished with those damned gloves.

"And your uncle?" she continued.

"Not doing as well, I'm afraid. He has a disease of the lungs. The doctors are not hopeful."

"Was that in the papers too?" A hint of surprise registered in her voice.

"No. I keep up on the latest with his health."

"Have a spy on it, do you?" she asked.

He glanced over. The first glove came off.

"Something like that." Mark hated to admit he cared enough about his mother's family to check on them, but it was true. According to his sources, his uncle was on death's door. Mark intended to visit him soon, to say good-bye. It was the least he could do but he wasn't about to admit that to Nicole. He'd checked on her too. Whenever one of his colleagues had been in France over the years, he'd asked them for a full reporting of Nicole's coming and goings. They'd failed to mention the orphanage. Or the *comte*. He needed to have a talk with them.

"I'm sorry to hear that your uncle's health is failing." Nicole's second glove came off and she carefully folded them together and set them on the seat next to her.

"Thank you," he intoned.

"Does he still not publicly acknowledge you?" she asked next. Yet another dig.

"At my request, yes," he replied in as unaffected a tone as he could muster.

She shook her head and sighed. "I'll never understand why you don't tell your superiors at the Home Office about your family. Besides, they're blasted spies, you'd think they'd have figured it out by now."

Mark pulled off his hat and let it fall to the seat next to him. "Some of them know. The astute ones do."

Her eyebrows shot up. "Do they?"

"Yes, and they also know I have little to do with my family."

"And the others?" she prodded.

He shrugged one shoulder. "The others are politicians, not spies. All they care about is themselves. They can't imagine someone being related to a man like my uncle and not claiming it. It's been a simple task keeping the truth from them."

She shook her head slowly. "And you want to be one of them."

"I want to be in politics, yes. But for very different reasons. I want to actually make a bloody difference." The anger in his own voice surprised him. He drew a deep breath to temper it.

Nicole lifted her eyebrows as she plucked at the

buttons to her pelisse. "Yet you refuse to use the connection to further your career? You'd rather chase me down in France and cart me back to England than publicly admit you're the grandson of a duke."

"If I claimed my grandfather and uncle, I'd be no better than the lot of them," Mark bit out. He stared out the window, contemplating her words. She knew how to rile him. In fact, she was one of the few people on earth who *could* rile him. Once, in the middle of the night after they'd made passionate love and lay naked and tangled in each other's arms, he'd told her he wanted nothing to do with his English family.

It had been the beginning of the end of their relationship . . . because that was when her lies had begun. At least the outright ones.

"Who is your family?" she had asked, all wide-eyed and innocent, blinking at him. She'd pretended she didn't give a damn about money or titles or lineage. And the entire time, she'd known. She had bloody well known who his grandfather was and merely feigned ignorance, like the scheming, lying member of the *ton* she was.

Mark met her gaze and gave her a calculated smile. "Seems chasing you down in France and dragging you back to England has an added benefit that claiming my family doesn't."

"What's that?" She shrugged off her pelisse from both shoulders.

He gave her a lazy smile. "I get to make love to a beautiful woman tonight."

CHAPTER SIXTEEN

Nicole woke from her nap when the coach hit a nasty bump in the road. She started and blinked, taking a moment to recall where she was. Her vision adjusted to the closeness and darkness surrounding her. Oh, yes. She was in a coach with Mark, heading back to England for the first time in ten years. She stretched her arms in front of her and let out a long sigh. Life was unpredictable. If, a week ago, someone had told her this is where she'd be, she would have informed them they were mad. Yet here she was, reposing in a rented coach not a stone's throw from her ass of a husband, of all people.

"Is it nighttime then?" she asked in a sleepy voice, sitting up and stretching her arms above her head.

"Nearly," Mark replied.

She couldn't see his features, but his eyes glittered like a wild animal's in the profound darkness.

She didn't have to ask to know he hadn't fallen asleep. He'd been on the lookout for highwaymen or trouble along the roadside. She didn't want to admit to herself that knowing he was there had made her feel safe enough to fall asleep. She'd had such trouble sleeping night after night in the big bed in her French country house. In fact, as she yawned and stretched more, she realized this long day in the uncomfortable coach was some of the best sleep she'd got in an age. "How much longer to the inn?"

"An hour, perhaps."

They'd stopped at midday at a roadside inn for a break and to use the conveniences. They'd changed horses and shared a lunch from the large picnic basket Cook had provided. Mark had informed Nicole they'd be staying at an inn tonight and would make it to the ship at Calais by tomorrow night.

Soon after their journey had recommenced, Nicole had fallen asleep against the side of the coach, using her bundled-up pelisse for a pillow. She glanced down at herself. There was a cozy blanket tucked around her. Obviously Mark had got it from his trunk and covered her with it. She couldn't help but smile. He could be considerate when he wasn't being a domineering ass. It reminded her of the time when they'd been together and she'd taken ill with an awful head cold. He'd made her chicken broth and tucked her in bed, coming to check on her periodically and feel her head for fever. He'd even mixed up some potent-smelling herbs he'd claimed would cure her. She suspected there was a great deal of garlic involved. He'd had to convince her to drink the vile liquid, and damned if she didn't feel right as rain the next morning.

Nicole sat up, pushing the blanket down to her lap. She was famished of a sudden. She leaned over to rummage blindly in the basket for more of the bread, meat, and cheese they'd discovered there.

Mark assisted by opening the window to let in the moon light.

"Want some?" she offered as she pulled a linen napkin, the loaf of bread, and what remained of the cheese onto her lap.

"Yes, thank you."

"How long have I been asleep?" She handed him a clump of bread and a lump of cheese wrapped in a second napkin.

"Hours."

It was on the tip of her tongue to tell him about her trouble sleeping, but what good could such a story serve?

"Did you nap too?" she ventured.

"No."

"You must be exhausted."

"I learned a long time ago to live without much sleep."

"I wish I could learn," she mumbled.

"What's that?" His brow furrowed.

"Oh, nothing. I sometimes have trouble sleeping. That's all."

He stared thoughtfully out the window into the darkness. "Me too." He smiled a humorless smile. "I don't think I've slept through an entire night since . . ."

She watched him carefully. "Since?"

He shook his head. "It doesn't matter." He turned to face her. "The *Duchesse de Frontenac* tells me you spend your time at an orphanage. Is that true?"

Nicole swallowed. Why had Louisa told him that?

What else had her friend told him? "I spend *some* of my time at the orphanage, yes."

"Why?"

She smiled and laid her head against the seat, closing her eyes. "I happen to like children."

"I never knew that." His voice was quiet, tender.

She straightened and concentrated on her meal. "I was much younger when we were together."

"She also said you're lonely. Is that true?"

A wave of anger rolled through her. Why had Louisa told him *that*? Nicole hadn't ever shared that news with her friend. Was it that obvious? She sighed and closed her eyes briefly. "I don't know."

"Even with the *comte* by your side?" Mark prodded.

"Let's not talk about the *comte*." She'd been thinking about Henri today during the long ride, before she'd fallen asleep. She'd written him a short letter that morning, telling him she was going back to England temporarily. She'd asked Jacqueline to ensure he received it. Of course Nicole hadn't mentioned the fact that she hoped to return *enceinte*. That would be a discussion for another time.

Henri had told her he loved her. He was a good man. The type of man she should have been happy to marry once. But she was already married and her heart did not belong to Henri. Henri was a dear friend. He'd been there for her during some dark days, but she could never return his affection the way he wanted her to. It was best that she'd left. She'd been relying on him too much of late. It wasn't fair to him.

"Very well, then," Mark replied, snapping her out of her reverie. "What would you like to talk about?"

She glanced over at him. His long legs were stretched out on either side of hers, the basket resting between them. His hair was slightly rumpled, but as tempting to the touch as ever, and he had an indecipherable look on his face.

"Why don't we discuss why you stubbornly refuse to let anyone know your grandfather was a duke and your uncle is one now?" she asked.

His body tensed. He clenched his jaw and turned his head to stare out the window at the shadowed trees along the roadside. "No. Next topic."

Why was he so stubborn? How could she convince him to tell her about his family? She contemplated the matter for a few moments while she chewed and swallowed a bite of bread and cheese. Then she snapped her fingers. "You continue to ask me about Henri, yet you aren't forthcoming about your family. How about for every question you answer about your family, I will answer one about Henri? Up to, say, three questions each?"

Mark batted his lashes at her. "*Henri*? His name's *Henri*?"

"Yes. There. That's one answer. Now you must answer a question of mine."

Mark groaned, laid his head back against the seat, and closed his eyes. "Fine."

"I already asked it. Why are you so stubborn that you won't use your grandfather's name? Surely it would assist you in your political career."

Mark poked his tongue into the side of his cheek. "Becoming the Secretary of the Home Office has nothing to do with my family."

"But it could," she persisted. "How do you know it might not help you secure the position?"

Mark rubbed his knuckles across his forehead and groaned again. "Fine. If you must know, I . . . promised my father I would never use my mother's familial connections to get ahead."

Nicole sucked in her breath. "Why did he ask that of you?"

Mark cocked his head to the side. "I believe it's *my* turn to ask a question."

Nicole sighed impatiently. "Very well. Go ahead."

"Do you love Henri?"

She narrowed her eyes on Mark. "You ask if I love him, not if I've *made* love to him?"

"That's a question and I'm the one asking at the moment." His voice had an edge to it.

"Fine. No, I don't love Henri. Not that way."

He lifted his head to look at her. Their gazes met. "And have you made love to him?"

She wagged a finger at him. "Ah, ah, ah, my turn to ask."

"I already know what you're going to ask . . . why did I make that promise to my father?"

"Yes, please answer," she replied, feeling smug.

Mark took a long deep breath. "My father was dying. I was fifteen."

"He asked you on his deathbed?" Her eyes filled with unexpected tears.

Mark clenched his jaw and looked out the window into the darkness. "Yes. My mother's family detested my father. They never accepted him and they barely accepted me."

Nicole gasped. "That can't be true." She covered her mouth with her hand, tears still burning her eyes.

"It's entirely true, I assure you. It's one of many reasons I have little use for the aristocracy. They're a lot of vultures who have no regard for the true meaning of love and family."

She took a deep, fortifying breath. *Merde.* She'd given him another opportunity to take a dig at her. "But why? Why did he ask it of you?"

Mark's eyes lost their focus. He was obviously remembering. "My father was proud. He believed a man should make his own way in the world, forge his own path. He disliked most Englishmen because they rely too heavily on their family names and fortunes. He warned me against it my entire childhood."

She cleared her throat. "And your promise to your father is worth more to you than your promotion?"

Mark's teeth flashed in his smile. "I have every intention of getting my promotion. I've got all of them to date without mentioning the Duke of Colchester once, and I intend to get this one the same way. On my own merit."

She ground her teeth. "But why don't you—"

This time he wagged a finger at her. "It's *my* turn to ask a question."

She sighed and nodded. "Very well. You want to know if I've been with Henri. But before I answer, think long and hard about whether you're going to be willing to tell me whom *you've* been with. What if that's *my* third question?"

He cocked his head to the side and gave her a look of sheer disbelief. "Are you serious?"

"Yes, quite. Think about it. Do you still want to know?"

"Are you planning to ask me whom I've been with?" he asked, still blinking in disbelief.

"I might. Be warned." She nodded vigorously, but her heart was pounding out of her chest. She didn't at all want to ask him whom he'd been with.

"Very well. Yes, I still want to know," he barked.

"Fine, but I've already told you, so you're wasting a question. No, I've never gone to bed with Henri." Was it her imagination or did Mark's shoulders relax a bit?

He propped one arm against the coach wall and regarded her down the length of his nose. "You want to know whom I've been with?" His tone was lazy.

"No," she said too quickly, lifting her chin and averting her eyes.

"No?" His voice held a note of surprise.

"That's right. That's not my question." She leaned to deposit the rest of the bread and cheese back into the basket.

"What is your question then?" He crossed his arms over his chest and slid further down in his seat, his legs encaging hers.

She shook her head. "I . . . I want to save my third question. For another time."

The sides of his firm lips quirked upward into a semblance of a grin. "That wasn't part of the agreement."

She raised her nose in the air. "I never said we had to ask all three of our questions now."

Mark sighed and shrugged. "Very well. Save your question then."

The coach rumbled to a stop and Mark drew open the curtains to look outside. "We're here."

Nicole nodded and leaned out the window to see a homey little whitewashed inn sitting in a circle of fat green hedges. The windows were open, candlelight danced inside, and the divine smell of some sort of stew cooking wafted from the place. After an entire day on the road, the inn looked like heaven. Even as an uncertain thrill shuddered through her, she tried not to think about the fact that she'd be sharing a room with Mark tonight. Was she ready? Would she ever be?

Mark pushed open the door and jumped to the ground. He helped Nicole down, grabbing her waist and swinging her to the ground.

The feel of his fingers made her shiver. He drew his hands away slowly. She swallowed and forced herself to turn and look up at the façade of the cozy inn. The coachman promised to ensure their trunks were brought to their room as he led the horses away.

They entered the inn together. Nicole waited near the windows, peering out into the darkness, while Mark spoke to the proprietor. Money changed hands and Mark was given a key. He turned to Nicole and gestured to a narrow flight of stairs with a well-worn bannister. "Shall we?"

Swallowing a fresh surge of trepidation, Nicole climbed the steps ahead of him. When they came to the first door at the beginning of the corridor, Mark slid the key into the lock, turned it, and opened the door.

"So, just the one room then?" she asked, her heart hammering.

He quirked a brow. "It's customary for married couples to share a bedchamber, or have you forgotten?"

Not for a second.

He allowed her to enter first. It was a simple room, but clean and well kept. A large feather bed dominated the center. Two small wooden chairs and an even smaller table sat in one corner. A wardrobe rested against the opposite wall.

Nicole stared at the bed, her heart still thumping like a hare's foot in her chest.

A knock sounded on the door and she jumped.

"Are you all right?" Mark asked as he made to open the door.

"Yes, I . . . I think I am."

The strapping coachman was at the door with Nicole's trunk. One of the lads from the stable was with him carrying Mark's trunk. The men placed the trunks against the wall nearest the door and Mark tossed each of them a coin. They grinned and hied themselves off.

Mark turned to Nicole. "I'll go down and get a tankard of ale, to allow you privacy to undress."

Nicole nodded, but as he made to open the door she said, "Wait. I'm . . . going to need . . . some help."

He hesitated. His Adam's apple worked in his throat. "Of course."

She took a long, deep breath and turned her back to present him with the buttons of her gown. "All you need do is unbutton them and loosen my stays. Do you think you can do that?" *Merde.* She wanted to kick herself for that last question. He knew *precisely* how to do that.

"I think I can remember." His voice held a note of sarcasm.

He started at her neck. His hands were warm and gentle. She trembled and bit her lip. At least he couldn't see her face. She closed her eyes. His skin against hers, even the barest hint of a touch, sent waves of pleasure through her.

His fingers took their time, slowly moving down her back, brushing her bare skin each time a new button popped free. This was torture. She struggled not to lean into his touch. Was he doing this on purpose? Jacqueline did it every day, quick and efficient. Perhaps he was slow because he was unpracticed? That thought sustained Nicole.

When the last button popped free, Nicole couldn't contain her sigh of relief. "Now my stays," she whispered.

"With pleasure." His warm breath brushed against the back of her neck.

The stays were more difficult. They were laced tightly in a crisscross fashion. It was painstakingly slow work to pull them loose, one by one. His fingers tugged first left, then right. As the laces loosened, Nicole should have been able to breathe more freely. Instead, she held her breath, her lungs aching. His fingers stroked her bare skin and she clenched her jaw, trying not to enjoy the feel of his hands slowly undressing her. Trying not to remember the nights they'd done this as a happily married couple, falling into each other's arms because they couldn't keep their hands off each other.

Finally, the stays were loosened. Mark's touch fell away. "Anything else you need, my lady?" he asked, his breath still a hot brush against the vulnerable skin on the back of her neck.

"No . . . no." Her voice quavered and she hated it. "That's quite enough. Th . . . thank you."

"Very well. I'll just go downstairs until—"

She swung around to face him, her heart hammering. "Mark?" Her voice was breathless.

"Yes?"

She cleared her throat. "I need time. To get to know you again. I cannot . . . couple with someone I don't remember. I want to wait before we . . ." She could not force the words past her lips. She desperately hoped he understood what she meant without her having to say it outright.

Mark's face fell. "I see."

"I hope you understand," she added, trying to muster a smile.

He quickly schooled his flash of disappointment into impassivity. "You're the one who wants the baby, or need I remind you?"

"I know." She nodded, her breath coming in short little pants.

"And there is only so long we intend to be in each other's company," he pointed out.

Another nod. "I know."

He studied her for a moment as though weighing whether her reticence was genuine, before he gave a soft sigh. "Very well. It's your choice. I will sleep in a hammock."

"Is there a hammock?" She glanced around the room.

"There's always a hammock. I'll find one." He left the room and the door slammed behind him.

Nicole watched him go and a relieved smile spread across her face. She could breathe easier. Now that she had time to contemplate it, she realized she'd managed to get a bit of her own back. He'd been the one to make the ridiculous demand that they make love, but she would be the one to decide when.

She'd told him she needed time, and that was true, but she was petrified that she'd never be ready. The trip to London would only take a few days. Would she be ready by then?

He was right. She was the one who wanted the baby. She was the one who wanted the sex. Now she was the one delaying it? It made no sense, but she needed time to come to terms with the fact that they would be intimate again. Time to steel herself against the emotions that would inevitably be stirred by such an intimate act.

Did she even remember how to go about it? What if she forgot everything about the act and made a fool of herself? Things were different now. Mark wasn't her loving husband as he had been the last time they'd been together. He was a stranger. A stranger who hated her, or at least didn't care. He was using her to further his political ambitions. Their coupling couldn't possibly be the same.

That frightened her the most.

Mark stood on the opposite side of the door he'd just shut behind him. He scrubbed his fingers through his hair. Damn it. He should have known she'd find a way to get a little of her own back. She had, hadn't she? He'd been hard half the day thinking about their night together. Just now when he'd been slowly undressing her, he'd been so damned hard, it had been painful. Then she'd gone and slammed the door on that by telling him she needed to get used to the idea of sharing his bed again?

Infuriating woman. Sex had been her idea, not his. He'd been prepared to never touch her again. She'd been the one to ask for a child.

He strode down the corridor and descended the stairs to the main room. The innkeeper was bound to have a hammock. He'd pay him for it and take it with him on the ship. How he would explain his need for a hammock while sharing a room with his own *wife* was another matter entirely.

An hour later, after procuring both a hammock and two tankards of ale, Mark returned to the room. He rapped once on the door before pushing it open. Nicole was snuggled up in the middle of the downy bed.

She lifted her head and nodded toward the tangle of rope bundled under his arm. "You found your hammock?" The look of relief on her face irritated him.

"I did." He let the thing drop and pulled the edge of it up to hang on a hook from one of the wooden beams that ran along the ceiling. He hung the other side from a beam across the room, shucked his boots and overcoat, and ripped off his cravat. He grabbed a spare pillow from the edge of the bed where she'd obviously left it for him, blew out the only candle in the room, and climbed into the hammock.

"Bonne nuit," came Nicole's soft voice from the bed. Was it his imagination or did she sound slightly smug?

"Good night," he grumbled, punching the pillow savagely with his fist. Score one for his infuriating wife.

CHAPTER SEVENTEEN

The next morning, Nicole awoke to an empty bedchamber. The hammock was gone and so was Mark and his trunk. She'd overslept. She winced. Mark was probably standing outside by the coach, tapping his boot on the ground and consulting his timepiece.

Nicole tossed on her traveling gown and flagged down one of the maids in the hall to help with her stays and buttons. She pulled on her pelisse and gloves and hurried downstairs to find Mark sitting at one of the tables in the great room, eating breakfast.

"Ah, there you are, Mrs. Grimaldi," he said with a bright smile on his face.

She stopped short and crossed her arms over her chest. "I thought you'd be waiting."

"And so I am. Would you like some breakfast before we leave?"

"Yes." She picked up her skirts to climb over the bench in front of the table where Mark sat.

Mark ordered her breakfast and asked the innkeeper to fetch the coachman to retrieve Nicole's trunk. She ate quickly, only too aware of Mark watching her, a smug smile on his face.

"Why are you staring at me like that?" she finally asked after she'd taken a bite of eggs.

"Am I staring?" he asked lazily, his chin resting on his propped-up hand.

"I'd say so," she retorted.

"You're quite beautiful, Nicole."

The eggs slid down her throat. What? Had he actually just said that? It was almost as if he was flirting. If he was going to *flirt* with her, she wasn't going to be able to withstand it. She'd be back in his bed in no time. The man could be downright charming when he chose to be.

Not half an hour later, they were ensconced in the coach. They'd purchased more bread and cheese from the innkeeper and Nicole had refilled the basket. The horses were hitched, the trunks had been packed in the back, and the coach took off at a steady clip toward Calais.

The morning was spent mostly in silence. They spoke only of things that did not bring up memories. The weather, their meals. Nicole carefully avoided any fraught subjects such as Mark's family and, oh, their failed marriage.

"What are your plans?" she finally asked him after they'd stopped for lunch and to change out the horses. They nibbled on the contents of the basket again.

"Plans?" Mark met her gaze and quirked a brow.

"Yes, for your new position as Home Secretary."

His face registered surprise, as if he hadn't expected her to ask such a thing. Good. She liked to keep him guessing. Being predictable was ever so dull. "Knowing you, I'm certain you have large and involved plans."

The hint of a smile passed across his lips. "I do."

"And?" she prompted. "What are they?"

He studied her as if trying to determine whether she truly wanted to hear about his plans. He must have decided she was serious because he took a deep breath and said, "I intend to implement a police force in London."

Nicole couldn't help her tiny gasp of surprise. "A police force?" she echoed.

"Yes. The city is sorely in need of one. It should start in London and eventually work its way throughout the country."

Nicole nodded. He never failed to impress her. "I see." She took a bite of sweet cheese.

"What do you think?" he asked. He'd surprised *her* this time. Did he truly care about her opinion on the matter?

"I think it's high time. Working with the runners taught me how little recourse people have when they're victims of crime. Especially the poor."

"I agree." Mark nodded. "The runners have been stretched impossibly thin. And while there are guards at the gates into town, a group of men whose sole job it is to enforce law and order is greatly needed."

"Only men?" She couldn't help her sardonic smile.

He arched a brow in her direction. "It'll be difficult enough to secure the funding from the government without my telling them that women will be a part of it."

"I was jesting," Nicole replied, nibbling on a bit of bread this time. "Secure your funding first. Women can be the future detectives. We're more clever anyhow."

Mark shook his head at her. He knew she was trying to bait him.

"I do think it's a brilliant idea, Mark," she said softly after she'd swallowed the bread. "Bow Street works on bounties. A paid police force will have the means to investigate a host of other crimes that go unheeded today."

"Precisely," Mark replied. "But it won't be easy to convince Parliament."

She gave him a tentative smile. "If anyone can do it, it's you." She glanced away. Why did those words seem so intimate?

"Thank you," he replied, sounding pleased.

"If you need any help from a clever woman, don't hesitate to ask." She winked at him, restoring the light mood.

Mark's smile was bright. "I'll keep that in mind, my lady."

Three days later, they arrived in London. They'd spent their time while traveling to Calais and on the packet to England discussing the particulars of the plan for the police force. Nicole had pointed out a few improvements on his ideas and he'd readily agreed with her. To her surprise, he asked her opinion on several details and seemed to listen intently to her answers, asking follow-up questions and nodding when she made a particularly salient point. The time passed quickly and pleasantly. After Nicole's declaration at the inn, there had been no more awkward moments spent wondering whether they would go to bed together. Mark slept in the hammock and Nicole took the bed. The one night they spent in an inn on their way between Dover and London, Mark had slept on a mattress bundle on the floor, clearly willing to allow her to make the choice as to when and if they'd spend the night together.

Nicole hadn't asked after their accommodations here in London. When they'd been married before, they'd lived in a modest flat above a shop in Kingshead. That was what they could afford on the wages of a corporal. Mark had steadfastly refused any help from Nicole's wealthy family to secure better lodgings and she'd been only too happy to agree with him. So, it was surprising when the coach they'd rented in Dover pulled to a stop in front of one of the finest town houses in Mayfair.

"Yours?" she asked, bewildered as she stared up at the grand four-story whitewashed stone building. The front door was lacquered in black and a large brass lion's head knocker dominated the center of it.

"Ours," he intoned, tilting his head to the side. "In case you're wondering, I haven't taken a shilling from my family."

"I never thought it," she replied, her tone still amazed as she stared up at the grand mansion.

Mark had certainly done well for himself. She'd always known he would, but to see this magnificent building and know he'd purchased it himself without any assistance from his family was impressive, indeed. She couldn't wait to get inside and discover what sort of furnishings he'd chosen. It was a silly thought, but she couldn't help herself.

The door was opened by a friendly, efficient-looking butler who introduced himself as Abbott. Nicole stepped inside and turned in a wide circle to take in the magnificent foyer. The home was even more impressive than she'd expected. Marble covered every bit of the floor and walls, with large columns of it holding up the grand staircase, which was also made of the stuff. The entry was sparsely but finely decorated in hues of whites and grays and blues. A Chippendale desk graced the foyer, solid gold candlesticks and a simple gold clock resting upon it. Nothing here was fussy. Just like Mark. No ormolu or knickknacks for him. It was pristinely clean and sparkling with a hint of lemon wax in the air.

She barely had time to hand Abbott her bonnet and pelisse before she found herself whisked up the sweeping staircase by a duo of giggling housemaids—Louise and Susanna, she soon discovered. The upstairs corridor was spare and neat as a pin too. A costly looking painting rested on one wall, but otherwise there were no adornments. While the maids bustled ahead, Nicole paused before the painting. It depicted a man facing away from the artist, looking across an empty field. Something about it made Nicole melancholy. She shook her head. She was just missing home. Cook and the butler. She sighed. The truth was, no one in France was her real family. She had more real family in this town (in this house) than she had spent time with in all her years in France. Which was why she wanted a baby.

Her heart ached at the thought of a soft warm bundle cuddled against her breast. She certainly wasn't doing a good job of getting to it by refusing Mark her bed. It was his condition, though. That was it. She couldn't hop back into bed with him as if nothing had happened the last ten years. She needed time to get to know him. Remember him. Come to terms with the fact that they would be sharing such intimacies again. They didn't even like each other. Let alone love each other. That was a great deal to contemplate.

She took a breath as the housemaids opened one of the doors and ushered her into a magnificent bedchamber.

"It's been waiting for ye, Mrs. Grimaldi, all these years," Louise said, a giggle escaping her lips. "The general asked us to keep it pristine for ye."

"It's been empty all these years?" Nicole couldn't keep herself from asking before blushing for what must have been the dozenth time since Mark had reentered her life.

"Of course," Susanna chimed in.

Nicole blinked. *That* was surprising news. How long had he lived here? He'd kept up a room for a wife who until recently he'd had no intention of seeing again? Nicole briefly wondered what his mistresses thought of that. Or did he not show them this room? The thought of Mark's lovers made her stomach twist in knots. On one hand, she desperately wanted to know, but on the other, much stronger hand, she couldn't bear to hear it. It would make her ill. "Did he tell you I'd be coming back with him?" she asked the maids.

"Yes, madame." They nodded vigorously. "That's why we aired out the space and added the flowers."

Nicole glanced over to see that the windows were both wide open to allow light and fresh air into the room. A huge vase of white roses sat on the silver table next to the bed. She shook her head. Of course Mark had been confident enough when he left to tell his servants she'd be back with him. Did she expect anything different of him? The man's middle name was arrogant.

She spun in a circle to take in the bedchamber. It was decorated in pale lavender, white, and silver. Her favorite colors, but he couldn't possibly have known that, and they certainly hadn't lived here the last time they'd been together. It had to be a coincidence. She couldn't bring herself to ask the housemaids. They were probably already confused by the state of affairs between their master and mistress as it was. She didn't want to contribute to any gossip below stairs.

The bed was raised on a dais, a four-poster dark cherry piece that was understated but obviously costly. It was precisely the type of bed she would pick for herself. In addition to a large silver-painted wooden wardrobe, and a cozy sitting area with two lavender-upholstered chairs and a small bookcase filled with books, the room also boasted a painting that looked suspiciously like a Lawrence and a gorgeous silver-painted dressing table with a small lavender tufted stool. Silver grooming items sat atop the table, including a hairbrush, a rouge pot, and a glass vial for perfume.

Mark had actually decorated this room for . . . her. They'd said a wife and that was her. She still couldn't comprehend either the fact that it was hers, or the fact that it was so tastefully decorated. Had Mark planned to find her one day after all? No. That couldn't be. It was unthinkable.

There was a knock at the door and the housemaids

scurried over to open it. Two footmen marched in with Nicole's trunk, their arms straining with the weight.

"Over here, please." She quickly guided them to a large space against the wall near the wardrobe. It would be more convenient for the maids to unpack it there.

"Merci," she said to the footmen before remembering where she was. She laughed softly to herself. "I mean, thank you."

The two young men blushed, bowed, and rushed off.

"They're smitten with ye, missus," Susanna said, giggling.

"What?" Nicole's eyes widened. She pressed a hand to her chest. "Them? With me?"

"Yes, I heard them when they saw ye getting out o' the coach. 'Oy, but who knew the stone man would have such a mighty fine-lookin' wife?' they said."

Louise nodded and giggled again too. "It's true. They both said it."

Nicole shook her head. It was pure silliness to think such young men would be enamored of her, but it did soothe her confidence. Did Mark think she was "mighty fine-lookin'?" She certainly thought he was, which made it more difficult to contemplate hopping into bed with him. If he'd become old and scarred and ugly over the years, she might be able to close her eyes and get it over with, but the man made her knees weak even still. Just like he had the night they met . . .

When she saw him again, she sucked in her breath. There he was, her soldier from the mews, standing near the refreshment table, surrounded by a group of her friends. For some reason she'd been startled to see him. He should have been a figment of her imagination, conjured from thin air and her vivid thoughts of what a truly handsome dashing young man would look like. But there he was again in the flesh. His hair was just as dark and ruffled as it had been outside. His eyes seemed darker when countered with the bright light of the ballroom. He was even more handsome than her memory.

He glanced over at her and raised his glass in silent salute. She blushed and turned away. So he did recognize her. At first she'd wondered how well he'd been able to see her outside. Now she had her answer. Soon she would have another answer . . . to the question he'd refused.

"Mother?" she asked, turning toward the older woman next to her. "Mother, who is that?" She nodded across the ballroom to the group he was in. He'd returned his attention to the many young women who were vying for it. Suddenly, Nicole was inexplicably jealous of the other girls.

"Who?" Mother said, scanning the room. She pushed a blond-gray curl away from her forehead.

"The soldier in the middle of that group over there. The one Lady Elizabeth is standing next to."

Mother narrowed her blue eyes. "I've no idea. No one of importance, I daresay." Mother turned away to speak with friends.

Not to be deterred, Nicole dodged the Marquess of Tinsley's small entourage and made her way to the other side of the ballroom where her grandmother held court. She wiggled into the middle of Grandmama's circle.

"Ah, Nicole, darling, there you are. Aren't you a vision?" Grandmama dropped her voice to a whisper. "Has the marquess asked you to dance?"

"Not yet, Grandmama." She left out the part of how she hadn't allowed him to see her long enough to ask her to dance. That would only worry the older woman.

"Well, off with you then. He's not likely to find you over here with all of these decrepit old things. Go, enjoy yourself with the youngsters."

"I will, Grandmama, I promise, but I came to ask you something first."

"What is it, dear?" her grandmother asked, turning her purple-silk-turbaned head in Nicole's direction.

"Who is that man standing in the group near the refreshment table? The soldier?"

Grandmama narrowed her eyes and squinted across the room. She plucked her golden-handled eyeglass from her bosom and squinted through it too. "Oh, that's Corporal Grimaldi."

Grimaldi? Nicole blinked. The name surprised her.

"Doesn't sound very English, does it?" Grandmama sighed.

"No."

"His father's Italian. Just met the lad tonight. Clever young man." She gazed after the soldier with a fond smile.

Nicole pursed her lips. "Hmm. Do you know anything else about him?"

Grandmama shifted her attention from the handsome corporal and gave Nicole a mock-stern stare. "I'm afraid not. Now off with you. You're keeping the marquess waiting."

Reluctantly, Nicole turned back to the other side of

the ballroom. She danced with the marquess as she was bid, but mostly because she'd never hear the end of it if she did not have at least one dance to speak of later when her mother and grandmother asked. The entire time they waltzed, she tried not to stare at the portly man's wet bottom lip but she couldn't seem to help it. It was like looking at a carriage accident. One didn't want to see anything truly heinous but one couldn't help but glance from time to time.

After the dance ended, the marquess deposited her back on the sidelines. She'd long ago learned that the best way to dodge his further advances was to send him in search of a refreshment and then become scarce.

"Would you care for a glass of punch?" the marquess asked right on cue.

"Oh, yes, please. That would be lovely." No it wouldn't. Punch was never lovely. Unless it was spiked with wine, which, sadly, tonight it was not, but the marquess seemed pleased with her when she said such inane things. She smiled at him and watched him waddle off. As soon as he disappeared into the crowd, she grabbed her skirts, turned . . . and ran smack into a wall. Or it seemed like a wall, but it turned out to be Corporal Grimaldi's chest.

"Enjoying yourself?" his deep smooth voice asked from above while she blinked and rubbed her smarting nose.

Corporal Grimaldi grinned down at her. In addition to the wideness of his shoulders and the darkness of his eyes, she was starkly aware of the fact that he was nearly a foot taller than she was. He also looked like a dream in his red coat and form-fitting white breeches. "Ah, it's you, Corporal Grimaldi," she said, smiling at him. "My apologies for running into you, but at least you've given me a chance to thank you properly."

"My fault entirely," he said with a bow. "I was standing far too close. You've learned my name, I see."

"I have." She smiled up at him.

"And I have learned that you are Lady Nicole Huntington, granddaughter of the dowager Countess of Whitby and daughter of the late earl."

"Yes," she admitted. "But then you already knew that."

"I didn't know your given name."

She glanced around, worried that the marquess might return and find her if they didn't leave the area quickly. "Come and take a walk around the room with me?"

One dark eyebrow arched. "Won't it cause talk?"

"It might, but if I stay here I'm in danger of having to drink the punch the Marquess of Tinsley is fetching for me, and I find that more tedious than talk."

"We can't have that," the corporal said with a laugh.

"No, we can't. Because the punch is bad and so is the company."

They strolled toward the French doors that led out to the balcony, but didn't go outside. Instead, Nicole propped her back against the wall next to the doors and surveyed the room. Mark joined her.

"If you dislike the marquess so much, why do you dance with him?" Mark asked.

"Because my mother and grandmama bid me to."

"You can't tell them no?"

She withheld a snort. "You don't know my grandmama. It's much easier to do what she asks than argue the point with her."

"A formidable woman, your grandmother?"

"Yes, quite formidable. She was the one who told me your name, however."

"Really?" He arched his brow again. "I'm surprised she remembered me."

"Oh, yes. You made an impression, Corporal. Grand-mama tells me you're Italian."

"Half Italian." He tugged at the throat of his uniform.

She found it difficult not to stare at the sharp-edged line of his jaw. "So, your mother is English?"

"Yes."

"What was her family name—"

"I'm much more interested in why a young woman like yourself decided to chase down a rogue in the mews." He met her eyes again and smiled disarmingly. "Why don't you tell me that story instead?"

She sighed. "I've never been good at sitting still and doing what I'm told, I'm afraid. I'm always watching people, noticing things."

"Like what?"

She gave a cursory glance around the room. "Like how Sir Winstead has a handkerchief sticking out of his pocket with lip paint on it that is decidedly not the same color as his wife's. Lady Hidemore is desperately try-ing not to stare at Lord Pengree, who is with his new wife after tossing over Lady Hidemore last Season, and Lord Markham is fighting off a case of hives, which happens each time he loses too much whilst gambling, and he has just come from the study where gambling is no doubt in full swing."

The corporal glanced around. Even though he obviously didn't know the people she was speaking of, he narrowed his eyes and regarded her down the length of his nose with a newfound respect. "Did anyone ever tell you, you would make a fine spy?"

"Actually, I—"

Her words were lost as Grandmama came sweeping up to them. "Corporal Grimaldi," the older woman said. "It's good to see you. There's someone I think you should meet. Lord Warren, the head of the Home Office, is here and he's asked about you."

Corporal Grimaldi's eyes widened with obvious interest. "I've been trying to catch the ear of Lord Warren for weeks," he whispered, looking at Nicole with obvious regret. She nodded and said, "Go on then," not willing either to keep him from meeting Lord Warren or to defy her grandmother. Grandmama was obviously trying to free Nicole's time in favor of the Marquess of Tinsley, who was even now headed her way with a half-full glass of no doubt lukewarm punch.

"Until we meet again, Corporal," Nicole said with a bright smile, before darting through the crowd to escape the marquess.

Another knock scattered Nicole's thoughts and her memories faded, but this time the knock was from a door in the sidewall of her gorgeous new bedchamber. "Come in," she called.

The door opened and Mark strolled in. He'd changed from his traveling clothes into buckskin breeches and a blue waistcoat. The skintight breeches left little to the imagination. Nicole glanced away.

The maids, who had been unpacking Nicole's trunk, both giggled and rushed off through the main door to the corridor.

"How are you settling in?" Mark strolled to the vase of flowers and plucked off a dead leaf.

"It's a lovely room," Nicole murmured.

"I'd hoped you'd like it."

"Louise and Susanna said you'd told them I'd return with you."

He turned to face her. His grin was wicked. "Confidence never hurt anyone."

"Least of all you." She couldn't help smiling a little. She gestured to the painting on the wall. "Is that Lawrence?"

"Of course not. I'm a spymaster, not the prince."

Nicole walked up to the painting and studied it. "It looks quite a bit like a Lawrence." The one she'd told him years ago was her favorite, actually.

"I don't know what you're talking about," he said, averting his gaze when she glanced over her shoulder at him. "I don't know much about art. I found that at a market and decided it would match the room."

She decided to let it go for the moment. She gestured to the door he'd come through. "Is that your room?"

"Yes."

She swallowed. "And you want me to stay . . . here? Next door?" She gestured to her room.

"It is customary for a husband and wife to have adjoining rooms, or have you forgotten that during your time in France?"

"I hadn't forgotten," she managed to force past her suddenly dry lips.

"It's especially convenient for a husband and wife who intend to create a child," he added with a sly grin.

All she could do was nod.

"Do you like the flowers?" He turned to regard the vase again.

"White roses are my favorite," she said softly, watching him caress a petal with a single fingertip. She couldn't help but remember the last time he'd purchased white roses for her. She swallowed hard.

"Are they?" He sounded as nonchalant as she'd ever heard.

She narrowed her eyes on him. It couldn't possibly be a coincidence that all of these things, her favorite things, were gathered here in this room. What in heaven's name did it mean that he'd gone to all this trouble to prepare them for her? She wasn't about to ask him. He'd simply deny they'd been chosen with purpose.

This was their first night in London and she'd all but told him this was the night they would make love again. Was she ready? She would have to be. She wanted a child, after all, and delaying the means by which to get one any longer was only foolish.

Mark took a step toward her, grasped her hand, and bowed over it, lightly kissing the delicate skin. "I'll leave you to rest and prepare for an evening out. We are going to a dinner party at Lord Allen's house. It's time for you to begin playing the role of my loving wife."

CHAPTER EIGHTEEN

Everything was riding on this dinner party. Before leaving for France, Mark promised Lord Allen he would be here tonight. He'd barely made it back in time. If Nicole had hesitated just one day longer, he would have missed it. Lord Tottenham would be here as well, and he'd be watching Mark closely to size him up as a potential candidate for Secretary of the Home Office.

Mark glanced across the coach at Nicole, who reposed in serene silence. She was dressed in a gown of costly peacock-blue silk with lace trim and her glorious hair was piled atop her head. Long white gloves and a beaded reticule completed her ensemble. She looked more like a goddess than a mortal woman. She was the perfect companion tonight; a member of London's elite *haute ton*, she knew exactly how to comport herself at such events. She would never be an embarrassment to him. On the contrary, her being the daughter of an earl would be nothing but advantageous to Mark's cause, although he had no intention of telling Tottenham who her family was.

Their coach pulled to a stop in front of an imposing town house not far from theirs. The footmen let down the stairs and Mark alighted, then turned to help Nicole. When he lifted her, his hands around her waist, the scent of her lavender perfume filled his nostrils. He set her on the ground next to him, his grasp lingering to steady her. She glanced up at him and smiled, and white-hot heat shot straight to his groin. He clenched his jaw. Would they make love tonight? He was more than willing, but after his first failed attempt on the journey to England, he wasn't about to push her. His pride was too great to be rebuked again. She would need to give him some sign that she was ready.

Her gaze lingered on his mouth. "Ready?" she asked. The question emerged low and throaty.

He widened his eyes, his heart hammering. Surely, she didn't mean . . .

"To go in to the party," she clarified, obviously responding to the confused look on his face.

He shook away the momentary pang of lust. "I've been ready for this for years. Are *you* ready?"

"I might be slightly rusty on the proper decorum at an English dinner party." Her smile turned rueful. "But it's certain to come back to me quickly."

He returned her smile. She certainly looked the part. She'd always been at home among these people. She was the perfect wife for a man with political aspirations.

Lady Nicole's grandmother's ballroom was bright and raucous. The dance floor was filled with couples dancing, the refreshment table overflowed with sweets and drinks, and the noise and temperature rose along with the number of drinks consumed by the crowd. It was downright stifling in the enormous room.

Mark waited for a break in the crowd before darting over to stand next to Lady Nicole on the sidelines of the dancing. She had a smile pinned sweetly to her face, but he could tell she was fantastically bored. Her eyes weren't sparkling. The smile hadn't reached them.

He'd never met anyone like her. She was irreverent about the aristocracy. She seemed to scoff at a marquess and she clearly had a sense of both humor and adventure. He'd never met a delicate young miss who was so forthright. Nor one who would chase down a thief in the mews while wearing her ball gown.

He leaned down to whisper in her ear. "Having fun?"

Her smile widened when she realized it was him, but she kept her gaze pinned on the crowd. "Loads of it," she drawled.

"It's hot in here," he said next.

"Yes." Her smile reached her eyes now. "I'd adore a stroll in the gardens."

Ah, she'd said precisely what he hoped she would. "If you're not worried about talk, then meet me there in ten minutes."

He left, confident she would meet him, but also slightly apprehensive. If she was as adventurous as she seemed, she would be there. If she wasn't, he'd probably leave after waiting a few minutes, and never see her again.

He waited an excruciating fifteen minutes by the count of his pocket watch before she arrived. She'd sneaked around the side of the house from the other end and met him under the rose arbor. The moonlight cast a glow on the glossy rosebushes and neat hedges that surrounded them. The sweet smell of jasmine floated on the night air.

"I did a sweep before I came. No one is out here but us," she informed him with an impish smile.

A sweep? That was an odd phrase for a debutante. She sounded more like a spy. "Is that good or bad?" he asked with a grin.

"Good. Very good. We don't want any talk."

He crossed his arms over his chest and looked down at her. She was positively adorable. "What would your grandmama say if she knew you were out here with a corporal?"

Lady Nicole's lip curled ever so slightly. "She'd tell me to get back inside to the marquess, of course."

"And why don't you?" Mark couldn't stop himself from asking.

"Because the marquess has a bulbous wet lip that makes me shudder, and you—" She blushed a glorious shade of pink.

"I what?" He stepped closer and dropped his voice.

"Don't," she finished sheepishly, examining a rose.

"How would you describe my lips?" He studied the delicate, plump curve of her mouth, dying to hear the answer.

She tilted up her head to look at him. "Firmly molded?" She took a breath. "Enticing."

He arched a brow. "Enticing?"

"Yes," she breathed.

His mouth quirked, aching to smile. "How so?"

She took a step closer to him. "I've never wanted to kiss a man before."

There it was again, that refreshing forthright honesty. "Have you ever been kissed?" he asked, ensuring that his tone remained conversational, as though they discussed the evening's temperature. The last thing he wanted was to scare her off.

She shook her head slowly, her eyes wide and liquid, shining in the moonlight.

"Well, then, we must rectify that situation." He pulled her into his arms and his lips crushed down on hers.

The door to Lord Allen's house swung open, shaking Mark from his memories and loosening his grip on Nicole. The memory of their first kiss had made his fingers curl more tightly around her lower arm. She gave him a questioning look and he released her, straightening his coat and clearing his throat.

A butler showed them into a well-appointed drawing room that held a variety of guests from both the aristocracy and the political arena. A footman offered them glasses of champagne. Mark exchanged greetings with several guests before both Lord Allen and Lord Tottenham emerged from the crowd to greet them.

"Grimaldi, there you are. I heard you left the country. Was wondering if you'd make it," Lord Allen said, with a friendly, gap-toothed smile.

"I just returned last night," Mark replied. "Gentlemen, may I present you with my wife, Nicole?"

Nicole executed a perfect curtsy and extended her

gloved hand first to Lord Tottenham, who bowed over it, and then to Lord Allen, who did the same.

"*Mrs.* Grimaldi," Lord Allen said. "So nice to finally meet you. I would love to tell you I've heard all about you from your husband, but I'm afraid he's earned his 'stone man' moniker. I had no idea you existed until a few weeks ago."

"Nicole has been in France for some time," Mark replied quickly before Nicole was forced to invent an excuse.

"Yes, so I've been told," Allen replied, eyeing Nicole with obvious approval before taking a sip from his own champagne glass.

"Family issues," Nicole interjected. It was the safest thing to say. They had discussed their story in the coach. The fewer details the better, they'd agreed.

"Grimaldi," Lord Tottenham boomed. "Good to see you again." Mark shook the older man's hand. "I had no idea you were married. And to such a beautiful woman. Why on earth have you been hiding her?" He waggled his bushy eyebrows in Nicole's direction.

"You know me," Mark replied, clenching his glass in his fist. "I prefer to keep my private life private."

"You spies and your secrets." Lord Tottenham shook his mane of gray hair and laughed. His generous belly bounced. "I must say, I'm pleased to learn you're a family man."

Nicole shot Mark a quick, ironic glance before turning her attention to Lord Tottenham and giving him a warm, genuine smile. "It's a pleasure to meet you, my lord."

"How in heaven's name did this blighter manage to convince a gorgeous woman like you to marry him?" Lord Tottenham asked, laughing heartily.

"He had his ways," Nicole replied dryly.

Mark could feel her looking at him sidelong. He cleared his throat.

"Yes, well," Allen said, directing his words to Lord Tottenham. "You know Grim here is my first choice for Secretary of the Home Office."

"Yes," Mark interjected. "I'd like nothing more than to steal a moment of your time, Lord Tottenham, so that I might share with you my ideas for the position. I have many—"

Lord Tottenham waved his hand in the air. "Yes, yes, there will be plenty of time for that, General. At the moment, my champagne glass feels a bit light." He lifted the nearly empty glass in the air and turned to locate a footman to give him another.

Lord Allen snapped his fingers and a footman rushed to provide a new glass.

"Mark has a great many ideas I'm certain you'll be eager to hear," Nicole said to Tottenham. "His plans to organize a police force are particularly impressive."

Tottenham, who seemed much happier with a full glass of champagne in his hand, looked at the couple and sighed. "Yes, well, Grimaldi, we've never had an Italian in the position, you know."

Mark wanted to snap his glass in two. Only a man who was preoccupied with things like people's lineage would mention his father's heritage. He was about to bite back something about overbred snobs when he felt Nicole's soft hand on his. She gently squeezed his wrist.

A spark shot straight to his groin. God, she had touched him—and of her own accord—at last. To help him maintain his temper, perhaps, but suddenly the barriers between them felt . . . surmountable. He stared down into her tender, stormy eyes and temporarily forgot what Lord Tottenham had said.

Mark took a deep breath. It wouldn't do to say something reckless to the man who would determine his future. Nicole knew his temper. He kept it in check most of the time, but there were a handful of issues, one being his bloodline, which brought it to the surface with frightening speed. She'd saved him already. She understood him.

Nicole's hand slid away from his and Mark took a sip of his champagne to afford himself time to both think of a more appropriate reply and allow his cockstand to subside.

"He's half English too, of course," Nicole said for him judiciously. "And has spent his life in service to the Crown."

"Yes, yes, of course," Lord Tottenham replied. "And he has an utterly charming wife." He smiled approvingly at Nicole, his bright blue eyes sparkling.

"Shall we go in to dinner?" Lord Allen said to the room at large.

The guests lined up two-by-two up in front of the double doors. Once everyone was in position, the procession made its way into the dining room.

"Thank you for that," Mark leaned down and whispered to Nicole as they slowly walked together toward the dining room still clutching their champagne glasses.

"You're welcome," Nicole whispered back.

"Know anyone here?" he asked, his eyes scanning the queue.

"No one stands out. London's changed quite a lot since I was last here."

"It has, indeed." Suddenly, the fact that he hadn't seen her in ten years seemed incomprehensible to him. Their brief romance was another life. Many things had happened since then. Many things had changed. He'd changed. Had she?

They took their seats side by side toward the middle of the long rosewood table in Lord Allen's grand dining room. Candlelight danced in golden flickers along the bright butter-yellow walls, playing shadows across the imposing portraits of Allen ancestors along with some great historical Englishmen including Henry VIII and Charles II. The dour faces seemed to stare down at them while the guests situated themselves.

Mark and Nicole made small talk with their tablemates while the footmen rushed forward to place napkins on the guests' laps and pour the first course of wine. The guests had barely been sitting five minutes when the butler entered carrying a silver salver with a note on it. The man stalked to Lord Allen's side, leaned down, and whispered into their host's ear.

Lord Allen's eyes widened and he glanced down the table at Mark and Nicole. "General Grimaldi, it seems an urgent message has arrived for you." Lord Allen motioned for the butler to deliver the note to Mark.

The butler made his way down to him, and with a frown, Mark plucked the missive from the salver. Nicole watched him from behind her wineglass, apprehension in her eyes. Mark ripped open the note and scanned the words. He hadn't seen the handwriting in years, but he recognized it. It belonged to his uncle.

"Please come quickly. I need your assistance. Your cousin John is dead."

CHAPTER NINETEEN

Nicole studied Mark's face. Something was wrong. He'd gone a shade paler and the lines around his mouth had tensed. What did the note say? Something to do with his work, most likely.

He pulled his napkin from his lap and stood. "We must go."

"What is it?" Nicole asked from his side, standing too.

"Everything all right?" Lord Allen asked from his perch at the end of the dining table.

"A family matter." Mark glanced at her. "Some bad news. I fear we must leave immediately."

"Of course," Lord Allen replied. He ordered the butler to have Mark's coach brought round.

Mark and Nicole said their good-byes to the other guests, including Lord Tottenham, who looked especially sorry to see them go. They made their way to the dining room door. Lord Allen accompanied them, leading them down the corridor to the foyer.

"Are you quite all right, Grimaldi?" the minister asked as they marched toward the front door.

"My cousin is dead," Mark intoned, his profile like stone.

Nicole gasped, but the look on Mark's face told her she should not say more in front of the minister. It had to be John who had died, but Mark wouldn't want that side of his family discussed in front of Lord Allen.

"Good God, man. Anything I can do?" the minister asked.

Mark's face was grim. "No, but thank you for your hospitality. I do hope we can reschedule. Next time at our house?"

"Yes, yes, of course," Lord Allen replied.

The butler handed Mark his hat and the moment their coach pulled to a stop in front of the minister's house, Mark opened the front door, clutched Nicole's hand, and led her quickly down the stairs toward the coach.

Once they were settled inside the conveyance, Nicole said, "It's John, isn't it?"

One terse nod from Mark. "I must go to my uncle's house immediately."

"Of course." She nodded too. "When's the last time you saw John?"

Mark leaned forward and braced his forearms on his thighs, staring down at his booted feet. "I've seen him . . . in passing."

"I know you haven't seen Regina in at least seven," Nicole added. Regina was Mark's other cousin. She was the granddaughter of Mark's grandfather's sister, Lady Harriet.

Mark narrowed his eyes on Nicole. "How do you know that?"

Nicole shrugged one shoulder. "Regina and I have kept in touch."

"I see." Mark opened the small door behind his head that connected to the driver. He turned back to face Nicole briefly. "I can drop you at our house first."

She shook her head. "No. I'm coming with you."

"That is not necessary," Mark intoned.

She crossed her arms over her chest. "It may be unnecessary, but I'm coming nonetheless."

"Very well." Clearly he didn't want to argue with her at a time like this.

Mark hadn't grown up close to either of his cousins, Nicole knew that, but blood was important to him. Even his blue blood. John was only thirty years old. What in heaven's name happened? Had he got sick? A carriage accident?

Mark gave the driver his uncle's address. Not a quarter of an hour later, they pulled to a stop in front of the grand Mayfair town house of the Duke of Colchester. Mark helped Nicole alight yet again and they hurried to the front door.

Mark pounded the brass doorknocker, but minutes passed before an elderly and somber butler opened the wide black-lacquered front door.

"His Grace isn't taking visitors at the moment," the butler informed them in a nasally tone, blinking at them with wide-eyed somnolence.

Mark pushed his way into the foyer, pulling Nicole

in with him. "I'm General Mark Grimaldi," he said in his most authoritative voice. "The duke's nephew. He asked me to come."

The butler raised his thick eyebrows and looked down his nose at the taller man, his skepticism thinly veiled, perhaps because no such nephew had ever shown himself at this residence. However, he clearly wasn't about to argue with a man of Mark's size and confidence. "Very well. Come with me," he intoned.

They followed the slender man up the massive staircase and down the upper corridor. The butler knocked twice on the imposing door to his uncle's bedchamber. "Your Grace, a General Mark Grimaldi is here to see you. He *claims* to be your nephew."

"Show him in," came the duke's reedy voice.

Nicole glanced at Mark. His nostrils flared. Uneasiness lurked in his dark eyes. He wasn't looking forward to this, but was doing it out of duty. Duty was always on his mind.

The butler pushed open the door and Mark stepped inside with Nicole right behind him. The room was dark and smelled of peppermint and turpentine. A nurse who'd been sitting in a chair in the corner quickly stood and excused herself.

Nicole nodded to her as the woman swept past. Once she was gone, Nicole hovered near the door while Mark strode to his uncle's bedside. The bed was strewn with handkerchiefs and a great many papers.

"Thank you, Bigsby. You may leave us," the duke said to his butler.

The butler bowed and retreated, giving Nicole a disapproving once-over before he left.

Mark crouched down beside his uncle's bed. "What happened?" he asked, his voice low.

The duke seemed to be studying Mark's face. "It's good to see you, Mark."

Just like he did with any sort of emotion, Mark shook off the words. Nicole could almost see him physically do that. "What happened?" he repeated.

"It's John." The old man's voice was withered and full of sadness. He apparently recognized that his nephew wasn't in a mood for a family reunion or special memories.

"He's dead? What happened?" Mark asked.

His uncle coughed piteously. He struggled to sit up. Mark leaned to help him. "Yes. Apparently he collapsed at the dinner table this evening. I received word not an hour ago."

Mark ground his teeth. "Jesus. He was young. Do they suspect a heart ailment?"

"I suppose so," the duke replied. "What else would cut down a man in the prime of life? Dear God. I truly cannot believe this is happening." He closed his eyes.

Mark's profile eased a bit. "I'll go to his house in the morning. See if I can learn any of the particulars."

"Thank you, dear boy." The duke opened his eyes again and lapsed into another wheezy coughing fit.

When he recovered, he reached out and patted Mark's cheek. "It's nice to have a spymaster in the family." Nicole couldn't see his face but she could imagine how difficult that small bit of tenderness was for Mark to accept.

"It is good to see you, Mark," the duke repeated. "Even if under such awful circumstances."

"I heard you were sick. I've been meaning to pay a call." Mark's voice was strained.

"Of course. Of course," came his uncle's reply.

"I had no idea John was ill too. I—" Mark stopped and clenched his jaw.

The duke shook his head. "He wasn't. But perhaps he was keeping it from me, given my condition. He recently became betrothed, you know. To Lady Arabelle Dunwoody. Lovely girl. They'd hoped to have the wedding before I curl up my toes."

"Don't say that," Mark scolded.

"More convenient, don't you think? Needn't wait a year for mourning and all that. I didn't blame him. I've been struggling to hold on for precisely that reason." The duke's hand fell to the bed. "Now I have nothing to live for."

"Please don't say that, Your Grace." To anyone else, Mark's voice would have sounded normal, casual even, but Nicole heard the strain in it. Sadness and angst lingered just below the surface. This was difficult for him. He'd loved his mother, and this man was his only living connection to her. Besides Regina and his great-aunt Harriet, the duke was Mark's only remaining family in England . . . save for Nicole.

The duke lapsed into another coughing fit. Once he regained his voice, he looked past Mark into the shadows where she stood. "Nicole," he croaked. "Is that you?"

Nicole started. She'd done her best to remain silent and fade into the background. She felt like an intruder. "Yes. Yes, Your Grace. It's me."

He raised a withered arm and motioned for her to

come forward. "Come here, dear girl. I never thought I'd see you again."

Tears filled her eyes as she made her way to the duke's bedside. "I didn't know if I'd see you either."

She bent over the bed and gave the elderly man a hug. She'd only met him a time or two, and never with Mark, but the duke had always been kind to her, and she'd heard from her mother that he'd been pleased by his nephew's choice in a wife. He'd sent them a gorgeous silver punch bowl as a wedding present. One they'd never used, one Mark had never acknowledged because the duke was his uncle. Mark had sold all the extravagant wedding gifts they'd received and given the money to injured war veterans. He'd said the veterans needed the money more than he and Nicole needed useless costly things. She'd agreed with him and had been happy to relinquish the gifts.

"As beautiful as ever," the duke said, smiling kindly up at Nicole. "I'm pleased to see you two made amends." He turned his rheumy gaze to Mark. "Your mother would have loved you together."

Mark remained silent. Nicole knew it was because he didn't have the heart to tell the sick old man that they hadn't made amends at all. More tears filled her eyes. Why was that thought so sad? She wouldn't be the one to tell the duke. His son had just died for heaven's sake. She wasn't about to take away the one bit of happiness he seemed to be enjoying.

Mark's mother had died before Nicole met Mark, but he kept a miniature of her on his nightstand. Her name was Mary and she had had dark hair and bright blue eyes. She'd looked a great deal like Mark's cousin Regina.

Mark cleared his throat. "I'm sorry, Your Grace. I truly am. It goes without saying that I'll help you with anything you need. The funeral arrangements or anything else. I'm happy to notify the next in line to the dukedom as well. I assume you'll want my help with that."

Typical of Mark, he'd already begun trying to fix everything. His power lay in his ability to get things done and exert control. In a situation like this, he was doing the only thing he could, taking charge of the mundane details, the things he could control. Nicole doubted the duke was in a mood to discuss funeral arrangements, or the next heir for heaven's sake. But that was what Mark could offer.

The next heir was some distant cousin on Mark's grandfather's side. Nicole didn't know the man's name.

"No, no, my dear boy." The duke coughed again. "That's why I've called you."

Mark's brow furrowed. "Yes, I understand. I can help. Just tell me who—"

His uncle's coughing fit worsened. He was obviously agitated. They waited in silence for it to subside.

"Don't upset yourself, Your Grace. We're here to help." Nicole stroked the man's sweaty hair away from his forehead and searched his haggard face.

"Mark doesn't understand." The old man addressed his words to Nicole. He clutched at her wrist. "He *is* the next in line."

CHAPTER TWENTY

Mark went hot and then cold all over. A chill ran down his spine. He tugged at his cravat. It felt like a garrote tightening, tightening, choking him to death. The room spun and the smell of turpentine made him ill.

No. What his uncle said was not true. Titles like that of duke didn't run to the female side of the family. The old man was mistaken. He was sick and old and mistaken. Nicole would tell him. She would know. She knew the rules of the aristocracy.

"No, it's someone on Grandfather's side, of course," Mark said, to convince himself as much as his uncle. He gave Nicole a desperate look, begging her with his eyes to explain to his uncle the error in his thinking.

"Yes," Nicole said, still stroking the old man's forehead. "Isn't the heir a man distantly related to your father? Some second cousin or some such?"

Mark expelled his breath. There. Nicole knew. Nicole

was right. Dukedoms didn't pass down to the sons of duke's daughters. It wasn't possible that he was the heir.

"Listen to me," his uncle said, clutching Mark's hand with his cold, bony one. "The Duchy of Colchester is a title unlike any other. It was bestowed upon my great-great-great-grandfather by the King. The King and my grandfather were quite close. They went to war together against the Scots. My grandfather saved the King's life. The King only had a daughter at the time. He was especially worried about his own heirs, his legacy. As a result, when the contracts were signed granting my grandfather a duchy and the land and entailment that went with it, the King ensured there was a codicil that allowed for the duchy to be passed down via a female heir *if and only if* a male heir existed on that side. You're the male heir. Now that John is gone, you're the next in line to the duchy."

Sweat broke out on Mark's brow. "No." He shook his head emphatically. "There must be some mistake." He stood and backed away from the bed, numbness spreading through his limbs.

Nicole rested her hand reassuringly on Mark's shoulder. "Hear him out," she whispered.

Mark swallowed hard. This couldn't be happening. This wasn't real. Inheriting a title wasn't something he'd ever considered. His uncle had been the duke since his grandfather had died, and his uncle had a strong healthy son. Even if they both died, the normal line of succession didn't pass down through a daughter. The possibility of becoming the duke had never been a threat.

Mark may not have grown up knowing the details of

the aristocracy the way his uncle, cousin, and mother
had, the way Nicole had, but he knew enough to know
that. There was no chance *he* would be the duke one
day.

His uncle glanced at the paperwork strewn across the
bed. "My solicitor brought this to me the minute I asked
for it. The minute I heard John was dead. There is no
mistake. See for yourself." He clutched the stack of papers and held them out to Mark with trembling hands.

Breathing heavily, Mark hesitated before taking a
step forward and reluctantly accepting the papers. He
let his hand fall to his side, the papers still clutched in
his fist. He didn't want to look at them. "It cannot be."

"Give them to me." Nicole slid the papers from Mark's
numb fingers.

She went to stand near a brace of candles on a nearby
table and scanned the pages, settling on the page that
held the relevant information. She read for several seconds, mouthing the words on the page. "It's true," she
finally said, looking up at Mark, her eyes wide. "It says
here the next in line is the next *male* regardless of his
connection to the duke being from a male or female de-
scendant."

"Fine." Mark, paced away from the bed and ran a
hand through his hair. "I will renounce it. That's been
done before. If and when the day comes—" He glanced
hesitantly at his obviously gravely ill uncle. "I will simply declare myself no longer the duke and give the title
to whoever would be next after that, given that I have
no heirs." He glanced at Nicole. They would have to
talk about it, obviously, but she could hardly object to
their child not inheriting the duchy. She hadn't known

when she'd married him that *this* was a possibility. He hadn't even known. Or had she?

"You cannot," his uncle whispered through dry, cracked lips.

Mark continued pacing. "Of course I can. Even a king can abdicate a throne if he so chooses."

"Mark, we tried to contact you all those years." The old man's voice was even weaker. "Your aunt and I, your cousins. Your mother refused us. She was a proud woman. But we never stopped loving her . . . or you."

Mark turned away from his uncle and closed his eyes. His pulse pounded. Nausea roiled in his middle. He didn't want to hear this. "I don't see what that has to do with—"

"Listen to me, Mark. Mary and I made amends. When she was dying, you were in Spain, fighting. You couldn't come home."

"I know that," Mark ground out. He didn't need to be reminded of any of these awful things.

"What you don't know is that I promised your mother on her deathbed, if this moment ever came to pass, I would convince you to take up your birthright. For her sake. That's what she wanted, Mark. That's what she asked for."

Several moments ticked by in silence. He clenched his fists so tightly they ached. His jaw did too. He wanted to smash something. What the hell was happening? How had his life been turned upside down in less than one hour? Damn his uncle and his deuced deathbed promises.

Bloody hell, he'd made a deathbed promise of his own and he intended to keep it. Mark had promised his father he'd never rely on his mother's side of the family to get ahead in life, and a blasted duchy was a leg up in life if ever there was one.

Mark swiveled on his heel to face the older man. "I can't. I absolutely cannot."

His uncle's watery eyes searched his face. "Why not? Even now, you're unofficially the Marquess of Coleford."

His cousin John's title. "No. That's not true." No. No. No. This wasn't happening. He was used to controlling things and he would control this too, by God. He had to.

His uncle cleared his throat and his frail body shook as he struggled to sit up higher. "You can deny it all you like, but it doesn't make it any less true. Why are you so hell-bent on refuting it?"

"There are a score of reasons," Mark said bitterly, shaking his head. "I doubt you'd understand any of them."

"I understand, Mark. I truly do, but you must promise me for your mother's sake that you'll at least consider it. I have a letter from her. It's—"

"No more, please." This was excruciating. He'd rather be back in France being tortured. At least physical pain was the kind you could absorb. When it was over, it was over. This was the type that gnawed at you endlessly, never relenting.

"He'll consider it," Nicole said firmly, crossing to Mark's side and laying a hand on his coat sleeve.

The room closing in on him, Mark whirled around, turning his attention back to his uncle. "Uncle, you know as well as I do that Grandfather wouldn't have wanted this."

"Why do you say that?" His uncle's brow furrowed.

"A half-Italian Duke of Colchester? Grandfather would roll over in his grave."

"No, dear boy. Father had high ideals about our way of life but he loved you, Mark."

Mark knew that wasn't true. "No, he loved my mother. He tolerated my existence because of her."

"He knew about the codicil. He knew this was a possibility."

"A possibility, perhaps, but a highly unlikely one," Mark shot back.

The old man paused as if considering his reply. He looked at Mark with tears shining in his eyes. "I never had a second son. Nor any daughters. It was always a possibility that John would die as a child. He's gone now, Mark. I'm asking you to do your duty."

Duty. Mark clenched his useless fist against his side. The one word he could never resist.

The ride back home began in silence, Mark splayed across the seat opposite Nicole in obvious exhaustion. Nicole ran the conversation with the duke over and over in her mind. She could guess that Mark was doing the same.

"Your mother never told you about the codicil?" Nicole finally ventured.

Mark rubbed his eyes with the heels of his hands. "Never," he ground out, narrowing his eyes on her.

The coach came to a stop in front of Mark's house and they alighted in turn as they had so many times already this evening. They slowly made their way up the front steps and into the foyer. They walked up the marble stairs together just as slowly.

They reached the top of the stairs and made their way down the corridor toward the bedchambers. Nicole stopped outside the door to his room. Given the events of the evening, it obviously wasn't the right time to begin their other "condition," but she felt closer to him tonight. Closer than she had since she first saw him in France. He'd allowed himself to seem vulnerable in his uncle's bedchamber and in the coach when he'd looked so tired. He wasn't entirely made of stone.

"Are you going to take the duchy?" she half whispered.

"Aiming to be a duchess, are you?" His voice was tight, cruel.

Ouch. She snapped her head to the side as if she'd been slapped. He was hurting and lashing out, but there was no blasted way she'd let him get away with it. "I don't give a toss about being a duchess, you dolt," she snapped. "This is about your duty to your family."

The pain that swept across his stonelike features was unmistakable.

"And there is more to consider than just us." Her voice wavered. "Our son . . . would be the next in line to a dukedom."

Surprise flared briefly in Mark's eyes. "Ah, have you decided it's time to demand your one condition, then?"

She straightened her shoulders, drew herself up, and met his eyes. "If you . . . like."

He reached out and slowly traced her cheekbone with a finger. She shivered. "Did you know about this? Is that why you want a child?"

She sharply drew away from him. "What? You're not serious."

"You've always cared too much about titles and social standing."

She lifted her chin. "That's not fair. No, I haven't. Besides, have you ever considered that perhaps your problem is that you've always cared too little about them?"

He drew his hand away and stared her in the eye. "Fine. You may not have known about the codicil, but are you *still* going to pretend you married me for love and not because you knew the entire time that my grandfather was a duke?"

She glanced away. Yes, she'd known. For some reason she still didn't understand, he hadn't wanted to tell her who his family was. If it were up to him, he'd have pretended he was the son of a shoemaker, with no ties to the aristocracy, for their entire marriage. He'd deliberately withheld information from *her*.

It had been a fateful day indeed when, three months into their marriage, he'd confronted her with the fact that she knew who his family was and had kept it from him. He obviously still distrusted her.

"You know I knew," she replied simply, turning her head to the side, not looking at him.

"Yet you pretended to marry me for love." His voice was tight with anger.

"I never pretended," she whispered through clenched teeth.

He opened the door to his bedchamber, stepped inside, and turned to face her. "Our bargain will have to wait longer, I'm afraid. I don't have it in me to bed you tonight."

CHAPTER TWENTY-ONE

The next morning, Mark sat in his study attempting to get some paperwork done, but all he could think about were two things: the fact that his cousin was dead and the fact that he'd stubbornly refused Nicole's bed last night. Both seemed incomprehensible.

John was dead. Why did the notion arouse Mark's guilt? Because he'd never publicly acknowledged they were cousins? They ran in completely different social sets. John was a darling of the *ton*, running about town to dinner parties and balls, attending the theater and frequenting his club. Meanwhile, Mark had been *working*. He'd spent his years ensuring the country wasn't overrun by the French, been on the frontlines of the wars, nearly died a handful of times, and when he was in London, spent his time with members of the Home Office and the people he worked for and who worked for him. He'd never given a toss about balls and dinner parties, unless they might be politically advantageous. Even then, they were just more work.

He'd seen John from time to time. More than once, John had looked as if he'd like to speak to Mark. But he never had and Mark told himself that was the way he liked it. Now there would never be a chance to know his cousin. Mark might be known as the stone man, but he didn't wish death upon anyone. It had been heart wrenching seeing the horrible effect his cousin's death had on his uncle. The man had lost his only son, his only child. Mark could not imagine that type of pain.

Mark tossed down his quill and scrubbed his hands across his face. It only made things worse that his cousin's death meant he would have to renounce a duchy of all blasted things. Could he do it quietly, without anyone finding out? He'd have to discreetly inquire about that as well. Blast. Blast. Blast.

Meanwhile he'd acted like a complete arse to Nicole last night. What the hell was wrong with him? She was here to get with child. He'd agreed to do the job. After so many nights spent alone, he should have jumped at the chance to end his self-imposed celibacy. He tried to tell himself he'd refused her because of the news of his cousin, and that was certainly part of the reason, but it would be disingenuous to blame it entirely on that. It wasn't because he was in mourning. He barely knew the man. He was sorry his cousin was dead for his uncle's sake. The poor man was near to breaking over it. Mark wasn't made *entirely* of stone.

He leaned back in his chair and rested an arm atop his head. If he was honest, he was also sorry his cousin was dead for his own sake. Why couldn't John at least have sired an heir first? It was an unkind thought, but Mark wasn't in a kind mood.

He hadn't been angry with Nicole last night because of that. He'd been an arse because the fact that he was suddenly a marquess brought up too many of the feelings he'd had early in their marriage, when she left. After she admitted she'd known all along that his grandfather was a duke, Mark realized she'd indeed married him for his connections, while allowing him to think she'd married him for love. Love? Ha. That's what he got for spending time with the daughter of an earl. Such young ladies had only one thing on their mind: marrying advantageously. Still, refusing to bed her last night had been idiotic. It punished him as much as her. He wouldn't make that mistake again. He picked up his quill again, determined to finish his paperwork before midday.

A knock at the door interrupted him. Abbott opened the door and cleared his throat. "A man is here to see you, General."

Mark looked up and narrowed his eyes at the butler. "Who is it?"

"He says his name is Oakleaf. Daffin Oakleaf."

Mark knew that name. "Show him in."

Daffin Oakleaf was a friend of Cade and Rafe Cavendish, two of his best spies. He was also the best of the Bow Street Runners, a small private police force that solved cases in return for bounties.

Oakleaf strolled into the study, whistling. "Good morning, General."

The man was tall, broad, and blond. He even looked like the Cavendish twins, only while their eyes were blue, Oakleaf's were bright green. Mark had heard that Cade Cavendish, a privateer with more aliases than a Drury Lane actor, had pretended to be Oakleaf a time or two. The man standing before him was definitely Oakleaf himself.

"Oakleaf," Mark said, glancing up from his paperwork. "Take a seat. To what do I owe the pleasure?" His tone was jovial, but a skitter of apprehension worked its way down his spine.

Oakleaf settled himself into a chair in front of Mark's desk. "I'm here to talk to you about your cousin's death."

Mark nodded. He'd suspected as much. Oakleaf knew exactly who his family was. "I plan to visit John's house today. My uncle told me he collapsed at dinner, a heart condition."

Oakleaf shifted in his seat. His astute gaze met Mark's. "He collapsed at dinner, that's true, but it was no heart condition."

Mark dropped the quill and eyed the other man carefully. As he'd feared. Bow Street Runners didn't involve themselves in deaths unless foul play was suspected. "What do you mean?"

"We suspect it was murder. Lord Tottenham asked me to come and find you."

Mark arched a brow. "Am I a suspect?"

Oakleaf grinned. "On the contrary, he wants you to assist with investigating the case. You, apparently, have an airtight alibi, you were at dinner with Tottenham and Allen when John died, were you not?"

"I was," Mark intoned, but it still seemed odd that Tottenham would ask for his assistance. Why would Tottenham care about this case? Mark shook his head.

No doubt it was because the heir to a dukedom was involved. Bluebloods always garnered attention. Damn. It would be difficult to keep the fact that he was related to the family a secret. Especially now that he was legally the heir. Bloody inconvenient.

"Will you help?" Oakleaf asked.

"Of course," Mark replied, resigning himself to the fact that he would have to navigate this investigation with extreme care. "My uncle—he doesn't yet know you suspect foul play, does he?"

Oakleaf shook his head. "No. We haven't told him. We know his health is precarious."

Mark nodded. "Good. Let's investigate first. If it comes to that, I will tell him."

Mark stood and made his way around the large mahogany desk to escort Oakleaf out.

"I heard Nicole is back. Think we should bring her with us to investigate?" Oakleaf gave him an innocent look, blinking as if he didn't know what a sore subject it was.

Mark growled under his breath. "Of course you've heard Nicole is back. You damn runners and your damned nosiness."

Oakleaf's crack of laughter shot across the room. "That's ironic coming from a spy. Besides, Nicole is a damn fine investigator."

"Nicole will not be coming with us," Mark grumbled.

"Retired from that line of work, has she?"

"No, actually. She was helping the police in France, but I'll be investigating this particular case on my own."

"With *my* help, of course." Oakleaf winked at him.

"Of course." Mark grinned. He swung open the door

and gestured to the other man to precede him into the corridor. "Lead the way."

Not half an hour later, Mark and Oakleaf stood in the dining room at John's town house. His cousin's body had been removed to one of the drawing rooms to be prepared for burial, but from the looks of the dining room, little else had been touched. The meal from the night before still lay on the table, chairs were pulled away at haphazard angles as if their occupants had left in a hurry, and the seat at the head of the table, where John no doubt had sat, had plates and glasses scattered on the floor.

Mark glanced around the scene, taking in every detail. He nodded toward the head of the table. "John's place?"

"Yes, have you never been here before?" Oakleaf asked.

Mark shook his head, keeping his face carefully blank. "No. And I'd prefer if you would keep the bit about him being my cousin to yourself, at least for the time being."

"Understood," Oakleaf replied. He crouched down to study the items on the floor next to John's chair.

Mark eyed the cutlery, plates, and two glasses scattered on the rug. "What do you think happened?"

"We have reason to believe he was poisoned," Oakleaf replied.

Mark scanned the area. A wineglass had rolled under the table and stained the rug a dark red that looked nearly black.

"His friends who were sharing the meal with him

report that he took a drink of wine just before he col
lapsed," Oakleaf continued.

Mark crouched down on the balls of his feet to study
the wine stain on the rug. There was a dark ring around
the stain. He carefully lifted the glass and sniffed it. "I
has a metallic odor."

"Precisely," Oakleaf agreed.

"Who else was here last night?" Mark glanced up a
the table to count the places.

"Eight diners total," Oakleaf replied. "John, his in
tended, Lady Arabelle, and her mother, Lady Eloise
Mr. Matthew Cartwright. Miss Molly Lester and he
mother, Tabitha. Lord Anthony Rawlins, John's clos
est mate, and Lord Michael Hillenbrand, another o
John's friends."

The name Matthew Cartwright seemed familiar, bu
Mark couldn't quite place it. He'd never heard of the la
dies, nor their mothers. Lord Rawlins and Lord Hillen
brand were peers. He'd met them both in passing a tim
or two. "We'll want to speak to each of them."

"Of course," Oakleaf replied.

Mark stood and examined the wine bottle the glass
had most certainly been poured from. It sat in front o
John's place at the table. Odd that one of the footmen
hadn't taken it away. In the course of a normal dinne
party, the footmen would pour the wine for all of th
guests and retreat with the bottle. Mark lifted the bottle
and sniffed. It had a metallic odor, too. "Any idea wh
would want him dead?"

Oakleaf had moved to the sideboard to examine the
contents of the covered dishes there. He shrugged. "The
man's father is gravely ill and he stands to inherit

dukedom. I'd say we find the next in line and we have a good suspect."

Mark cleared his throat, turning to face Oakleaf. 'Normally I would agree with you, but there is only one problem with that theory."

"What's that?" Oakleaf replaced the lid on a silver tureen and met Mark's gaze.

Mark scratched his cheek and expelled a deep breath. No use hiding the facts from the best of the Bow Street Runners. "Turns out *I* am the next in line."

"What!" Oakleaf's eyes looked as if they might bug from his skull. "How in the devil's name?"

"It was a surprise to me as well. My uncle just informed me last night, shortly after he told me about John's death."

The runner's eyes narrowed suspiciously. "You didn't *know* you were next in line to a dukedom?"

"My mother was the duke's sister. These things are not normally passed down by female bloodlines. In our case it's an exception." Mark paced toward the dining table and ran a hand through his hair. "Again, I ask for your discretion with that news as well." There was no use not telling Oakleaf. His investigation would turn it up eventually. By telling him now, Mark was staving off an awkward moment later and the risk of making Oakleaf think he was purposely hiding information.

"As you wish," Oakleaf replied, his tone measured. "For the record, who did everyone *think* was the next in line?"

Matthew Cartwright. That's where he'd heard that name before. The detail snapped into place in Mark's memory. "Mr. Cartwright, I believe. We'll need to confirm that, though. I gave little thought to my mother's side of the family. None of these details were at the forefront of my mind until last night."

"I see," Oakleaf replied, still examining the contents of the sideboard. He bent to sniff another dish. "I must ask, did anyone else know you were next in line?"

"I don't think so," Mark replied.

Oakleaf straightened and stared at him for a moment as if turning everything over in his mind. "If your uncle suspected you, I daresay he wouldn't have made you privy to the details."

"He trusts me," Mark replied. "And he doesn't yet know John was murdered."

Oakleaf's eyes narrowed. "May I ask why he's never claimed you as his nephew?"

"On my request," Mark said. "He knows that the last thing I've ever wanted was the dukedom, or any ties to my family's name on my mother's side. We've never been close."

"You don't say." Oakleaf shook his head. He raised a brow at Mark. "Anything else to declare before we continue this investigation, Grim?"

Mark scratched the back of his neck. Oakleaf was being damned reasonable, given the circumstances. Though having a flawless alibi didn't hurt. "No, that's it."

"Normally, I wouldn't allow someone with such close ties to the family to help investigate," Oakleaf said, pursing his lips. "But Tottenham specifically asked for you and doesn't know you're related."

"I promise to be impartial," Mark replied soberly

"And I promise to inform Tottenham . . . when the time is right."

"Fine." Oakleaf gave him an efficient nod. "Meanwhile, we'll have to study each of the people who were at the dinner party last night."

"And the servants," Mark added. "Are they still here? We need to ask them some questions."

Oakleaf nodded and left the room to arrange for the servants to come speak to them. Not ten minutes later, a worried-looking butler and a stricken-looking housemaid were lined up in the dining room near the wall.

"Did anything unusual happen last night? When the guests were arriving?" Mark asked the butler.

"Like what, sir?" The sweating man looked completely miserable.

"Like did any of the guests leave the drawing room? Do anything unusual?"

"No, sir. Not a one," the butler replied, wringing his hands.

"Did your master say anything to you last night to make you think anything was different?" Mark asked the butler next.

"Not that I can think of, sir. Lord John was in high spirits. He was always happy to see Lady Arabelle, if not her mother."

"Mother bothered him, did she?" Oakleaf asked with a smirk.

"As much as anyone's future mother-in-law is bothersome, I suspect, sir," the butler replied, his voice cracking.

Mark pulled his card from his inside coat pocket. "If

you think of anything, anything that happened that was out of the ordinary, don't hesitate to contact me."

"Yes, sir." The butler nodded profusely.

Mark dismissed the butler and smiled kindly at the maid. The poor woman had obviously been crying and now she had the look of a person headed for the hangman's noose. Her face was pinched and pale.

"Who was here last night? Serving, I mean?" he asked.

The housemaid looked startled and shook her head. "The usual servants wot serve. Both footmen, Matthew and Timothy."

"They're not here at the moment," Oakleaf explained.

Mark narrowed his eyes. "Where are they?"

The maid's face grew paler. "They went out with a few o' the other servants to have a pint, sir. Ta toast Lord John. They were all frightened something awful. And Mr. Cartwright gave them money."

"Mr. Cartwright? He was one of the guests last night?" Mark asked.

"Yes, he's the one wot's rumored ta be takin' Lord John's place as the marquess. Seems ta be a generous man."

Mark and Oakleaf exchanged a look.

"And the usual cook prepared the meal last night?" Mark prodded.

"Yes," the maid replied. "Mrs. Whately. She's down at the pub wit the others."

"I see." Mark flashed a bill to the maid and handed her another card. "When they return, ask the footmen and the cook to come to this address later today. There will be money for them if they arrive."

"Yes, sir," the maid said, bobbing a curtsy and rushing out of the room.

Mark crossed back to the table where Oakleaf stood.

"Do you know this Cartwright man?" Oakleaf asked.

Mark placed a fist on his hip. "Never met him."

Oakleaf crossed his arms over his chest. "Seems to me he should be first on the list of possible suspects."

"Agreed," Mark replied. "I'll meet you at your offices this afternoon."

Oakleaf nodded. "Where are you going?"

Mark took a deep breath and blew it out, hanging his head. "To perform the unsavory task of telling my uncle his only son was murdered. We need his help."

CHAPTER TWENTY-TWO

Nicole once again stared at a blank piece of vellum. She couldn't summon the will to write her mother and tell her she was in London. Mother was in the country this time of year. There was no chance Nicole would run into her, but there was *every* chance her mother would hear about her appearance at Lord Allen's dinner party last night. Still, she didn't want to write her. There would be too much explaining to do, that, at the moment, Nicole was not prepared for. She didn't intend to *lie* to her mother, but she couldn't tell her the entire embarrassing truth either, and frankly it was none of her mother's affair.

She'd been keeping things from her mother for years, hadn't she? What did a bit more hurt? She'd never told her mother about the time she sneaked out to the stables when she was fifteen years old and rode her horse in the darkness. She'd never told her mother about her work with the Bow Street Runners. She'd certainly never told her mother about the time she kissed Corporal Grimaldi at Grandmama's ball.

It was true. Nicole had never been kissed before and now she was certain she'd never recover from it. Corporal Grimaldi's mouth claimed hers. His lips pushed hers open and his tongue plunged inside, exploring every bit of her mouth. It was like drinking from a fountain on a hot day. She couldn't get enough of him. Her arms moved up to wrap around his neck and he pulled her against him, hard. She gasped into his mouth as he continued his gentle assault. His lips twisted to meet hers, her hips lifted to meet his. By the time he grabbed her upper arms and pushed her away, they were both gasping.

"Why did you stop?" She blushed for asking such a bold question, but the words had flown from her lips.

Letting go of her arms, he bent over and rested his palms on his knees, still breathing heavily. "Sweetheart, if I didn't stop, we'd end up doing far more than you bargained for."

She vaguely understood there was more, much more that went on in private between a man and woman. That had to be what he was referring to, but the kiss had been so magnificent, she hadn't wanted it to end.

She blew out a breath. "I didn't know we'd be kissing when I agreed to meet you out here."

"Neither did I." He stood up straight and flashed a grin at her.

She took a tentative step toward him. "Since we've already done it, might we not do it again?"

He seemed to contemplate her words for a matter of seconds before he reached for her and pulled her to him again and then oh, that delicious, dangerous mouth was claiming hers again, drawing a moan from her throat even as passion drew the breath from her lungs. She wrapped her arms around his neck and stood on tiptoe to capture more of his lips. He lifted her in his arms, molding her against him to better position her to receive his kiss. She'd never known a man's body was so unyielding. His arms were like a cage she never wanted to escape.

The crack of a twig behind the mews made his head snap up. A different type of tension tightened their embrace, one of alarm. He carefully, reluctantly set her on her feet. His hands lingered at her waist long enough to ensure she was steady, then he stepped away from her, his breath coming in hard pants, staring at her as if she was a magical being.

She lifted her hand to touch her bruised lips and stared back at him in a similar state of wonder. "Thank you," she said inanely.

His smile returned, slowly, this time with the smallest hint of shyness to it. "I should be thanking you."

"I've never been kissed before," she continued. "And that was quite . . . quite . . . extraordinary."

He was quiet for a moment, his gaze darting above her head before he focused on her face again. "I wasn't joking when I said I didn't come out here to kiss you."

"Neither was I." She took a deep, fortifying breath. She wasn't certain she would ever be the same again after that kiss.

They stared at each other and exchanged smiles as if they'd both discovered something astonishing.

"I should take you back into the ballroom now," he said at last. "You'll be safe there."

She studied the sharp, handsome lines of his face. "I feel perfectly safe here with you."

Nicole sighed. Her first kiss with Mark had been unexpected and magnificent. They'd kissed once more before she'd rushed back into the ballroom, asking him to call upon her the next day. He had.

She closed her eyes tightly and when she reopened them she refocused her attention on the blasted empty sheet of vellum in front of her. She decided to take a break from the exhausting task of writing and go down to the kitchens to see if there were any more of the delicious raspberry tarts she'd been served for breakfast. As she stood from her desk, a sharp knock on the door interrupted the silence.

"Come in," she called, expecting to see Louise or Susanna. She'd asked Susanna to serve as her personal maid and all morning the girl had been making excuses to come by and ask how she liked her hair and her wardrobe. The young maid was obviously pleased with her new position. Nicole thought it was adorable.

The door opened and Mark strode inside. The look on his face told Nicole something wasn't right. She studied him, clutching the back of her chair with white knuckles. "What's happened?"

"I need your help." His voice was tight.

She rushed over to him to study his face more closely. "Of course. Anything."

He took a deep breath and scrubbed the back of his

arm across his forehead. "Bow Street suspects John was murdered."

"No," Nicole breathed. She clasped her hand over her mouth, bile rising in her throat.

"Poison," Mark said grimly.

"Oh, God, no." Nicole shook her head. Then she clenched her jaw and turned up her face to look him in the eye. "Do you have a list of suspects?"

A muscle ticked in Mark's cheek. "Yes, and by God, I intend to find out who did this."

"What do you need from me?" Surely he hadn't come to ask for her assistance in the investigation, but a glimmer of hope remained. Did he want her help?

"I need to inform my uncle." Mark cleared his throat. "I'd like you to come with me."

The glimmer died a short death, replaced with the determination to help him share this awful news with his poor uncle in the kindest way possible. "Yes, of course."

It was touching, actually, that Mark had stopped by to bring her with him. He had *some* faith in her. Either that or he didn't want to face his uncle alone. She discarded that thought. Mark was no coward. He'd asked her to accompany him for his uncle's sake. He knew the man liked her and felt comforted by her presence.

She lifted her skirts and rushed toward the wardrobe. "I'll get my pelisse and meet you downstairs."

Half an hour later, Mark's coach again pulled to a stop in front of the duke's house. The same somber butler opened the door for them. "His Grace has been waiting for you, my lord."

"No, not 'my lord.' I am *not* 'my lord,'" Mark insisted, glowering at the servant.

The butler's long face darkened into a frown. "There must be some mistake. His Grace specifically told me you are now the Marquess of Coleford."

Mark brushed past him into the foyer. "Not yet. Not officially. I'm not a lord."

Nicole watched the exchange with ill-concealed amusement. Strictly speaking, Mark was correct. He would not *officially* be the Marquess of Coleford until the paperwork had been reviewed and approved by the House of Lords and signed off on by the Lord Chancellor. His uncle had obviously seen fit to begin using his title before all that happened, however, which was not uncommon.

In heavy silence, Nicole and Mark followed the butler up the stairs and down the corridor to the duke's bedchamber. The butler rapped only once upon the thick wooden door before pushing it open and stepping inside.

"The Marquess of Coleford," the man announced while Mark narrowed his eyes at him and growled under his breath.

Nicole swept in behind them. This time the sickroom held more light. The heavy dark curtains had been pulled back and the windows had been opened. The room still smelled of peppermint tea and turpentine, but there was also a lemony scent as if the furniture had been freshly waxed.

"Come in, my boy," the duke said from the middle of the bed. He was sitting up, with pillows propped behind him, motioning for both Mark and Nicole to come closer.

A nurse, different from the one who'd been there last night, stood from a chair in the corner and marched toward them. "Nothing to upset him," she whispered with a stern glare as she left the room. Mark and Nicole gave each other an uneasy glance.

"Come in, come in," the duke repeated, waving for them to sit in the two chairs placed next to his bed.

Nicole took a seat closest to the duke, a knot tightening in her chest as she contemplated what the old man was about to hear. Mark remained standing, his hands clasped behind his back.

"Have you any news from the doctor? Do they know what caused John's attack?" the duke asked eagerly before launching into a coughing fit. He feebly held a handkerchief to his lips.

Mark cleared his throat, waiting for his uncle's fit to subside. "Yes," he said simply. He was not one to sugarcoat such news. "I spoke with Bow Street this morning. There's no easy way to tell you . . . they suspect foul play." His voice was clipped and direct.

"Foul play?" The duke repeated the words in a confused whisper, his breath rasping from his lips.

Mark straightened his shoulders. "They believe John was poisoned, Your Grace."

"No." The old man's craggy voice was broken. He screwed his eyes shut and tears dripped from the sides of them.

Nicole dug a fresh handkerchief from her reticule and held it out to the old man. She leaned forward and grasped his hand. "I'm so sorry, Your Grace. So very sorry."

"I intend to do everything in my power to find out

who is responsible," Mark promised, his voice edged with anger.

The duke opened his eyes again and took three heaving breaths. Nicole waited on tenterhooks, worried he might have another attack himself. Finally, the old man's eyes focused, a determined look in their blue depths. It was a look she'd seen many times in Mark's eyes. "You must promise me you'll avenge him," the duke whispered.

Mark nodded curtly. "I promise I will find his killer and bring him to justice."

"What can I do to help?" the duke asked, a faint blush tingeing his pale cheeks. He was old, but he was still a man. It had to be difficult for him to be so near the end of his life and confined to a bed during such a fraught time. Nicole lightly squeezed his frail hand.

"Our investigation will proceed more quickly if we can gather everyone who was at John's dinner table last night in one place," Mark replied without missing a beat. It warmed her heart to see him trying to give his uncle something to feel proud about, something to grasp onto, something to do.

The duke struggled to sit up straighter. Nicole stood to help him. She rearranged the pillows behind his back and helped him settle himself.

"You want me to bring them together?" the duke asked. "Here?" Another coughing fit ensued.

"No," Mark replied after his uncle stopped coughing. "We'll need to question them over a period of time. A few days or more. The sooner the better. You should invite them all to your country house for a memorial."

"Perfect," the duke intoned. He clutched Nicole's

handkerchief to his chest. "But what if any of them re fuse?"

"I've been thinking about that," Mark replied. "I sug gest you also inform them that after the memorial, yo intend to . . . name the next heir. You must imply it ma come as a surprise."

"Brilliant," the duke breathed.

Nicole faced Mark. She spoke quietly. "Do you thin such an event is wise, given your uncle's health?"

"I'll be fine," the duke replied stubbornly, though hi coughs belied his words.

Mark stared down at his uncle, pity in his eyes. "I won't be easy, but if you can make it to Surrey, I thin having everyone there together will make a difference in the investigation."

"Why not invite them here to His Grace's Londo home?" Nicole asked. "That way your uncle won't hav to travel."

"If we invite them here, they can leave if they choose In the country they'll be forced to stay and answer ques tions for a few days at least. Besides, they'll all expec John to be laid to rest at Colchester Manor. It's the per fect reason to invite them. The naming of the heir at th end will ensure they stay."

"Yes, yes, of course," the duke insisted, waving th handkerchief in the air. "I agree. Just tell me, who shoul I invite?"

"Four ladies and three gentlemen. Everyone who wa at the dinner last night, including some of the servant if I cannot cross them off the list of suspects in time." Mark rattled off the list.

The duke rang for a footman. When the young ma

arrived at the door, the duke ordered him to send for his secretary posthaste. "We'll get the invitations out immediately," the duke said. The old man seemed strangely energized. Nicole couldn't help but wonder if the determination to avenge his son's murder had given him the impetus to go on. She patted his hand.

Mark folded his arms behind his back and gave the duke a curt nod. "We'll leave you to it."

Mark and Nicole entered the coach again in silence. They were well on their way back home when Nicole finally asked, "You don't think it will be too much for your uncle's health to host a house party in Surrey?"

"It's not as if he'll be doing any of the work. He has myriad servants. Besides, he said it himself. He has only been hanging on for John's sake. I suspect now he'll hang on to discover who killed his son. We need his help."

"I understand," Nicole said quietly. "Only it's such a pity that a sick old man should be forced to play host to a group of people, one of whom is his son's murderer." She shuddered.

"I agree." Mark stared out the coach window. His profile was stonelike. His jaw was set. "All we can do is discover the truth as quickly as possible. For my uncle's sake."

Nicole pressed her fingertips to her temples. An awful headache had begun to form behind her eyes. "Of the people who were there that night, who, do you suspect?" She couldn't help it. The investigator in her was eager to help determine the culprit.

Mark slapped his gloves against his thigh. "As of now they're all suspects, but Mr. Cartwright is the man who believes himself to be the next in line to the duchy. Mark tapped a finger against the window. "That is strong motivation for murder."

"You're right," Nicole replied, before venturing, "What of your plans for securing the position of Secretary of the Home Office?"

"For now, they are on hold. Before we leave for the memorial, I must pay a visit to Lord Tottenham to let him know I'll be out of pocket for a bit. He shouldn't mind. Apparently he asked for my assistance on this case."

Nicole met Mark's gaze. "What if he discovers you're the marquess?"

"I'm *not* the marquess," Mark ground out, clenching the gloves in his fist. "I intend to ask my uncle to keep the news to himself for the time being. I haven't decided whether I'll renounce the title, but if I *am* going to be a bloody marquess, I want my promotion first."

CHAPTER TWENTY-THREE

The next few days passed in a haze of preparations. The invitations to the memorial were sent by liveried messenger. No mention was made of the fact that murder was suspected. All seven accepted.

Mark was reading a letter from an operative in the north of England when the butler knocked on the door to his study.

Mark glanced up. "Yes."

"Excuse me, sir, but a trio of people are here to have a word with you. Servants by the looks of them. They say you asked them to come." The butler's raised eyebrows proved his skepticism.

A trio of servants? They had to be John's cook and two footmen.

"Thank you, Abbott. Please show them in, one at a time."

Abbott bowed and left, and not three minutes later, a

round, middle-aged woman with bright blue eyes and a mobcap on her head arrived at the study door.

Mark stood. "Come in," he intoned.

The woman tentatively moved into the room. Her face was bright red and her eyes darted about nervously.

Mark gestured to one of the chairs in front of his desk. "Please take a seat. I am General Grimaldi. And you are?"

The woman scurried to the chair and slowly lowered herself into it while keeping her eyes on Mark's face. "I'm Mrs. Whately. I'm Lord John's cook, er, I was his cook. Now I suppose I'm no one's cook." Her eyes filled with tears.

Mark's felt a pang of regret for the poor woman. "Thank you for coming, Mrs. Whately. I have a few important questions for you."

"Of course, sir," the woman replied, swallowing hard. "Go ahead." She nodded.

"You prepared the meal the night Lord John died. Is that correct?"

"Yes, sir." The woman nodded more. "It were a terrible tragedy, ta be sure."

Mark pressed his lips together and nodded back at her. "Who served the meal?"

"Timothy and Matthew." Her voice wavered. "They both came wit me today but yer butler asked me to come in first."

"Yes, thank you," Mark replied. He cleared his throat. "Who prepared and served the wine?"

"The wine?" Mrs. Whately scratched at her mobcap, a frown on her face. "The wine usually comes from the cellar, sir. I remember seeing Timothy sneak a sip o' it before he took it up to the dining room. He's a bit o' a drinker, but otherwise, a fine footman, sir."

Mark leaned back and steepled his fingers over his chest, watching the older woman. "And Matthew? Did you ever see him with the wine?"

She shook her head vigorously. "No, sir. At the start o' the meal, Matthew was helping me because like a fool, I had knocked over the soup tureen and had ta clean it up."

"Matthew was with you the entire time then?"

"Yes, sir." More nodding.

"What did you think of Lord John?" Mark asked.

Mrs. Whately's eyes filled with more tears and she dabbed at them with a handkerchief she extracted from her sleeve. "He was a fine man and a fair employer, sir. We'll certainly miss him."

Mark bit the inside of his cheek. His experience told him John's cook, at least, truly liked him. "What do you know of Mr. Cartwright?"

"Mr. Cartwright, sir?" The cook blinked at him.

"Yes. He was at the dinner, was he not? The man rumored to be the next in line to the marquisate?"

The cook's eyes widened. "Oh, Mr. Cartwright, o' course. He seems like a right nice young man. He gave us each some coin."

"How much?"

"One pound each, sir."

"That much? Did he say why?"

"No, sir. He never mentioned that he was next in line. We heard that rumor from one o' the housemaids. But we all assumed he gave us the monies to tide us over while the will and whatnot is worked out."

Mark pressed his lips together. "Thank you, Mrs. Whately. That will be all. Will you please send Matthew next?" Mark pulled open the desk drawer, retrieved a coin purse, opened it and tossed the cook a pound. "Thank you for your help."

The cook grasped the coin and smiled. Her face was full of relief as she scrambled out of the chair and rushed out the door. "Ye're welcome, sir. Ye're quite welcome."

A few minutes later, Matthew poked his head through the door. The young man was in his early twenties with dark hair and eyes. He held his hat in his hand.

Mark began questioning him the same way, confirming that he'd been there the night John had died. "Did you serve the wine?" he asked.

"No, sir," the footman replied. "Timothy served it, sir."

"You're certain?" Mark narrowed his eyes on the servant.

Matthew tugged at his collar. "Yes, sir. I . . . I saw him sipping a small glass of it before he brought it upstairs."

"You're certain of that?" Mark narrowed his eyes further.

"Yes, sir." The servant tugged at his collar more. "It's . . . it's something Timothy does most nights, I'm afraid. Though he's an excellent footman, sir. Truly."

Interesting. Both Mrs. Whately and Matthew seemed eager to defend Timothy despite his penchant for nibbing the wine. He was obviously their friend. Most importantly, if Timothy had been drinking the wine, it stood to reason that neither the cook nor the other footman would have poisoned it. They'd have known their friend would drink it. It ruled Timothy out as a suspect as well. Unless he poisoned the wine after he drank it and before he'd taken it into the dining room. It seemed unlikely, but his discussion with Timothy might uncover the truth.

"What did you think of Lord John?" Mark asked Matthew next.

The servant's face crinkled into a smile. "Aw, he was a good man, sir. The very best. Not a cross word out o' him ever."

Mark considered that for a moment. "Where were you when you saw Timothy drink the wine?"

Matthew's cheeks reddened.

"What is it?" Mark asked, leaning forward in his seat.

"I was in the kitchen, sir." He paused and took a deep breath. "And in the corridor just outside the dining room."

"Pardon?" Mark frowned.

"Timothy likes ta sneak a sip below stairs *and* just before he takes it into the dining room, he sneaks another. He took his own cup upstairs for that purpose."

Mark leaned back and raised his eyebrows. "Really?"

"Yes, sir," Matthew replied, nervously glancing around the room. "Please don't tell Mr. Cartwright, sir. Timothy may sneak a sip o' wine now and then, but he needs his position. He takes care o' his sick mother and young sister. If he got tossed out on his ear, ain't no telling what would happen to his family, sir."

Mark nodded. "Don't worry. I have no intention of telling Mr. Cartwright, but speaking of him, did he say anything to you?"

"He gave us one pound each, sir," the footman replied. "Me, Cook, Tim, and the maids. I think he gave the butler and housekeeper a bit more, sir, but ye'd have to ask them."

Mark inclined his head. "Did he say why he gave you the money?"

"No, sir," Matthew replied. "But one of the maids said she heard one o' the ladies wot visited that evening say Mr. Cartwright was the duke's heir after Lord John, sir. We assumed he's ta be our new master."

"I see." Mark pulled another coin from his purse and tossed it to Matthew. "Thank you for your help."

Matthew gave him a gap-toothed smile and headed toward the door. "Should I send Timothy?"

"Please," Mark answered.

Timothy's story was much like the others'. He also informed Mark that Mr. Cartwright had given him money without mentioning he would be the new marquess. When Mark asked the footman what he thought of Lord John, Timothy replied, "Oh, he was the best, sir. The very best. He knew me penchant for drinking and he never tossed me out, sir. Even gave me a bit o' a nip here and there."

"Did he?" Mark raised his brows and bit the inside of his cheek to keep from smiling. Seems his cousin had been beloved by his servants. It made Mark feel guiltier for never knowing him.

"Yes, sir," Timothy continued. "Even when he caught me sampling the dinner wine." A chagrined look crossed the footman's face. "Lord John didn't say a word."

"About that," Mark replied. "Did you take the wine

directly into the dining room that night? After you took your last sip, that is?"

Timothy gulped but looked Mark in the eyes. "Yes, sir. I did. I poured a splash into me own cup, took a nib, and then hurried the rest directly into the dining room like I do every evening, sir."

"Thank you, Timothy," Mark replied. He'd seen a lot in his day, but a servant who couldn't keep his hands off the wine thereby providing his own best alibi was a new one. This time Mark pulled three pounds out of the coin purse. He slid them across the desktop to the servant.

"What's this, sir?" Timothy asked, eyeing the money with wide eyes.

"One for you, one for your mother, and one for your sister," Mark replied.

The servant gathered the coins into his hands and nodded vigorously. "Thank you, sir. Mighty kind o' ye."

Mark quirked a brow. "If I hear you spent so much as a shilling of it on alcohol, I'll beat you myself."

The footman shook his head. "No, sir. No. I wouldn't dream of it, sir." The young man jumped from his seat and nearly ran from the room, the money clutched in his fist.

Smiling and shaking his head, Mark sat back in his chair and considered the servants' stories. He'd got no inkling from any of them that they'd been responsible for poisoning their employer's drink. He doubted they even knew it had happened. Besides, the two footmen and the cook had no reason to kill John. They obviously liked him and he was responsible for their livelihood.

Most importantly the three servants had served as

each other's alibis, which made Mark's job less complicated. He no longer needed them to attend his uncle's event in the country. But that didn't put him any closer to knowing who *had* poisoned his cousin's wineglass.

Mark absently flipped through the papers in front of him. He'd only ever been able to do such mundane tasks for so long. He wanted to get to Surrey and begin the investigation. His trunk was packed and he and Oakleaf had carefully discussed their strategy. A surge of energy flowed through him. He always felt invigorated before he went on the hunt for someone, whether spy or killer.

He stood and paced to the window where he looked out onto the street in front of the house. Yes, he was more than prepared for the investigation to begin. What he wasn't prepared for was spending several days in the same bedchamber as his wife.

He groaned and scrubbed his hands across his face. He and Nicole had barely seen each other in the last few days, let alone touched each other. They were like strangers sharing a house. She'd spent her time shopping, exploring the house, and talking with the maids, while he'd been planning the investigation with Oakleaf and performing his duties managing the country's spies. There was less work to do these days than there once had been. With the wars with France over, the last few years had been much less taxing. Of course there had been the odd attempt at restoring Napoleon to the throne. A grim smile curled his lips. One such attempt he'd thwarted with the Cavendish brothers last year, but for the most part, Mark had been working to stop smugglers, thieves, and others who threatened England's shores.

He wanted to move into the political arena, and effect change through policy. The country needed a police force. The Bow Street Runners were stretched too thin. Nicole agreed with him.

Nicole?

Nicole probably thought he'd lost his bloody mind. She'd all but offered herself to him the other night and he'd turned her down out of spite . . . to himself. Which was stupid for more than one reason. First, he was denying himself the obvious pleasure, and second, he'd promised the woman he would impregnate her. Not only was he being an ass, he was being a dishonorable one, not holding up his end of the bargain.

He braced a forearm above his head against the wall and continued to stare unseeing out the window. Now things were simply . . . awkward between him and Nicole. It was about to get worse because they'd be going to Surrey to be glared at and dissected by the duke, the duke's sister, Aunt Harriet, and his cousin, Regina, Harriet's granddaughter, and God only knew who else. Damn it. He needed to get it over with and bed Nicole before things became even more difficult. Hell. It wasn't as if it would be a chore. Spending time with Nicole had never been a chore.

The weeks after meeting Nicole at her grandmother's ball had passed in a haze of stolen moments and even more stolen kisses. On leave from the army, Mark used every moment he could spare to court the lovely Lady Nicole Huntington. Curiously, her mother and grandmother allowed it. At first he'd been prepared for them to forbid it, but Nicole explained they'd told her they were confident she would make the right choice. The right choice obviously being the Marquess of Tinsley.

For his part, the marquess continued to arrive at Nicole's grandmother's town house with the same frequency that Mark did, only the portly older man increasingly found himself outwitted by the corporal. Each time the marquess arrived asking to see Lady Nicole, it seemed Mark had already been there and taken her off to go riding in the park, or to get an ice at Gunter's, or to do myriad other things that didn't matter as long as they were together. It was exactly as Mark had planned it. He reveled in outsmarting the marquess and was often rewarded with a kiss from the fair Lady Nicole.

Less than a month after they'd met, they took a walk in her grandmother's gardens. The sun had just slipped out of sight.

Nicole sighed. "I'll have to go back inside now. Mother will be looking for me."

They'd come upon the rose arbor where they'd shared their first kiss. Without saying a word, Mark stopped and turned to face her. He tugged her beneath the arbor and pulled her into his arms. The scent of roses perfumed the air. His lips swooped down to capture hers. She tasted like sunlight and strawberries.

Nicole wrapped her arms around his neck and kissed him back so passionately he'd have to take a cold bath later.

When he finally pulled his lips from hers, she rested her forehead against his chest and sighed again. "I always hope Mother will catch us doing that."

"What?" he half laughed, half gasped.

"You know. So I'll be ruined and you'll be forced to marry me." She pulled back and studied his face, a mischievous smile on her lips.

He chuckled. "That's not necessary."

"It isn't?" She blinked at him.

"No." Mark dropped to his knee, grasped her hands, and looked up into her beautiful face. "Lady Nicole Huntington, will you do me the great honor of becoming my wife?"

Her silence made his stomach drop. Had he misread her? He'd assumed she was falling in love with him as deeply as he was falling for her. She'd said a number of things that indicated she'd welcome a proposal and didn't seem to give a toss that he was merely a corporal in the army. Had he been wrong? Did she truly care about such things more than she seemed to?

The silence seemed to drag on for minutes until Mark realized her eyes were slowly filling with . . . tears.

He leaped to his feet and pulled her into his arms again. "Don't cry, sweetheart. If you don't want to—"

"No!" She nearly shouted. "I mean, yes. Yes, of course I'll marry you. I've been waiting for you to ask for days."

He smiled at her, kissed her, and several moments later when they were both able to talk again, he said, "I intend to make you the happiest woman in the world."

He picked her up and swung her around while they both laughed.

"That's good," she replied when he set her down again, his hands lingering at her waist. "Because I intend to make you the happiest man in the world. Let's go tell Mother."

Mark's stomach clenched at the memory. At least they hadn't *promised* to make each other happy. They'd both be damned liars.

Surprisingly, Nicole's mother and grandmother had agreed to the union. Mark had secretly thought they knew how stubborn Nicole was and didn't want to go up against her when she'd set her mind to something. Or perhaps they'd realized he was on his way to greater things. Mark knew the countess's solicitors had been asking questions about him to his colleagues. Had they discovered his relationship to the duke? He doubted it. Surely, they would have said something.

The banns were read the next three weeks in Nicole's family's church, St. George's of Hanover Square. Exactly two months to the day after they met, they were married. Mark managed to secure an extension on his leave in order to remain in town the rest of the summer. He and Nicole spent the long hot days in bed and preparing their new flat. It had been one of the happiest times of Mark's entire life. Before it had all been destroyed.

Mark blinked. He turned sharply away from the window and forced himself back to his desk, back to his work. No use remembering such things. The past was in the past, and that's precisely where it belonged. He glanced around his study. There was just one thing left to do before he traveled to Surrey for his cousin's memorial.

One hour later, he beat the knocker against Lord Tottenham's door. When it opened, Mark was ushered into the study by a regal-looking butler.

He didn't have long to wait before Lord Tottenham's voice came booming into the room. "Grimaldi, so good to see you. Come by to reschedule our dinner party, did you? Allen told me you intended to."

Mark stood to greet the large older man and held out his hand for a shake. "Unfortunately, no. Not yet. As you know, I've been helping with the investigation into the death of the Duke of Colchester's son."

Lord Tottenham gestured to Mark to take a seat before settling his girth into a large chair behind the desk. "Ah, yes. Bloody shame. John was a young man. I'm pleased you're on the case. Any suspects yet?"

Mark took a seat and crossed his booted leg over the opposite knee. "We have a few, but part of our strategy is to gather everyone who was there that night at the duke's country house. We want to see them interact. The duke has asked them all to Colchester Manor for a memorial. As a result, I'll be away for a few days."

Lord Tottenham lit a pipe and puffed a smoke ring before saying, "Yes, I know. I'll be attending as well."

Mark blinked. "My lord?"

Another smoke ring floated into the air. "Colchester intends to name his heir. Rumor has it the name may be a bit of a surprise. The duchy was not entailed normally, or so I've heard. It's certain to be one of the biggest pieces of news the *ton* has got in years. I asked the duke if I might attend. I'm a distant relative of his so he allowed it. I wouldn't miss it."

"You'll be in Surrey?" Mark asked stupidly.

"Yes." Lord Tottenham blew a third smoke ring. "And I do hope you'll be bringing your lovely wife. I look forward to getting to know her better."

Five minutes later, Mark grabbed his hat from the startled butler and nearly flew down Tottenham's front stairs to his coach. Lord Tottenham was coming to Surrey too? Perfect. Not only did that mean Mark would have to admit the truth to him about his family sooner than later, it also meant he and Nicole would have to pretend to be a loving couple the entire time and convince none other than the man who held his entire future in his hands.

CHAPTER TWENTY-FOUR

They left for Surrey early the next morning. Nicole wore a dark blue traveling gown, matching pelisse, and a new bonnet that she'd gone shopping for on Bond Street. Mark and Nicole had agreed not to wear the customary black of mourning to maintain the façade of not being related to the Colchester family, but they still wore dark clothing as a sign of respect.

Nicole's shopping outing had been a disappointment. She'd hoped to meet old friends, run into acquaintances. Instead, no one recognized her. She shouldn't have been surprised. She'd been gone for ten years. The debutantes she'd known were married ladies . . . with children. Apparently they weren't shopping at the same time she happened to be. Still, it had been bittersweet, strolling with Susanna and one of the footmen through London's shopping district. She hadn't realized how much she missed the teahouses and the good English milliners. It was lovely to speak in English and have no one turn up their nose.

Her outing was filled with memories and no one to share them with. She'd purchased a few items and come home to stare at the blank piece of vellum that *should* contain a letter to her mother. She'd almost hoped she'd run into her mother on Bond Street. At least that way she'd have been spared the need to write her. But Mother was in the countryside this time of year. The empty page had haunted Nicole until she finally tossed it into a drawer and slammed it shut. She would write her mother when she returned from Surrey.

Nicole glanced across the coach at Mark. She couldn't read his emotions. He was the stone man today. Was he sad to have lost his cousin so early? Even though he barely knew the man, John had been family, after all. Did Mark regret not having known him before his death? Was he kicking himself for not having visited his uncle until after the news? Probably not. Mark wasn't one to regret things. It begged the question, however. Did he have *any* regrets? If so, what were they?

She traced a finger along the coach's windowpane. These were the sorts of questions she would have asked him if things were different between them, but she didn't know where she stood with him. He'd made no attempt to touch her in all these days. She wasn't about to press the issue. He was dealing with a lot and it hardly seemed right to demand sex from a man whose uncle was dying and cousin had just been murdered.

But how was Mark feeling? He didn't need comforting. The man never had. She studied his features. He was reading the paper, the set of his wide shoulders dwarfing the seat on his side of the coach. No. He wasn't sad. He was more . . . angry. Angry at the killer. Mark would discover who had taken his cousin's life. Nicole had no doubt. He was not a man who suffered blows to those in his inner circle without retribution. Whoever had done this had done it to the wrong man. She greatly looked forward to the reckoning.

Nicole pulled her hands back into her lap and folded them, trying to think of something simple to speak to him about. His head was bowed over the paper. She watched the curve of his lashes against his cheeks, giving him a hint of vulnerability that she rarely saw. The silence was becoming unbearable. The safest subject would probably be the investigation. He liked to talk about clues. So did she.

Nicole cleared her throat. "In addition to the people who were at the dinner party the night John died, who else will be in Surrey?"

Mark glanced up from the paper he'd folded into a neat square. He hesitated, as if thinking, before answering. "In addition to Lord Tottenham, Daffin Oakleaf will be there."

"Daffin?" Nicole's eyes widened. A wide smile spread across her face.

Mark glanced at her and his mouth set in a line. "I didn't realize you were on a first-name basis with him."

Nicole merely shrugged. "I've always greatly admired him."

"Yes, he mentioned his admiration of you too," Mark drawled, focusing his attention back on his paper.

"He remembers me?" Nicole's smile remained plastered on her face. Her memories of Daffin were fond ones.

"Of course he remembers you. It's not as if he hires debutantes to run investigations for him every day." Mark's perturbed voice came from behind the paper.

"Perhaps he should," was Nicole's laughter-tinged reply. Already she wanted to change the subject. She'd always liked and respected Daffin, but Mark sounded annoyed. She wished that meant he was jealous. Of course, nothing romantic had ever taken place between Daffin and herself. Their relationship had been strictly professional, if a bit unusual. But jealousy from Mark would mean he cared more about her than he obviously did. Whatever he didn't like about the Daffin discussion, it would be best to talk about something else.

She scratched her forehead. "How long do you think you can keep the secret of your familial relationship with the duke from Lord Tottenham?"

The paper lowered to Mark's lap. "It will be difficult, but I want to keep the secret at least until my uncle makes the official announcement."

Nicole tilted her head to the side. "For the heir, you mean?"

He nodded.

"But surely you must tell him before that? You cannot let it be a complete surprise to him."

Mark merely shrugged and lifted the paper again. "I intend to see how it goes."

Nicole traced her fingertip along the embroidered edge of her pelisse. "You're still hoping for a miracle, aren't you? Some way out of it?"

"I have a few discreet questions in to colleagues at

Whitehall. I'm certain there must be a way to quietly renounce the duchy."

Nicole nodded, trying to make sense of the thing in her head. She'd never known anyone who'd renounced a duchy, or any title for that matter. "If you don't take it, who would get it? Mr. Cartwright?"

"I don't know. Probably." Mark folded the paper and tossed it on the seat next to him. He glanced out the window at the rolling green landscape. "If only Regina could take it."

"Regina?" Nicole blinked rapidly. "She's female."

Mark's lips twitched. He met Nicole's gaze. "Yes, I'm aware of that."

"And she's unmarried," Nicole continued.

Mark's eyes temporarily narrowed on her. "How do you— Oh, that's right, you said you two have kept in touch."

Nicole lifted her chin. "My mother also keeps me informed in her letters. About some people. The ones I like, and I've always liked Regina."

"What about Lady Harriet?" Mark asked, his lips twitching suspiciously.

"Harriet is a dear and you know it," Nicole replied.

Regina's grandmother, Lady Harriet, the duke's aunt, was a flighty little bird of an old lady with a big heart and a bigger mouth. Her granddaughter was clever, with a sensible head on her shoulders, and had refused all marriage offers because she was convinced they were all from fortune hunters and men looking to increase their prestige in the *ton* by hitching their wagon to a duke's niece. Regina and Mark actually had a great deal in common, only Regina hadn't rejected her family and pretended not to be a part of it. At the age of twenty-nine, Regina was an outspoken, confirmed spinster and Nicole liked few people more.

"Regina would be a sight better at being a duchess than I would a duke," Mark said. "Blasted unfair rules granting all the rights to men."

"How very progressive of you," Nicole said with a snort.

"You know I've never been one to discount women."

Nicole's stomach clenched. "Really? You could have fooled me. I recall you being none too pleased about my unconventional position with the runners."

Mark clenched his jaw. "I was none too pleased about your involvement with the runners because—"

"Let's not argue." Nicole snapped her head to the side to glare out the window. Nothing good could come from this conversation. She uttered a small sigh. "We're going to be in close quarters for several days in a row. I agree. Regina would make an excellent duchess. Though I also believe you'll make a fine duke." She tentatively met his gaze.

"I'm not meant to be a duke." His tone was strong and certain.

Nicole pressed her lips together. "Sometimes life calls upon us to be the things we never thought we were meant to be."

Mark's gaze caught and held hers again for a fraught moment.

She shook her head and continued, "I still think you should find a way to tell Tottenham before your uncle does."

Mark nodded. "I will, but not right away. I need to

find the perfect way to couch it. Not to mention explain why I've never revealed it before."

"Yes, that is sticky."

Mark picked up the paper again and unfolded it. "In the meantime, you and I must remain the image of the loving couple."

Nicole swallowed a lump that had formed in her dry throat. She needed to voice a thing she had been thinking for days. A thing that made her stomach churn. "You know, if you accept the marquisate, you might not need me. If Lord Tottenham knows you're part of the illustrious Colchester family, it may help your candidacy."

"Nonsense." Mark didn't look up from the paper.

"You and I both know that's not nonsense." She wanted to snatch the damn paper from his hands and toss it from the coach.

Mark looked up at her. "Then it's a damn good thing for you that the last thing I want to do is claim my heritage. Besides, you're wrong. Your being with me *will* help. Tottenham wants a family man. I still need you, Nicole." Their gazes met again.

She took a deep breath. "I still need you too."

She said no more. Mark returned his attention to the paper, while their words lingered in the silence.

CHAPTER TWENTY-FIVE

When Colchester Manor came into view, Mark clenched his jaw. The huge estate was an undeniably magnificent property with expansive, sweeping lawns, parks of trees, and a meadow filled with wildflowers that overlooked a lake. The property went on for acres and acres and was one of the finest in the land. Mark had only been here twice as a child; both times, his mother had brought him without his father. His father had never been welcomed here.

The place had always seemed ridiculous to Mark. Too big, too imposing, too opulent, too much of everything. It made him uncomfortable to see the eyes of his ancestors staring at him from the walls, forever captured in heavy oil paintings. He'd never felt at home here.

His grandfather had peered down at him as if he were a bug, glaring at him with menacing dark eyes and a face rife with disapproval. The cook had been nice to him. She'd given him a biscuit and patted him on the head. That was his most pleasant memory here. The other memories were . . . less pleasant.

The second time they'd visited, his mother had asked him to play upstairs in the old nursery while she spoke with her father. Mark was a lad of nearly eight and had grown easily bored, a condition that plagued him his entire life. He'd left the nursery and wandered about the enormous house, opening doors and peeping into the keyholes of locked rooms. He'd finally made his way to the ground floor, where he'd meandered around until he heard his mother's voice coming from his grandfather's study. Mark's fingers were on the door handle and he was about to enter the room to ask his mother when they'd be leaving, when his grandfather's angry words struck his ears.

"He's clearly half Italian," Grandfather barked.

"My husband is Italian, Father, or do you forget that too?" Mother's voice was sharp and defensive, unlike Mark had ever heard it.

"He's not your husband," Grandfather countered.

"You're mad. Of course he's my husband. We're married and I love him," Mother retorted.

"Bah. Love has little to do with marriage." Frustration sounded in his grandfather's voice. "I will never know why you have failed to comprehend that."

"No, Father, love has *everything* to do with marriage." His mother's voice was still angry, but there was an undercurrent of determination that Mark would never forget. "Love is the most important part of marriage. I'll never understand why you refuse to believe that."

"It's not too late. You can seek a divorce. We can have

the marriage annulled," his grandfather countered. "Besides, you're only married in the Catholic church. It's not even a *real* marriage."

His mother's shocked gasp frightened Mark. His fingers tightened involuntarily on the door handle.

"It may not be your chosen religion," Mother said, "but I assure you our marriage is quite real."

There was a sharp rap, as if his grandfather had slapped the top of the desk. "You're not thinking about this logically, Mary. If you denounce your marriage, we can still fix this."

"I have an eight-year-old son, Father, or did you forget that?" His mother's voice was tight.

"You can keep him," Grandfather replied. "We'll send him off to Eton. He won't be the first bastard to go there."

His mother's gasp was sharper this time and a scraping sound made Mark think she'd stood from her seat. He pulled his hand from the door handle where it had been frozen and took a step back.

"Bastard? How dare you? Mark is *not* a bastard and he never will be." The rustle of her skirts swept closer to the door. "And if you refuse to accept my husband or my son, then I am no longer a part of this family."

"You don't mean that," his grandfather intoned.

"Yes, I do. I'm leaving now and won't be back." The door handle turned. Mark held his breath.

"If you leave here, you won't be welcomed back."

"Good-bye, Father."

Mark scrambled away from the door. He ran down the corridor several yards to pretend he'd been examining an oil lamp on a nearby table.

When his mother opened the door to the study and stepped into the corridor, there were tears shining in her blue eyes. "Come now, Mark," she said, opening her arms to him. "We're going home."

That had been the last time he'd seen his grandfather. The last time he'd been to this palatial estate. His grandfather hated him. The man had made no excuses for it. Mark had heard it with his own ears. He'd called him a *bastard*. His uncle might claim that his grandfather had softened in his old age. That he and his mother had reconciled. That all three of them had agreed Mark was worthy of the title of duke, should it come to that. But Mark knew he had no business as the Duke of Colchester. He was in this house in one capacity, that of an investigator. He was doing his job. He refused to allow the memories to haunt him.

CHAPTER TWENTY-SIX

Nicole stared out the coach window and blinked, in awe of the splendor that was Colchester Manor. She'd heard stories about the estate but she'd never been here. It was even grander than what her imagination had conjured.

Regina and her grandmother, Lady Harriet, stood on the front steps of the enormous Palladian manor house as Mark's coach pulled to a stop in front of it. The two women hurried out to greet them.

The coachman hopped down and lowered the steps. Mark opened the door and helped Nicole alight and then he jumped down behind her.

"Mark and Nicole, I never thought I'd see the two of you again," Lady Harriet exclaimed as she made her way toward them, hoisting up her black skirts. "Especially not together." The old woman waved a black handkerchief in the air. It looked nothing so much as a bat circling her black-turbaned head.

Nicole gave Mark an amused look. "Prepare yourself," she whispered. Nicole had known Lady Harriett and Regina through Society functions after her debut.

Lady Regina, also dressed in a black gown, reached them first and held out her arms to give Nicole a hug. Regina's dark hair and blue eyes shone in the afternoon sunlight. "I must say I'd hoped for this day, but I never quite expected it." She squeezed Nicole tightly then stood her at arm's length, still grasping Nicole's elbows, so they could see each other.

Nicole's gaze traveled fondly over her old friend's features. Regina was even more gorgeous than Nicole remembered. The last ten years had only served to heighten her beauty. She looked a bit thin and tired, but no doubt that was due to the fact that her beloved cousin had just died.

"Regina." Nicole clasped the shorter woman's hands and squeezed them. She couldn't help the tears that sprang to her eyes. "It's so lovely to see you."

Lady Harriet shook her head. "Isn't it a pity that we should all meet again under such sad, sad circumstances?" She dabbed at her eyes with her handkerchief before opening her arms to hug Nicole also.

"Lady Harriet," Nicole intoned, giving the older woman a kiss on her papery cheek. "After all these years."

"You could not be more gorgeous, my dear," Lady Harriet said, reaching up to pat Nicole's cheek.

Mark cleared his throat and shifted on his feet. Neither lady hugged him. He was in full stone-man stance, his legs braced apart, his arms folded behind his back. If he was trying to keep his relatives at a distance, he was doing a fine job of it.

Nicole shook her head. So that was how it was going to be for their stay here: Mark refusing to acknowledge his family and serving only as an impartial investigator, while pretending to be in love with his estranged wife. *Such* a normal family.

Of course neither lady was a suspect in John's murder. They'd both been here at Colchester Manor the night John died and a slew of servants had already verified that via letters, according to Oakleaf, who had researched the whereabouts of all the family members. Mark had told Nicole that neither Lady Harriet nor Regina had been informed of the foul play suspected in John's death. Lady Harriet, because she wouldn't be able to keep the news a secret, and Regina, because it would only upset her.

"Cousin Mark," Regina finally said, curtsying to him.

"Lady Regina," Mark intoned, bowing. "And Lady Harriet." He offered a similar bow to his aunt.

Regina smiled warmly at Mark. "I must say I never thought I'd see you set foot back at Colchester Manor."

"Believe me, neither did I," Mark replied, his hands still firmly crossed behind his back. "You're looking lovely as ever."

"Thank you," Regina replied. "I hear you're in the running for the Home Secretary position."

Mark narrowed his eyes on the petite woman. He glanced at Nicole, who shrugged and held up her palms.

"How did you hear that?" he asked, returning his attention to his cousin.

"I hear many things," Regina replied, her blue eyes twinkling.

"It's not in the papers, is it?" Nicole asked.

"Not yet," Regina replied.

"The Home Secretary?" Lady Harriet craned her neck to stare up at Mark. "Why in heaven's name would you want that awful responsibility?"

Mark bit his lip to hide his smile. "It's a position I've aspired to for some time now, my lady."

"You young people and your ambition. Makes no sense to me." Lady Harriet fanned herself with her handkerchief, then pointed toward the house. "Let's all go inside and have some refreshments. You are the first to arrive."

Exactly how Mark had planned it, of course.

The ladies ushered Nicole and Mark inside, across the vast marble-floored foyer, and into a light blue drawing room that was the most magnificent space Nicole had ever seen. It was at least twice as big as the drawing room at her family's estate and was filled with priceless antiques, heavy rich carpets, and luxurious tapestries.

"Please sit." Lady Harriet took a seat on a delicate rosewood chair in the center of the room. She plucked at her dark skirts, her black-slippered feet barely grazing the rug-covered floor. Her turban sat haphazardly atop her head as if it might topple at any moment.

Regina chose a Chippendale chair near her grandmother, which left Nicole and Mark to sit next to each other on the dark green settee across from the ladies. They left a conspicuous gap between their bodies when they sat.

Regina and her grandmother shared a glance.

"You must tell us all about how you two finally made it back together," Lady Harriet said, the black handkerchief taking to the air again, like a bird to flight.

Nicole cleared her throat. "I decided to return. I've missed England and . . . well, it was time." She and Mark had talked about the potential pitfalls of this conversation during the long coach ride. They'd agreed that the less specific they were, the better.

"I, for one, couldn't be happier for you both," Regina said. "I'm merely surprised. You never mentioned anything about it in your letters, Nicole."

Nicole glanced down at her slippers. "It was . . . rather a sudden decision." She looked back up at Regina. "And you know how awful I am at keeping up with my correspondence." Both things were true. Why did she feel so guilty for saying them?

Regina smiled at Nicole. "I don't blame you. It's not my favorite pastime either."

"Yes, well, it's high time you two reunited," Lady Harriet interjected. "And none too soon." She punctuated each word with a flap of her handkerchief. "You must get about the duty of making babies. Immediately."

"Grandmama!" Regina plunked her hand on her hip and eyed the old woman warily.

"Don't you Grandmama me, miss." Lady Harriet crossed her arms over her chest and glared at her granddaughter. "It's bad enough you've refused to marry and provide me with great-grandchildren. At least I can hope for a grandniece or- nephew from these two." She waved the handkerchief in Nicole and Mark's direction.

"You've refused to marry, Regina?" Mark asked, cocking his head to the side. Nicole had to admire how smoothly he avoided more questions about his own life and lack of heirs.

Regina smoothed her dark hair with one hand. "It's not so much that I've refused, really. It's more that I have yet to find anyone I particularly *want* to marry. Not to mention, I have the ludicrous notion that you should only marry if you fall in love and actually *want* to spend the rest of your life with the person you're marrying." She rolled her eyes. "Call me mad."

Nicole reached over and squeezed Regina's hand. "I don't think you're mad at all."

"You sound like my mother," Mark said to Regina.

"Yes, I think I take after Aunt Mary quite a bit. Grandmama even says I look like she did at my age."

"I've only ever seen a miniature of her," Nicole admitted quietly.

Regina clasped her hands together and gave Nicole a bright smile. "Oh, we'll have to rectify that. There is a grand painting of her in the east wing. I'll show it to you while you're here."

"I would like that very much," Nicole replied. She dared a glance at Mark. He was staring out the window, clearly lost in his thoughts.

"Well, I'm certain you two are exhausted," Lady Harriet said, taking a long deep breath. "I'll show you to your room. We picked out one at the end of the corridor. It's large and comfortable and far away from the others." She beamed at them and batted her eyelashes. "You know, so you'll be at ease getting to the business of producing an heir, which is even more important, I'm afraid, now that our poor dear John is gone."

Nicole barely had a chance to contemplate *those* surprising words before the old woman added, "In fact, we don't have any plans till dinner. Now's the perfect time to begin."

CHAPTER TWENTY-SEVEN

An hour later, having refreshed himself with a change of clothing and a stiff drink, Mark knocked on the door to his uncle's study. He and Nicole had gone up to their bedchamber together and silently laughed after Lady Harriet left them, waggling her eyebrows. If they'd expected the older woman to be proper because she was in mourning, clearly they'd been mistaken. Lady Harriet didn't know the meaning of the word "subtle."

Mark and Nicole agreed they'd change clothing and rest for a bit, allowing Lady Harriet to think what she would. Nicole had actually fallen asleep, her light breaths filling the air. Mark had lain on the bed next to her, his body stiff as a board, until he gave up the pretense of resting. It was not the time to pounce upon Nicole, even if the idea of lovemaking in the afternoon held a certain appeal. Mark had sneaked out the door quietly so as not to disturb her, in search of a drink.

He scowled at the door to the study, the same room that had once housed his pompous ass of a grandfather. The door seemed smaller now. It was no longer the dark imposing barrier that had hidden an awful, scary man behind it. It was just a door. Just wood. Nothing special.

"Come in," came his uncle's frail voice.

Mark pushed open the door and stepped inside, further banishing his painful memories to the shadows. The space smelled of wood and lemon polish. The room was not as imposing as he'd remembered. Ornate furniture filled the space. The desk was still large and centered in front of the mullioned windows, but it was just a desk, nothing but a piece of furniture. The man who sat behind it now was a much different man, in a *much* different set of circumstances.

Despite his illness, his uncle had managed to wheel his chair to sit behind the desk. He looked so pale and thin, hunched over the grand piece of furniture. The duke couldn't be much more than five and sixty years old, but his illness had taken its toll and his son's death hadn't helped. He seemed to have aged ten more years since Mark had last seen him.

His uncle raised his arms and spread them wide to indicate the room at large. His voice shook when he spoke. "This will all be yours . . . soon."

Mark clenched his jaw and stared out the windows into the flower-dotted meadow beyond. "Please don't say that."

"Why shouldn't I? It's true." His uncle lapsed into a coughing fit. He slowly pulled a handkerchief from his lap and covered his mouth.

Mark took a seat across from him on the other side of the desk and waited for the fit to subside. "Nothing's been decided yet and you promised—"

His uncle waved a thin hand in the air. "I know. I know. I promised not to tell anyone that you're my nephew . . . yet. But once I announce the heir—"

"Just a few more days," Mark replied. "For the sake of the investigation." Would he ever be ready to be named heir to a dukedom? No. No, he would not.

"Very well." The duke sighed. He carefully backed up his chair and pulled open the drawer in front of him. With painstaking slowness, he retrieved a small, aged letter from inside the drawer. "I want to show you something, Mark. Something I hoped I wouldn't have to." The old man deliberately pushed the letter toward him with a shaking, wrinkled hand.

Mark glanced at the parchment. Then he narrowed his eyes on it. His name was written on top in a bold scroll. "No." Had he said that aloud?

The duke nodded toward the letter. "It's from your grandfather. I never sent it to you before because I assumed you'd rip it up. Such acts done in anger cannot be undone. I hope you've matured enough to finally read it, regardless of how you respond to it."

Mark took the letter. Rage rose in his throat, threatening to choke him. He didn't want to read it, but he also had no intention of ripping it up.

"Read it, Mark. I think it will help you to understand your grandfather a bit."

"You're assuming I want to understand him," Mark said through clenched teeth.

"I only meant—"

"I already understand perfectly. I understand he disowned my mother because of me and my father."

"Read it," the old man repeated in an even tone, pointing feebly toward the letter. "Please."

A knock at the door interrupted them. The butler stood there with Daffin Oakleaf at his side. Daffin was dressed in the red vest his profession was famous for.

"Ah, Oakleaf." Mark stood and crossed the thick carpet to greet the Bow Street Runner. Oakleaf's arrival was a welcome distraction from arguing with his uncle about the letter sitting on the desk, untouched.

The butler left them and Mark introduced Daffin to the duke. "Your Grace, may I present Mr. Daffin Oakleaf? He works for Bow Street and is the best of the lot. Daffin, this is my uncle, the Duke of Colchester."

Daffin bowed to the older man. "Your Grace."

"So, you're claiming me now?" the duke asked Mark with the hint of a smile in his voice. Then the older man turned his attention to Daffin. "Good to meet you, Mr. Oakleaf."

Mark nodded. "Daffin knows the details about our family, but Lord Tottenham does not and I'd ask you to keep it that way."

"As you wish, Mark, as you wish," the duke replied. He turned his attention back to Oakleaf. "Thank you for helping us discover who killed John."

"I'll do everything in my power, Your Grace," Oakleaf replied. "Speaking of Lord Tottenham, he intends to arrive tomorrow morning."

"Ah, good to know," the duke croaked.

"Have you learned anything else, about any of the diners?" Mark asked.

"I have." Oakleaf pulled open his coat and slid a small notepad from his inner pocket. He flipped it open and scanned it as he spoke. "About Mr. Cartwright, the man who believes himself next in line to the dukedom. No word on why John invited him to dinner that night. From all accounts, they were not close."

"That's true. They barely knew each other," the duke replied.

"Miss Lester and Lady Arabelle are friends. Both made their debuts last Season. They were accompanied by their mothers," Daffin continued.

"Yes?" Mark prodded.

"Lord Anthony was John's closest mate," Daffin said.

"I cannot imagine how Anthony is holding up. It'll be good to see him," the duke said, his eyes misting.

"And the last person? Lord Hillenbrand?" Mark asked.

Oakleaf flipped the notebook shut and stuffed it back into his pocket. "Apparently, Lord Hillenbrand had asked for Lady Arabelle's hand earlier this Season. She turned him down before accepting John's suit."

Mark rubbed his jaw. "That's interesting. Hillenbrand is a viscount, is he not?"

"Yes, but is he a jealous one?" Oakleaf quirked his brow. "Jealous enough to kill?"

"I don't know him," the duke replied. "I've met him once or twice, but I cannot remember anything specific John had to say about him." The old man tapped his forehead as if it might help him recall.

"Is there anything else, Your Grace?" Oakleaf's astute gaze turned to the duke. "Anything John said about any of these people that might help us with our investigation?"

The duke stared unseeing at his lap for a moment or two before sadly shaking his head. "No. Nothing. If I do remember something, I'll send for you posthaste."

"Thank you, Your Grace." Oakleaf bowed his head.

"I'm going to rest now," the duke said in a weary voice. He rang a bell that sat upon his desk and two footmen arrived to push his wheeled chair out of the room.

Mark and Oakleaf watched him go in melancholy silence. Mark waited for the door to close behind his uncle before he turned back to Oakleaf. "Who do you think did it?" he asked in a clipped voice.

Oakleaf shook his head. "We've got at least two good suspects. Cartwright and Hillenbrand both had a reason to want John dead."

Mark rubbed his chin. "Cartwright stood to inherit a dukedom."

"Or so he thought," Oakleaf replied with a wry smile.

"And Hillenbrand may have been angry about losing his potential betrothed to a marquess," Mark said.

Oakleaf nodded once. "Precisely."

"What about the others? Anything?"

Oakleaf walked to one of the windows, and stared out across the meadow. "This place isn't too bad, Grim. Don't have a clue why you'd renounce all of this." He turned and waved a hand around the study, grinning at Mark.

"I have my reasons," Mark ground out. His father's face flashed through his mind.

"Yes, and I'm certain they make perfect sense . . . to you."

"I asked about the others," Mark reminded him, growing impatient.

Oakleaf continued to grin at him. "And you wonder why they call you the 'stone man'?" He laughed, but before Mark could bark out a reply, Oakleaf added, "I found no indication that Anthony and John had had any sort of falling-out. Seems the two of them were thick as thieves. I fail to see what either of the ladies or their mothers would gain in killing Lord Coleford."

"Understood." Mark leaned back in his chair and steepled his fingers over his chest. "Anything else?"

"Just that we examined all the food and wine. The only glass that was poisoned was Lord Coleford's."

"I see. And the others? They all intend to arrive to-morrow as well?"

"Yes, from what I understand." Oakleaf stretched and waggled his eyebrows. "Now where is that wife of yours, Grim? I haven't seen her in an age and I daresay she'll be a sight for sore eyes."

CHAPTER TWENTY-EIGHT

Nicole sat in the brightly lit sunroom with Regina, sharing a cup of tea. It was lovely to discover that while Regina had grown more beautiful with age, she hadn't lost any of her biting wit and wisdom. They'd already talked about Nicole's mother, the latest fashions in both London and Paris, and Regina's steadfast refusal to take a husband.

"Why did you never visit?" Regina asked Nicole, pouring herself a second cup of tea.

Nicole took a deep breath and traced her finger along the edge of her half-filled cup. "At first it was because I was needed in France. I was working . . . for the War Office while I was there."

Regina nodded. "Yes, I remember hearing something about that. And after the wars ended?"

"I don't know." Nicole hesitated. She looked down and bit her lip. "I suppose I stayed out of habit. I was used to it there. I'd made a few friends. I moved out to the country to live in the lavender fields."

"And to avoid Mark," Regina finished quietly, setting the delicate china teapot back down on the silver serving tray that rested on the table between them.

Nicole calmly lifted her cup and took a sip of tea. "He was in France dozens of times over the last ten years. He could have looked for me. He never did."

"He almost died there, you know." Regina's words were barely a whisper.

Nicole sucked in her breath and stared at her companion, the teacup frozen in her hands. "Pardon?"

Regina didn't look at her. She busied herself adding two lumps of sugar to her tea. "He was in a French prison camp for months. They nearly beat him to death. Broke his nose three times."

Nicole's stomach clenched. She lowered her teacup with a shaking hand and set it on the table. She felt as if she might retch. "I . . . didn't know." She pressed suddenly freezing fingers to her middle. Horror and the urge to cry burned her eyes as she lifted them to meet Regina's. "Oh, Regina."

Regina reached out and squeezed Nicole's numb hand. "It's all right. He's back, he's alive."

But Regina's words didn't help. Bile rose in Nicole's throat. She didn't want to contemplate it, but all she could do was picture Mark's fine features bruised and bloodied, his strong body broken under the enemy's brutal hands. The image tore a hole through her heart. To imagine him abused and helpless when he'd always been such a strong, unyielding force. Yes, he was the stone man, but he did bleed.

Where had she been when he'd been so close to death? She bloody well would have hunted him down and tried to help with everything in her, if only she'd known. He'd nearly died. Her *husband* had nearly died.

Their wedding had been a small, private affair. Surprisingly, her mother and Grandmama hadn't been against the match. Nicole had expected them to put up a fight. She'd expected them to argue with her, tell her she should marry the marquess. Instead they helped her plan the ceremony and even agreed to Mark's demand that it be a tiny affair. There were no invitations sent to members of the *ton*. The banns were read and posted in the newspaper of course, indicating that Corporal Mark Grimaldi was to wed Lady Nicole Huntington. If anyone thought anything of it, they didn't mention it to the happy couple.

It wasn't until a few nights before the wedding that Nicole learned the truth about who she was marrying. She'd been trying to track down any member of Mark's family to invite to the wedding. She knew his parents were dead and he had no siblings, but surely he had an aunt or uncle or some cousins to share such an important event in his life. She meant to surprise him with his family, but she'd only been able to locate the part of his family that lived in Italy. She'd written to them and they had wished the new couple well but told her it was too far to travel. She couldn't blame them. She'd saved their letters to share with Mark after the wedding.

A few nights before the wedding, she made the fateful decision to ask Daffin for help. She sat across from the Bow Street Runner in his office as she had a hundred times before. "I only want to find one person on his mother's side," Nicole explained. "Just one person. Surely, there is someone still in England he's related to."

Daffin barely glanced up from his paperwork. "Of course there is."

"What?" Nicole blinked. She leaned across the desk, folding her arms in front of her. "Who?"

"He's got an uncle, two aunts, and two cousins."

Nicole cocked her head to the side. "What are you talking about, Daffin?"

Daffin pushed aside his papers and regarded Nicole down the length of his nose. "His mother's side of the family. They live right here in London . . . when they're not at their estates."

"Estates?" Surely the runner was mistaken. "What in the world are you saying?"

Daffin dropped his quill and looked at her. His expression changed to surprise when he read her features. "Surely you aren't telling me that you don't know that Grim's family on his mother's side is the Duke of Colchester and his lot."

"The Duke of what?" She jumped from her seat and braced her palms on the desk, staring at Daffin in shock.

Daffin winced. "Damn. I never thought he wouldn't have told you. I probably shouldn't have said anything. You must promise me not to tell him that you know."

"Why wouldn't he have told me himself?" A thousand thoughts flew through her mind. It definitely explained why her mother and grandmother were fine with the match. Why hadn't *they* told her either?

"How exactly is he related to them?" she demanded.

"The duke is his mother's brother. The former duke was his grandfather. The Marquess of Coleford is his cousin."

Later, Nicole had asked her mother why she hadn't said anything. "Oh, darling, Corporal Grimaldi clearly didn't want anyone to know who his family was. We weren't about to be the ones to tell you. Frankly, we thought part of the reason you liked him was because he was a nobody. We feared if you knew you were marrying the grandson of a duke you might cry off."

"Did you always know?" Nicole asked, still baffled.

"No, darling. At first we thought he was a nobody too, but when you seemed so attached to him, your grandmama hired a man to do some investigating."

"You *spied* on him?" Nicole couldn't breathe.

Her mother waved a hand in the air. "I wouldn't call it spying, dear. We simply needed to know who you were falling in love with. We weren't about to allow you to marry just anyone, regardless of your affection for him."

Nicole had been forced to let that go. It bothered her that her mother and grandmother had been manipulative, but it would be silly to argue the point when she was madly in love with Mark and longed to become his wife. So she proceeded to the wedding without mentioning a word to her husband about his family, hoping he might tell her himself. He never did. She made a fateful choice by not telling him that she knew.

Mark was obviously pleased she'd kept the wedding small. Nicole's mother and grandmother were there, of course. The Duke of Colchester and his wife had sneaked into the back of the church. They'd quietly left before the ceremony ended. Nicole pretended she hadn't seen them. Mark pretended too. He hadn't said a word to them or her. She could not understand why her husband didn't want her to know. He married her with no other family present. Her heart had ached for him, but she would be his family now. She and the children they made together.

If there was one thing she'd been looking forward to, it was the method of producing children. Her heart raced each time she considered making love for the first time that night. Her mother had sat her down for an awkward conversation during which she told her the basics of what would happen. Nicole suffered through it with a blank look on her face, nodding at the correct parts and asking a question here and there. She wasn't frightened. She was eager. She and Mark had barely been able to keep their hands off each other during their engagement. She couldn't wait to share her body with him.

That night, after dinner at her grandmother's house Mark had taken her back to his flat. They'd walked together, silently, up the stairs to the small set of rooms. The place was sparse but clean and smelled like him, his delicious cologne. He gave her a tour of the small parlor, the tiny kitchen, the . . . bedchamber. She hovered in the doorway while he lit a lamp on the table next to the bed before coming back to take her hand and lead her into the room.

He faced her and clasped his hands over her shoulders, his thumbs drawing circles over them to help her relax. "Are you frightened?"

"Not at all." She shook her head. "I've been looking forward to this for weeks." She gave him a bright, saucy smile.

Mark laughed and pulled her into his arms. When his mouth found hers, all traces of laughter vanished. His fingers worked their way into her hair, where he began greedily sliding the pins from their places. Those clever fingers moved down to the buttons on the back of her wedding gown. She'd chosen a simple silhouette of white satin. She'd adored wearing it all day but now was eager to be out of it.

While Mark popped open button after button along her back, Nicole's hands moved to his cravat and ripped at the fabric. Untying the bow and knot, she pulled it from his neck and tossed it to the floor before moving her hands down to work on the buttons of his waistcoat. They ripped at each other's clothing in a frenzy.

She paused in their kissing to help him pull her gown over her head. Then he divested himself of his shirt. Their mouths locked together again, her fingers traced the outline of his muscled abdomen while he reached behind her and pulled hastily on the laces to her stays. When that contraption finally hit the floor, she leaned down and pulled her shift over her head, tossing it aside to stand completely naked in front of him, save for her stockings.

"Now you," she breathed, staring at the fall to his breeches. He moved quickly to the bed, shucked his boots, and lay back while she climbed atop him to help him remove his breeches.

Her fingers worked on the buttons to the fall while she leaned down and kissed him, her tongue exploring every part of his mouth. Once the buttons were undone, he sat up and she moved to the side while he pulled off his breeches. Then he turned and, smiling, tackled her to the bed, his chest coming down hard atop her, her legs parting of their own volition beneath him. He felt like silk and steel and she breathed in the heady scent of him, her head nuzzled in the crook of his neck while his mouth found the delicate spot beneath her ear. "You're gorgeous, Nicole," he breathed.

"It's funny," she gasped against him as he sucked her earlobe into his mouth. "I think the same about you."

He pushed himself away from her to gaze admiringly down her body while she did the same to him. Her eyes fastened on his large member jutting from between his legs, nestled in a thatch of dark, curly hair. She leaned down and grasped it in her fist, squeezing it out of instinct and the desire to feel every inch of it. Mark groaned and shuddered.

She smiled a catlike smile against his shoulder. "Do you like that?" she asked in a breathy voice.

"Very much." He nuzzled his way down her neck until his mouth hovered just above one of her breasts. She'd been forced to let go of him when he moved lower, but was temporarily distracted by his admiration of her breasts. "These are magnificent," he breathed, staring at them in obvious fascination.

He bent his dark head and took a nipple into his mouth. Nicole cried out and arched her back. Oh God. Her body hummed with desire, as if a cord had been drawn between her breast and the aching space between her legs, which was quickly becoming wetter and wetter.

She'd known that would happen. It happened every time Mark kissed her and it happened even more when she'd laid in bed, thinking about him night after night. Having him touch her, his rough hands gliding over her body, his teeth gently tugging at her nipple, made her wetter than she'd ever been. His hand moved down between her legs. His finger searched through the triangle of hair there. It found the bud of pleasure nestled in the center of her wet warmth. He stroked it with his thumb and she cried out again, grasping his dark head to her breast and shuddering with pleasure.

She tossed her head fitfully against the bedsheets as he continued to stroke the nub between her legs. Each time he did it, she cried out again, unable to control the building pressure and her body's response to his touch. When he slipped a finger inside her, she moaned deep in her throat.

His lips moved back up to her mouth to quiet her, and his tongue tangled with hers while his finger moved in and out of her with maddening slowness. She grasped his head with both hands and kissed him with all the pent-up lust she couldn't control. "Oh, God, Mark."

"Shh," he whispered against her lips. "Just feel it, Nicole. Let it happen."

Let what happen? She wasn't certain, but she desperately wanted to find out. His finger played with her more before his thumb returned to nudge the spot between her legs that made her legs tense and her thighs quiver. He moved his lips back down to her breast and tugged at her nipple once, twice, between continuing his descent to rain kisses along her trim belly and then . . .

he parted her thighs with both hands, his mouth a whisper away from the nub he'd made so swollen and wet.

She bit the back of her hand to keep from crying out. She knew what he was going to do, instinctually she knew, and she didn't want to move a muscle for fear he would stop. She held her breath, every aching sinew in her body tensed and ready to feel his mouth on the spot where she desperately ached for it.

When he lowered his tongue to her, she gasped. The tip moved through the springy hair to part her lips there and rub deliciously over the swollen nub that ached for him. She whimpered in the back of her throat. Her hands moved down to tug at his hair and hold him in place. "Don't stop," she begged.

"I wouldn't dream of it," came his deep, aroused voice. She felt his smile against her thigh.

His tongue plunged again and again, rubbing roughly over the spot where she needed it most until her legs shifted restlessly beneath him and she arched up on both hands, her breasts jutted out. Her head fell back, her hair dangling behind her to brush across the mattress.

"Oh, God, Mark," she breathed.

He slipped a finger inside her then and pressed upward against the inner wall of her sex, hitting a spot so perfect, so sensitive that she cried out again, and when he paired it with the brush of his tongue against that spot between her legs, she cried out one last time as shudders racked her body and tremors made her limbs quake. She fell backward against the mattress, her body deliciously limp, her breath coming in hard, fast pants, as she tried to make sense of what had just happened to her, an experience unlike any other.

"That was . . ." She tried to speak but words failed her.

"The most beautifully erotic thing I've ever seen." He pulled her hand to his lips and kissed her knuckles.

"But you're not . . ." She blushed and continued to pant.

"I'm not?" He arched a brow.

"Mother told me what happens in bed between a man and woman," she explained, too weak to rise up on an elbow and look him in the eye. "And that wasn't it," she finished with a wry smile.

"It wasn't?" he said with feigned surprise, lifting his eyebrows high.

She weakly pushed at his arm while he laughed, his wide shoulders shaking with mirth.

"Don't make sport of me," she said, in a mock-angry tone. "I'm new to this, you know."

He rolled atop her and covered her with his body again, his laughter fading. His lips covered hers, his hard probing length searching between her thighs.

"I believe the correct way to go about the actual act," he breathed into her ear, "is something like this." He circled his hips above her. She clutched at his thighs, wanting to guide him into the nest between her legs.

His length slipped against her wet warmth and she reached down to clasp him in her fist and lead him into place. He felt like heated silk, throbbing, reaching for her.

"Yes, sweetheart." He kissed her forehead, her neck, the delicate shell of her ear. When he was in place, he breathed in and out for a few moments while Nicole pre-

pared herself for the pain her mother had assured her
would be a part of this.

But when he slid inside, there was only the heat of
him, the wet warmth and the slick slide of him, pushing her open and filling her. She fiercely wrapped her
arms around his neck, her eyes widened with shock.

"What's wrong?" he asked, gazing down at her and
swiping a strand of her hair from her face.

"Mother said . . . it would . . . hurt." She winced, embarrassed to admit it to him.

"Yes, well, it doesn't have to," he replied, kissing her
forehead again. "If you have a partner who knows what
he's doing."

She didn't have time to think about that loaded reply
because he began to move and her breath arrested in her
throat. The hot length of him slid slowly in and out of
her, pausing so his fingers could glide down her body
and once again find the nub between her legs. He skill-
fully brought her to climax one more time before
pumping into her. Sweat beaded on his forehead as he
released himself inside her while calling out her name.

In the aftermath, he pulled her atop him and stroked
his fingers through her long hair. "I love you, Nicole,"
he breathed against her temple.

"I love you too, Mark," she replied on a long, satisfied sigh. "More than words can say."

They'd spent the next few days in bed, where he'd
proceeded to teach her a variety of different positions
and the places on her body that were the most sensitive
to pleasure. He'd taught her about his body too, what he
liked and where her touch caused his pulse to quicken.

They'd talked, laughed, and discussed all sorts of topics ranging from his love of horses, to her favorite Lawrence painting. Nicole had never been happier.

Regina cleared her throat and Nicole's tear-blurred gaze found her friend's across the table in the sunroom. Oh, how her heart ached when she thought of that man, the man who had awakened her to passion, being beaten mercilessly in a French prison camp.

"His imprisonment was a long time ago," Regina said softly, handing Nicole a handkerchief. "I never wrote and told you because . . ."

"Because I asked you not to mention him in your letters. I know." Nicole took a deep breath and wiped the tears from her cheeks. "But how did you know about his captivity? He doesn't keep in touch with any of you."

"Uncle Edward keeps tabs on him. There are stories in the papers. We know a great deal more than Mark thinks we do." Regina searched her face. "I didn't mean to upset you."

"I'm not upset . . . I'm . . ." God. What was she? Nicole didn't know anymore. She'd spent so many years trying to numb her emotions when it came to Mark. She'd spent so many days picturing herself reading the letter that would inform her of his untimely death, trying to prepare herself for it. To hear it had been a near possibility . . . it just . . . shattered her. She folded the handkerchief into a tight square and dabbed at her damp eyes again. "*Merde.* I'm not one to cry."

"Of course not," Regina said. "You are my fearless cousin who worked for both the Bow Street Runners and the War Office and I've been wanting to ask how you managed both. I may be interested in a similar path. So, please tell me."

Nicole smiled and tucked the handkerchief into her sleeve. Regina was a dear for changing the subject. "I don't know about the fearless part, but I wanted to do what I could to help."

"But how did you manage it? How did an earl's daughter become a female Bow Street Runner?"

Nicole laughed. "I was never officially a runner. I was an assistant. A helper. They weren't about to appoint me to the team." She stared out the window at the hawthorn trees, memories overtaking her again.

Nicole had walked into the office on Bow Street on trembling legs. Would they laugh at her? Throw her out? Both were possibilities. She forced the two thieves in front of her to march at the end of her pistol and they both did so, possibly because they were astonished by the fact that they'd been apprehended by a lady.

A young man with silver spectacles and a slight build sat behind a desk that looked far too large for him. "May I help you, lady?" he asked, his eyes widening at the sight of Nicole and her two prisoners.

"Yes, please." Nicole straightened her shoulders. "I am here to see one of the Bow Street Runners. I would like to turn in these two wanted men for the crime of stealing."

The young man's eyes darted back and forth behind the spectacles and he plucked at the haphazard dingy cravat at his throat. "Oakleaf!" he finally called out.

Moments later, a large, blond god of a man strode from one of the offices in the back. He was dressed in tight-fitting black breeches, black boots, a white shirt and cravat, and a red waistcoat. He must have left his overcoat in the back. When he saw Nicole, he pulled a cheroot from his lips and whistled. "Well, I'll be a son of a—"

"My name is Nicole Huntington," she interrupted, purposely leaving out the lady part. "I'm here to turn these two in. They are thieves." Her heart hammered in her chest and she eyed the runner warily.

The blond god named Oakleaf strolled up to the three of them and gave them each a once-over. "Good morning, Miss Huntington," he said with a wide grin. "My name is Daffin Oakleaf and I have a slew of questions for you."

"Are you a Bow Street Runner?" she asked, head still held high.

"I am." He tilted his head toward her in the semblance of a bow.

Nicole swallowed. "Then I shall be happy to answer your questions once we have these brigands squared away. I have a few questions of my own."

"Who are they?" Daffin asked, walking around the men in a wide circle, still clutching his cheroot between his fingers.

"The two thieves you were looking for in yesterday's paper," she informed him with a solid nod.

Oakleaf's eyes went wide and his mouth dropped open. "Parker and Smith? *You* found them?"

"Yes." A proud smile popped to Nicole's lips.

"Why bring them to us?" Daffin's eyes narrowed in suspicion.

Nicole summoned every ounce of courage she possessed. She concentrated on ensuring that her voice did not waver. "I want you to hire me."

"Oh, lady." His grin returned even broader. "I want to hear *all* about this."

And so her relationship with Daffin and the runners had begun. He hadn't liked the fact that she was female. He liked it even less when she admitted she was a lady. But she'd been able to convince him she could help. Many crimes were committed by and against the aristocracy, after all. Who better to be watching without being paid any mind than a young lady of the *ton*? Who better to sneak up on unsuspecting brigands in the streets than a woman no one would suspect was looking for them? This, and only this, had convinced Daffin to allow her to be a part of his tribe.

He would not allow her to call herself a runner. She was an assistant, and if that was as close to becoming a member of law enforcement as she could be, it was good enough for her. For the moment.

She'd prove her worth and convince them they needed her. They couldn't officially hire a woman, but they could accept her help and give her a share of the bounty. She readily accepted.

After working out the particulars, Daffin had set to work teaching her. He showed her techniques of watching people, questioning suspects, establishing alibis, tracking people down, and searching for clues. She'd had many good instincts on her own, but with his help she'd exceeded expectations. By the time she'd been working with him for two years, she was one of the finest of the lot, according to Daffin. Which was why the night she'd met Mark, she'd been chasing the servant out to the mews with nary a thought.

She'd hoped Mark would be proud of her accomplishments. She'd thought he'd look at her with more pride and respect. Instead, when he discovered her affiliation with Bow Street, it was just another strike against her. She'd been asked to work for the War Office through a connection of Daffin's, and after she and Mark had their falling-out, she took it. She had more reasons than one to leave England.

"I want to help too," Regina said, snapping Nicole from her thoughts again.

Nicole furrowed her brow. "Help with what?"

"I want to help discover who murdered Cousin John."

CHAPTER TWENTY-NINE

Mark provided Oakleaf the directions to the sunroom where he'd last seen Nicole. He was sorely tempted to go with him and witness his loving wife's reaction to seeing the Bow Street Runner again, but he didn't want to have to punch Oakleaf in the face when the man was doing his family a favor by being here. And at the moment Mark was even more curious about something else.

He stared at the letter that sat untouched on his uncle's desk. He slowly placed his hand atop the aged parchment, then snatched it away as if he'd been stung by a wasp. Damn it. How did a dead man still have this power over him? This was just a piece of paper. It meant nothing.

Drawing a deep breath, he pulled the letter toward him, carefully unfolded the parchment, and scanned the words. Bloody hell.

Mark,

If you're reading this then I am gone. Your parents are also dead. I am sorry. I know how difficult it is. The same thing happened to me when I was a young man in my early twenties. I had no idea how to be a duke then, Mark. The truth is, there are days I still think I don't know how. Your mother and I never had a simple relationship. She seemed hell-bent on defying every one of my wishes and I was too much of a fool to let it go. If I could go back now and see her again, I'd tell her that. Alas, I cannot.

I did not know your father well. I'm certain he was a good man. I do know that he adored your mother and while that should have been enough for me, at the time, it was not. I have lived with that regret all these years. I also know your father was a proud man. Your mother told me that he asked you to never rely on our side of the family. It's a sentiment I cannot blame him for. But what you don't understand is the importance of family to me too. I love both of my children more than my own life. The fact that I didn't always agree with your mother's actions is what pulled us apart and it is what I regret now more than anything.

I am asking you, Mark, to consider this side of your family now. Mary and I spoke just before she died. I told her I loved her. She said the same to me. Your uncle was there too. She asked both of us, should the need ever arise, to convince you to take up your rightful place in this family and become the duke. Hence, my writing this letter.

I know becoming the duke is probably the last thing you want to do, but think of your mother. It was not her fault that I pushed her away out of my vanity and need to control everything. I'm told that you're like me in that way, that you also like to control things. If so, I think you'll make a fine duke. I can only hope you learn from my mistakes. Do not push away the people you love and who love you because they refuse to be the people whom you think they should be. The duchy of Colchester needs you. Your mother, who never asked anything from you in life, needs you. Do not let her down.

Bloody hell. Frustration and rage roiled from the pit of Mark's stomach and soared up his throat. He wanted to yell. He wanted to punch his fist through the nearest wall. The only thing that could counteract his father's deathbed request was the same request from his *mother*. The papers slid through his hands and fluttered to the desktop. He pressed the heels of his hands to his temples and squeezed his eyes closed. He hadn't even been there to hear his mother ask him. He hadn't been there for her, to hold her hand and tell her he loved her as she died. He'd had to hear about it after the fact.

At least she hadn't been alone. Apparently, she'd reconciled with her family before she died. But damn it, why, why did this have to be the case? He'd had his life carefully planned for years now and none of it involved his taking up the duchy of Colchester. None of it.

His head still bowed, he opened his eyes and stared at the papers in front of him. Although his grandfather had signed his letter, there was another page. Squinting, he pushed the first page aside and stared at the last page for several seconds before it registered that it was written in another hand.

His mother's hand.

"No," he whispered, closing his eyes again briefly. Anything but this.

He took a deep, fortifying breath and forced himself to concentrate on the page. The vellum trembled like a leaf in the breeze in his unsteady hands.

My darling Mark,
You're in Spain now. My illness is progressing and I fear I will not see you again. There are things I must say to you. Things you don't know. Your father and I loved you dearly of course, but I was the one who pushed away my family. I rejected them when they tried to make amends. It wasn't the other way around. I regret that now, Mark, because I want you to know them. I want you to be connected to them. They love you. I know if you will give them a chance they will show you that. I regret that you grew up not knowing your cousins. I regret that you grew up not knowing your aunt and uncle. I sorely regret that you grew up not knowing your grandfather, due to my choices, not theirs and not yours. I know your father asked you to never rely on them. I would not ask that of you either. But what I do ask you, Mark, what I need from you, is to allow them to rely on you. If you're reading this it's because John is dead. I asked Edward to give you this letter. You've al-

ready proven yourself in this world, Mark. You've made yourself the man you are without any help from my family. The time has come for you to help them, however, and I am asking you, I am begging you not to turn your back on them. For my sake. I know you will do the right thing. Duty has always been important to you. Your duty now is to take up the title of Duke of Colchester when the time comes.

Love forever, Your Mother

Mark folded the letter and expelled his breath in a rush. Leave it to the members of the aristocracy to do things like write heart-wrenching letters to be produced in the event that an heir died. They were constantly planning to secure their titles.

Bloody hell. Part of him had hoped that his uncle had been lying. That his grandfather had been lying. That his mother hadn't really reconciled with them. It would make the entire thing much easier to deal with. He could reject them and feel right about the whole thing. But there was no mistake. The words he'd just read were in his beloved mother's handwriting. The tone of the letter was in her sweet voice. There was no way this wasn't real. His mother had died of consumption. She'd been of sound mind when she went. She knew what she was doing and she'd asked him on her deathbed to let her family rely on *him*.

He folded his arms across the desktop and let his head drop onto them. Damn it all to hell. This changed *everything*.

CHAPTER THIRTY

Nicole blinked furiously at Regina. "What? How did you—"

Regina leaned back in her seat and folded her arms across her chest. "Don't try to deny it, Nicole. John was murdered. I'm certain of it."

"How did you know?" The demand emerged breathless from astonishment.

"So I'm right?" Regina leaned forward again, an eager look on her pretty face.

Nicole drummed her fingertips along the tabletop. "*Merde.* Yes, you're right."

"I knew it!" Regina clapped her hands.

Nicole narrowed her eyes on her friend. "But truly how did you know?"

Regina set her teacup on the table in front of her and fingered the rim of the cup. She lifted one shoulder. "I read about his death in the paper and it simply didn't make sense to me. John had never had an attack. He was a fit and healthy young man. When Uncle Edward asked us all to meet, I knew my suspicions were correct." She leaned forward, her eyes wide. "There will be investigators here, won't there be? Bow Street and the like?"

Nicole glanced around to ensure they were alone. She lowered her voice. "Yes, Mr. Oakleaf will be here."

"Ooh, who is Mr. *Oakleaf*?" Regina asked brightly, rubbing her hands together in obvious glee.

"Mr. Oakleaf . . . Daffin is the best of the Bow Street Runners. He and I worked together years ago."

Regina's pretty blue eyes searched Nicole's face. "A *real* Bow Street Runner will be here? I cannot wait to meet him. The investigation, it's why you and Cousin Mark are here too, isn't it?"

"Yes," Nicole admitted. "I'm not supposed to be investigating of course, but I'd like to see them try to stop me." She grinned at Regina.

Regina laughed and clapped her hands. "Ah, that is why you're my favorite, Nicole. Spoken just like a true Colchester."

Nicole's smile was forced. It made her cheeks ache. She wasn't a Colchester and she never truly would be one. But perhaps . . . perhaps her child would be. If she and Mark ever managed to get to the business of creating one.

"What I don't understand," Regina continued, "is why you and Cousin Mark came back to London together before John was murdered. I mean, you were in London that night, weren't you? Which meant you had to have been planning to come back before John died."

Nicole's breath hitched. How much should she tell

Regina? "It's true," she said after a moment. "We were on our way back long before John died."

Regina watched her cautiously. "Care to tell me why you two suddenly made up after ten years?"

Nicole sighed and scrunched up her nose. "Suffice it to say your cousin came to France and made me an offer that was impossible to decline."

Regina's jaw dropped. "Oh, no, now you *must* tell me more. You cannot—"

A slight knock on the door snuffed the conversation. The two women's heads swiveled to see who was there.

Nicole jumped from her seat, hastily gathered her skirts in her hands, and hurried toward the door. "Daffin! It's so good to see you."

The Bow Street Runner seemed taller and blonder than ever. His green eyes sparkled, his square jaw was like the edge of a razor, and his muscles went on for miles. Nicole would be utterly infatuated if she had eyes for any man other than her own blasted husband. Daffin was a good man too. He'd give you the shirt off his back and could be called upon day or night to help in any crisis. She was honored to call him friend.

Daffin Oakleaf held out his arms and Nicole rushed into them, hugging him. "Good to see you too, Nic," he said with a laugh.

"You must come meet my cousin Regina." Nicole tugged him into the room. "She's Mark's cousin, actually, which makes her my cousin by marriage. She just mentioned how much she looked forward to meeting you."

Regina rose from the table, her eyes bright and cheeks flushed, as Daffin made a slight swerve around Nicole and beelined straight to her. He stopped before her, and for a long moment, neither spoke. Nicole glanced back and forth between the two. Was it her imagination or had sparks leaped between them? They stared at each other intently, each sizing up the other.

Nicole shook her head, realizing her failure to make the proper introductions. "Lady Regina Haversham, this is Mr. Daffin Oakleaf."

Regina picked up her black skirts with both hands and executed her best curtsy. "Mr. Oakleaf."

"Mr. Oakleaf, this is Lady Regina. She is the duke's niece."

Daffin took Regina's hand and bowed over it. "My lady, a pleasure. I'm sorry to hear of your cousin's death."

"Thank you, Mr. Oakleaf. I appreciate that, and the pleasure is all mine." Regina's blue eyes smoldered as she spoke.

Nicole continued to glance back and forth between them. Oh, yes, there was definitely a spark in the air.

"Are you still hiring ladies to be Bow Street Runners?" Regina asked Daffin, a saucy smile on her lips.

Daffin arched a blond brow. "Are you volunteering?"

"Yes," Regina replied. "Yes, I am. Especially if I get to work with you."

CHAPTER THIRTY-ONE

Mark tossed back the final finger of brandy in his glass. He'd been drinking with Oakleaf in his uncle's study for the last hour. In the shadows, the grandfather clock stirred to life, dutifully bellowing the midnight hour.

"What is it with women in your family and the desire to investigate crime?" Oakleaf asked him. He'd just finished relating the story of how he'd met Regina in the sunroom.

Mark shrugged. "I can't explain it. It must run in our line."

"Nicole told me I should hire her." Oakleaf shook his head.

Mark pushed his empty glass around the desktop in a circle as he considered Oakleaf's words. "Regina's clever. Always has been. I should have known she would guess the truth about what happened to John."

Oakleaf rubbed the back of his neck and groaned.

"Yes, well, both ladies peppered me with questions for the better part of an hour. Lady Regina agreed to keep the news a secret, however."

"Good." Mark nodded, then shifted in his seat. "And was my wife a 'sight for sore eyes' as you said?" He narrowed his eyes on the runner.

"She's a fine-looking woman." Oakleaf emptied his glass and set it down with a resolute thud on the desk.

Mark was about to reply to that loaded statement when Oakleaf added, "As is your cousin Regina."

Mark flicked the glass hard, making a pinging sound. He wanted to toss the bloody thing into the fireplace. Damn it. No good could come of arguing with Oakleaf. The man was obviously trying to rile him. No more brandy. It was time to retire. He and Nicole would be sharing a bedchamber tonight, and Oakleaf was right. She was a fine-looking woman indeed.

A hot jolt of anticipation streaked through Mark's middle and settled in his groin. Would she welcome him into the bed or ask him to sleep in a chair in the corner? It was bloody ridiculous to contemplate, but he'd put it off for long enough. The last time they'd been alone together, in the coach, she'd said she needed him too. He'd known what she was really saying. She'd lived up to her part of the bargain, now it was time for him to live up to his.

Yes. He needed to be a man and make love to his wife, but it stuck in his craw that she'd mentioned his being upset about her involvement with the runners when they'd spoken in the coach. First, she'd failed to reveal that bit of news before they married. Second, and most importantly, it was true he hadn't liked her involvement with Bow Street, but not for the reason she seemed to think.

The runners risked their lives on a daily basis, chasing down thieves and murderers. Nicole might enjoy the adventure, but she put herself at risk by working with Daffin. Mark had been scared witless every time he contemplated her being exposed to such danger. It wasn't because he didn't believe women could take care of themselves. Two of his best spies were Daphne and Danielle Cavendish, Rafe's and Cade's wives. He'd trust those women with his life. He would trust Nicole too. The difference was . . . God damn it, the difference was that he had *loved* Nicole. She was his family. The only family he had left. He'd watched his father die and he'd been absent for his mother's death. Losing Nicole would have been too much for him. He'd never said those words aloud. Now it was too late. He'd take his own life before he'd tell her that.

He'd already had to pressure her to allow him to make love to her, not tup her like a common whore. If she didn't want to call lying with him making love, she certainly wouldn't want to hear those other words from him now.

He groaned and scrubbed both hands across his face. She wanted a baby. A piece of him that would open him up to the fear of loss, the unimaginable pain. The notion of having a baby made his stomach clench. He hated the thought of losing a child. Seeing his uncle's reaction to John's death made it worse. But Mark had agreed to Nicole's condition. He would not go back on his word. Yes, tonight, he would keep his promise. It was time.

Mark stood and headed toward the door. "Good evening, Oakleaf."

"Evening, Coleford." The hint of a smile resided in the runner's voice.

Mark's only reply was a growl.

Nicole had asked Susanna to help her into the most risqué bit of lace and silk that could still qualify for a shift. She pulled her hair down and ran her fingers through it, brushing it until it shone. Next, she drank half a glass of wine to calm her nerves. Then she crawled into the middle of the fluffy white feather bed and kneeled in the center, waiting for Mark.

Not five minutes later, Mark opened the bedchamber door and strode inside as if on a mission. He headed for the antechamber where his clothing was, tugging at his cravat. He didn't even glance up to look at her. Her knees trembled and her heart pounded. Was the man even going to acknowledge her?

After several minutes passed, she crawled off the bed, stood beside it, and cleared her throat. She placed a hand on her hip to (hopefully) make herself a bit more enticing. Mark emerged from the antechamber, his coat and waistcoat off, his cravat gone, his boots removed, and his shirt opened to the waist, revealing glimpses of his muscled abdomen. He braced a forearm against the antechamber door frame and looked across at Nicole, his eyes hooded, smoky.

The moment their gazes met in the firelight Nicole realized he knew precisely what she was about. Dropping her hand to her side, she took a tentative step toward him, the slit in her shift coming all the way up to her hip, exposing her leg.

His throat worked when he swallowed. "You haven't . . . retired yet, I see."

"I have no intention of retiring." She lifted her chin. "Not without you."

Mark advanced on her. The determined set of his jaw and the heat in his eyes sent her pulse thrumming. He ripped his shirt from his shoulders and tossed it to the floor.

He backed her up to the wall behind the bed, his lips hovering a mere inch over hers, his hands pressed against the wall above both of her shoulders, caging her in with desire radiating heat from his body. He was so close to her. Could he see her heartbeat jumping beneath her breast?

"Are you certain this is what you want?" he asked, his tone even.

"I've never been more certain," she breathed.

Apparently, that was all Mark needed. One hand moved down to cup her jaw, while his mouth captured hers. The second their tongues met she wrapped her arms fiercely around his neck. It felt so good, his strong, unyielding body pressed to hers, to drink in the taste of him, to let her mouth soften beneath his. The feel of his hands on her was so right. Like coming home again. She hadn't experienced this sort of passion since she'd left England and she'd doubted she ever would again. She had to enjoy however many nights they spent together. Enjoy them and remember them forever.

He reached down and pulled up her shift to her hips in one swift, sure movement. He was as desperate as she was as they both ripped at the fall to his breeches. The moment he was free, he pushed boldly between her legs, so caught up in his passion that he didn't measure her readiness, but it didn't matter because she was more than ready for him.

He slid into her to the hilt and she sobbed, while he released a shuddering sigh. They stilled for a moment in their frantic squirming to get closer, each absorbing the unbelievable fact that their bodies still fit as perfectly as they used to. Then she tilted back her head and he rained kisses down the slim column of her throat. God, the way he filled her, the grasp of his hands on her hips, holding her tight. It had been too long. She'd missed it. She'd missed him. She wrapped her arms around the solidness of his shoulders, breathing in his heady scent as he slammed into her again and again, making her cry out in ecstasy.

Mark clapped one hand to Nicole's backside to keep her pressed tight. The other hand he braced on the wall behind her head—partly so her skull wouldn't hit the wall, and partly to hold himself upright, to keep his knees from giving way. Damn. He hadn't meant for their first time in years to happen like this. He'd planned to woo her, undress her slowly, take her to bed leisurely and make her call out his name, make her cry out for him. But here they were—she was making maddeningly seductive noises in the back of her throat, and he was pounding into her like a rutting stag. And he couldn't stop. The moment he touched her skin, smelled the lavender essence of her hair, felt the softness of her bottom lip against his tongue, he couldn't stop himself. He hadn't touched a woman this way in ten years, and the fact that he was touching the one who'd haunted his dreams since then made it all the more torturous. He couldn't get enough. If she wanted him to go more slowly, she didn't indicate it. Instead, her arms had a near stranglehold on his neck and she was all but eating him alive, her teeth biting at his shoulder, sweet stings of pain and pleasure that sent lust barreling through him. He clenched his jaw. God, he wanted to make this last, wanted to make her come first, but he couldn't. He was too far gone, too mindless with passion. "Sweetheart, it's been too long. I can't stop," he whispered into her ear.

Nicole had never heard anything more erotic than Mark declaring surrender. God help her, she didn't want him to stop. It had been too long for her too, far too long. With every hammering thrust he made, she met him with equal force, her legs leaving the floor to encircle his lean hips, his frantic movements sliding her back against the wall until she thought her flesh might burst into flame from the agony of friction and need. Of course it would be like this between them—just as it always had. Fire and ice, pain and pleasure.

She didn't want to hope that when he said it had been too long, that meant he hadn't been with anyone else in all these years. No doubt he only meant it had been too long without *her* . . . but she wasn't about to dwell on that while he was pounding into her.

"It's all right," she panted into his ear. "Come."

His hands tightened on her hips. His mouth moved back to hers, ravaging, demanding. He pumped into her once, twice, three times more and stilled. His big body tensed and shook, then trembled in the circle of her embrace as the warmth of his seed spilled within her. His mouth gentled on her, his kiss replaced by the hard rush of his breathing. His hands slipped away from her legs and he gulped in air, pressing his forehead against hers, hard.

"Damn," he murmured against her swollen mouth. "I did not mean for it to happen like that."

"I thoroughly enjoyed it," Nicole replied, her arms and legs still wrapped around him.

He picked her up and carried her to the bed, where he gently disengaged from her embrace and laid her there, her shift still wadded above her hips. He took a moment to drink in the disheveled, thoroughly ravaged sight of her. "God, I want to rip that thing off you," he breathed.

"Do it," she taunted. "But first, take off your breeches."

Mark glanced down. He'd been so ravenous for her, he was still wearing his breeches. They'd merely been pushed down below his hips. Such bad form.

He sat on the bed and pulled off his breeches. By the time he turned back around, Nicole had pulled her shift over her head and was sitting up on her knees, completely nude. His eyes scoured her body, her breasts, her slightly rounded belly, her thighs. She was as beautiful as ever. More so.

He crawled toward her and plunged his hands into the thick, rich depths of her silky hair. "God, you're gorgeous." He captured her mouth again in a long, drugging kiss.

"I'm glad you still think so," she murmured against his lips.

"Are you mad?" His mouth found a sensitive spot on the side of her neck and he gave it a gentle bite. "Of course I think so."

"You're looking quite fine yourself." She tried to laugh, but the sound was abruptly cut short as he pulled her beneath him and covered her with his hard, nude body.

"I want you again," he breathed into her ear, already pushing her knees apart with one strong leg.

"Yes," she whispered, closing her eyes.

"I'm going to make you come so hard you call my name." His lips glanced over her ear and breathed heat into its shell, making Nicole shiver in ecstasy.

"Is that a challenge?" she asked, trying to keep her wits about her and failing pleasurably as Mark's hand slid down between her thighs to play with her most intimate spot.

"No," he growled into her ear, "it's a promise."

He knew her body, knew exactly where to touch. His hand found the nub of her pleasure swiftly, as if ten years hadn't passed. His thumb flicked across it again and again while Nicole squirmed and ran her fingers through his silky dark hair. She'd wanted to touch him this way ever since she'd seen him sitting in her drawing room in France, taunting her. And oh did the man know how to taunt. His thumb left her and she cried out in protest.

"Shhh," he murmured against her lips. One long finger slipped inside her then, in and out, working her tight passage. Her hips twisted, wanting more. Finally, his thumb came back to rub the spot of pleasure between her legs and she arched against his maddening hand.

"That's it," he said, watching her face. "I want to see you come. I've waited so long."

She couldn't examine what those words meant, not when she was half mindless with pent-up longing. Her legs slid restlessly against the sheets, her hips twisting and arching, completely at the mercy of his skilled hand. She was close. Oh, so close.

"Say my name," he whispered wickedly in her ear.

"No," she said, just to be equally wicked.

His hand stopped and she cried out, "No!"

"Say it," he taunted, resuming his skilled maneuvers.

"Mark," she whispered.

"What do you want?" His dark head bent to her breast and he sucked her nipple into his mouth with unmerciful slowness.

"You," she replied, the breathless word drifting featherlike in the air. Her eyes were closed. Her legs tensed. Her entire body focused on the pleasure that was so near.

"What else do you want?" he murmured in her ear again.

"To come," she breathed. He'd taught her these things. All of them. He'd taught her to ask him for what she wanted. He'd taught her how good her body could feel when it was touched the right way, and he'd taught her the unrelenting pleasure he could give her.

Shifting over her, he pushed her legs apart with his knees and withdrew his finger from her, only to replace it with his cock. The hard slide of him inside her made her cry out again. "Mark!"

His thumb returned to the nub between her legs and he flicked and toyed with the spot while he slowly moved in and out of her. "I want you to come." He rubbed her in tiny circles. "Now."

As if his words had power over her body, she shattered around him while he pumped into her again and again. She sobbed his name against his ear, tumbling in ecstasy so intense, she was only vaguely aware when his body quickened and shuddered to its climax in her wake.

Oh, God, yes. She drifted as his dark head sagged against her breast, and she slid idle fingers through his damp, soft hair. She had missed this.

And she was in so much trouble.

CHAPTER THIRTY-TWO

The next morning, Mark rolled over and encountered the most enticing backside he'd ever seen. Memories from the night before came roaring back and he grinned to himself. He'd spent the night with Nicole again. Something he never thought would happen. Not in a hundred years. Her shoulders were bare and smooth and her backside . . . perfect. A vision of her in those breeches she'd worn in France flashed through his mind, making him hard again.

Their lovemaking had been better than he remembered it. There was something different about her. Not just her body, which was that of a more mature woman, but her manner. She wasn't the shy young woman she had been. Not that she'd been timid before, but it was as if her experience in the world made her more uninhibited in bed. He hated to think it was because of experience she'd had with other men.

It had been poorly done of him last night. He'd been eager as an untried lad. He cringed at the thought of how quickly he'd gone about it the first time. His pride smarted. He needed to make amends. Nicole had been a heavy sleeper. Was she still? Her deep breathing indicated she was asleep. He would wake her up . . . in the best way possible.

He began by carefully rolling her over. Her glorious naked body lay splayed beneath him. He kissed her neck, her ear. He worked his way down to her breasts, her belly, and then her thighs, to the thatch of bright red hair that veiled the tender, enticing center of her. He parted her legs gingerly with his hands and moved slowly down, down, down. He covered the nub of her pleasure with his mouth and his tongue worked on her until she stirred and her hips moved beneath his hands. She moaned. He smiled to himself but kept up the gentle assault.

Nicole had been having the most erotic dream of her life. She was used to them, these sorts of dreams. Normally they took place in a lush tropical forest with Mark. There was a waterfall and a huge stone basin with a large rock jutting out, heated by the sun. He laid her down on it and loomed over her, sucking her nipples and teasing her by refusing to enter her until she begged. When he finally gave her what they both wanted, she cried out and clutched him to her, while he slammed into her again and again and again. It was her favorite dream.

This time, though, something was different. She was there, lying on the hot rock, the gentle breeze caressing her heated limbs. But instead of Mark slamming into her . . . his mouth was on her—

She startled awake to see Mark's dark head moving between her thighs.

Oh, God, this was better than the dream. What Mark was doing with his tongue should probably be illegal.

He laved her again and again and a deep guttural moan emerged unbidden from her throat. She was torn between the voice of propriety telling her to protest and the wildness rising within her, which sent her fingers creeping into his hair to hold him to her. "Mark," she whispered.

His rough palms cradled her outer thighs as he held them apart, keeping her open and vulnerable to him. "Mark," she called again. She wanted him to kiss her, wanted to feel his body slide over hers, wanted to feel him buried deep inside of her, but she also didn't want him to stop licking her like that.

His mouth and tongue kept up their sinful assault until she shattered against his mouth and cried out, her orgasm bringing unexpected tears to her eyes. She felt his wicked mouth curve into a grin against her thigh. He slid up her body until the hot hardness of him rested against her most sensitive flesh. She quivered again when he smiled down at her and circled his hips against hers, without quite penetrating her, in a dance that felt oh, so promising. Her arms wrapped around him. The scars on his back reminded her of his time in the French prison camp. No doubt that's where he'd got them. Tears stung her eyes again. In that moment, the enormity of how much he owned her, body and soul, sent the tears streaking down her cheeks.

His grin instantly faded and he went still. Just like that he shifted from sensual tease to earnest lover. He wiped away the tears with his thumbs, kissed her forehead, and searched her face. "Sweetheart, what's wrong? Don't you want me?"

She swallowed a few times before she could choke out the confession. "I want you so much it frightens me."

His concerned features softened. He clasped her hands with his and slid oh-so-slowly inside of her. "I want you too." He pulled out and slid back inside. His gaze never left her face. "So much."

The pressure slowly built inside of her, tangled in the jumble of emotions in her heart. By the time he pumped into her one last time, her orgasm washed over her in a wave of sublime pleasure, wringing another unstoppable moan from her throat.

The man was a master. He'd given her four orgasms in one night, but it felt far too much like lovemaking and it wasn't supposed to be that. How had it all gone so wrong and yet so wonderfully right? How in the world was she going to survive this? She'd keep him chained to the bed if she could. Her sex slave for the next three months. The idea held a certain appeal. She smiled to herself and cuddled against him, limp and languid and ready to go back to sleep after all that delicious pleasure.

"Why were you crying?" he asked gently after he rolled to his side and captured her hand in his.

The tender rasp of his thumb over her knuckles brought her eyelids open. He was watching her face with dark, unreadable eyes, waiting for her answer. An answer he apparently cared about. Oh, God. What was happening between them?

She carefully disengaged her hand and noted his frown when she did so. She turned on her side to look at him and pulled up the sheet to cover her breasts. "It was nothing. Truly."

He studied her face for a moment and reached to push a lock of hair behind her ear. "I don't want to hurt you, Nicole."

She turned onto her back and stared at the ceiling, flinging her arm over her head to rest on the pillow. A hollow ache pulsed in her chest. "I was the one who demanded we do this."

"Yes, but I was the one who insisted it not just be an act. I—"

"It's fine, no need to explain." Her voice was more terse than she'd meant it to be. They could *not* start talking about their feelings. If that happened, there was no way she would survive with her heart intact.

He brought her knuckles up to his lips and kissed them tenderly. "I don't know how to do it any other way."

She swallowed hard and nodded, still staring at the ceiling. "I understand."

He lifted up on his elbow and grinned down at her. Then he leaned over and gave her a quick kiss on the tip of her nose. "And it was fun, wasn't it?"

She nodded again, a smile creeping onto her lips. "It was indeed."

He rolled toward the edge of the mattress. "I need to get the day started but I, for one, am greatly looking forward to doing this again."

She watched him leap from the bed and couldn't help but stare at his magnificent backside as he disappeared into the next room to dress.

"Me too," she whispered to herself. "And that's the problem."

CHAPTER THIRTY-THREE

"They've all arrived," Lady Harriet told Mark later that morning in the breakfast room. "I've shown them to their rooms, but per your instructions, asked that they all meet in the blue drawing room at half past eleven."

"Very good," Mark replied, leaning back in his chair. Regina had already eaten and Nicole had ordered a tray brought up to their room. His uncle was too ill to come down to breakfast, so Mark and his aunt were there alone.

Lady Harriet had a smug little smile on her face too, which made Mark wonder if she had some way of knowing what he and Nicole had done last night. The old woman kept glancing at him and smiling. She was humming sporadically too. Mark couldn't blame her. He rather felt like humming himself this morning.

During breakfast, he had tried to concentrate on preparing for the interviews he would conduct today, but

all he could think about was last night with Nicole. It
wasn't his imagination. It *had* been better than he remembered. Wild, passionate, unencumbered. Nicole
was fiery in bed and she drove him mad with the sounds
she made in the back of her throat. She'd given herself
to him entirely, holding nothing back, and he was mad
for her. Damn it. How long did it take for a woman to
know whether she was with child? A month at least,
possibly less? He hoped to hell she wasn't with child yet.
He'd like to continue the method of producing an heir
as long as possible.

He finished his eggs and coffee, stood from the table,
and excused himself from Lady Harriet's presence. "I'll
be in the drawing room at half past eleven. See you
there."

The drawing room was full of somber faces. Lord
Anthony looked particularly solemn, spine erect, on a
stiff-backed chair in the corner, his face drawn and
pale. Lady Arabelle, blond and fragile, held a handkerchief in her fist and dabbed at her wide wet blue eyes
repeatedly. Lady Arabelle's mother, looking downcast,
heaved sigh after sigh as she sat perched on the settee
next to her daughter, patting her hand and murmuring
to her. Lord Hillenbrand was stoic. Mr. Cartwright looked
perturbed. Miss Lester sat next to Mr. Cartwright, her
mother on the other side of her. They looked somber
too. Everyone was dressed in black with nary a smile
among them.

Oakleaf stood in the front of the room next to Mark,
arms clasped behind his back. Lord Tottenham had arrived, but had not been asked to join the group in the

drawing room. Oakleaf wanted only the people who'd been at the dinner that night to be there.

The duke arrived shortly after, wheeled in by two footmen. All the guests stood and bowed to the old man. He feebly lifted his hand in the air. "Sit, sit, please."

"I'm glad you've come," the duke began as they all took their seats again. "It's important for me to honor John here at the family estate. The memorial service will be tomorrow afternoon at the family cemetery over the hill. The naming of the heir shall be the day after. In the meantime, I hope you will all relax and enjoy yourselves as much as you are able, given the circumstances. If you need anything at all, please let one of the servants know."

The group nodded and murmured their agreement.

The duke continued, waving his arm toward Mark and Daffin. "These fine gentlemen are investigators. I'm told it's standard when a member of the aristocracy dies for an investigation to take place."

Another murmur ran through the room, this one carrying a surprised tone.

"General Grimaldi and Mr. Oakleaf will be asking each of you some questions about the night John died," the duke said. "I request that you share any details you have with them, for my sake."

A general nod and murmur of approval went through the group again. Mark, one elbow braced on the mantel, watched their faces. No one seemed particularly alarmed or uncomfortable. They'd planned this little announcement with everyone present so he and Oakleaf could see if any of them appeared anxious when they realized an investigation was taking place.

"We're happy to help," Lord Anthony said from the corner, his jaw clenched. "Ask me anything."

"Yes, yes," Lord Hillenbrand added, pushing a shoe along the edge of the fine rug. "Quite."

The others murmured in agreement.

Mark stepped forward and crossed his arms over his chest. "I'd like to begin by speaking with Lady Arabelle, if that's all right with you, my lady." He smiled patiently down at Lady Arabelle.

Arabelle nodded and dabbed at her eyes again. Her mother made to stand and come with her but Mark said, "Alone, if you don't mind. I assure you, I will be nothing but kind to her."

"That's hardly proper," Lady Arabelle's mother said, her mouth turned down in a frown.

"I will accompany them." Lady Harriet shot to her feet with alarming speed for someone of her age, her turban tilting haphazardly.

While Lady Harriet righted her headpiece, Lady Arabelle's mother looked as if she might continue to argue the point, but Arabelle patted her mother's arm and said, "It's all right, Mama. I'm certain I won't be long."

"Not at all," Mark replied, bowing to both ladies.

He escorted the lovely blonde out of the room and down the corridor to the next room over, a smaller drawing room decorated in hues of green. Lady Harriet, looking like the cat who swallowed the cream, trailed behind them.

"Can I get you anything?" Mark asked as they entered the room.

"No, thank you." Lady Arabelle shook her head and held the handkerchief to the tip of her nose. Although

she was serene and composed, the black she wore made
her pale features even paler. Dark circles ringed her eyes
as if she hadn't slept much of late.

"I'm sorry for your loss," Mark said, gesturing to her
to take a seat.

Lady Harriet hurried to grasp the young woman's
hand and to sit next to her on the settee. Mark waited
until the two ladies were settled before he pulled up a
wooden chair before them, sat, and leaned forward, elbows braced on his knees.

"How long did you know John?" Mark asked her, his
tone gentle and sympathetic. He would not use a notebook. That might make the young woman nervous. He
wanted her to feel as comfortable as possible. That was
important when interviewing sources, especially if he
wanted them to remember important details.

"Since April," Lady Arabelle said quietly. "He and I
met at a ball. The Baxters' ball."

"The Baxters always host the most lovely balls." Lady
Harriett patted the young woman's hand.

Mark gave his aunt a reproving glare.

"Oh, yes, dear, back to the point," Lady Harriet murmured, casting down her eyes and turning pink.

"You had your debut this Season?" Mark asked Lady
Arabelle next.

"That's right." The quiet blonde nodded.

"And how soon after you met did John propose?"
Mark asked.

The hint of a smile floated across the young woman's
pretty face. "Not until early July."

"July is a lovely month for engagements," Lady Harriet said with a sigh.

Another reproving glare from Mark.

"Oh, quite right. I shall just lock up my lips and toss the key. Such a bother, my mouth sometimes." Lady Harriet made a show of using an imaginary key to lock her lips.

"John courted you until then?" Mark asked Lady Arabelle.

Lady Arabelle nodded. "Yes, some of the time. Before that he seemed as if he might be keen on Molly."

Mark furrowed his brow. "Molly? Molly Lester?"

"Yes, he'd danced with Molly a few times and we both thought he might offer for her."

"I'd never met Miss Lester before today," Lady Harriet interjected. "She seems like a fine girl."

"Oh, she is," Lady Arabelle replied with the hint of a smile on her otherwise sad face. "I've known her for years."

"Did you have other suitors?" Mark asked, pointedly ignoring his aunt this time.

A blush stained Lady Arabelle's pale cheeks. "Yes. I had another offer, actually."

"Two offers in one Season?" Lady Harriet's mouth formed an O. "Good for you, dear." She patted Arabelle's hand again and smiled at her approvingly.

Mark cleared his throat and his aunt looked properly chastised again. He steepled his fingers in front of his face. "Who was your other offer from, Lady Arabelle?"

"Lord Hillenbrand." She uttered the name so quietly that Mark barely heard it.

"Hillenbrand? My, he's a good-looking one." Lady Harriet pulled her black handkerchief from her bosom and fanned herself with it.

Mark didn't need to say anything this time. Lady

Harriet put her handkerchief over her lips and mumbled, "I'm so sorry. I'm rubbish at keeping my mouth shut."

Lady Arabelle gave Harriet a patient smile.

"And you turned Hillenbrand down because of John?" Mark continued.

"Oh, no." Lady Arabelle sat up straighter. "Not because of John. I mean, I fancied John, of course, but I didn't want to interfere with his pursuit of Molly. It wasn't until I realized he didn't fancy Molly that I truly allowed myself to care for him."

"Wise, dear." Lady Harriet nodded sagely, briefly closing her eyes. "Quite wise."

Mark narrowed his eyes on Lady Arabelle. "How did you know he didn't fancy Molly?"

Another blush from Lady Arabelle. She glanced away. "He told me."

Lady Harriet gasped before covering her mouth (and her eyes this time) with her handkerchief.

"And that's when you refused Hillenbrand's offer?" Mark prodded.

"No. I'd already refused it," Lady Arabelle replied. "Lord Hillenbrand is quite nice, but I feared we would not suit."

"Also wise," Lady Harriet mumbled from behind the mass of her handkerchief.

"Was Hillenbrand angry with your refusal?" Mark continued.

Arabelle twisted the handkerchief in her hands. "I'm certain he wasn't pleased, but he never seemed angry."

Mark leaned forward and searched the young woman's face. "He didn't say or do anything that made you think he was displeased with either you or John?"

"No." Lady Arabelle shook her head and her curly golden locks bounced. "We all remained friends. I hoped he might fancy Molly. I thought perhaps they might suit." Arabelle took a deep breath. "You don't think anything untoward happened to John, do you?" she asked breathlessly.

Lady Harriet made a funny sort of strangled noise, but otherwise kept her lips sealed. She'd lowered her handkerchief to her mouth again. Mark was convinced her next move would be to stuff the thing inside of her mouth. He would not object.

Mark shifted in his seat. "I need you to think back to the night he died. The dinner party. Did you see anything out of the ordinary that night? Did John say anything? Mention anyone?"

Lady Arabelle's bottom lip trembled and her brow knitted. After several moments, she shook her head. "No. I . . . Mother and Molly and Mrs. Lester and I all arrived together."

Lady Harriet had been rendered speechless apparently, because now she was simply staring at Lady Arabelle in awe, waiting for her answers, her turban also tipped forward as if it was on tenterhooks.

"And did you stay together all evening?" Mark asked.

"Yes. Of course." Lady Arabelle nodded.

"None of you left one another's company?"

The young woman's face clouded with confusion. "No. We were in the dining room most of the night. Why?"

"Did Lord Hillenbrand or Mr. Cartwright do or say anything out of the ordinary that night?"

She sat quietly for another moment. "No. We were all

talking and laughing and having a good time until . . ." She drew a long, shaky breath. "Until John collapsed."

Tears filled Lady Harriet's eyes too. She dabbed at them with her handkerchief and squeezed Lady Arabelle's hand.

Mark finally pulled a notebook from his coat pocket. He opened it to a blank page, then stood and crossed to the writing desk in the corner where he found a quill and ink. He quickly drew a large oval on the blank page. He put the initials *JC* at the top. He strode back to where Lady Arabelle sat. "John was sitting here, correct?" He pointed at the diagram on the page.

"Yes." Lady Arabelle nodded.

"Where was everyone else?" Mark asked.

While Lady Harriet hovered over her shoulder, Lady Arabelle took the quill from Mark and added initials to indicate where the other diners had been. "I was to his right. Then Mother. Then Molly and Mrs. Lester. Lord Anthony was to his left, then Lord Hillenbrand, then Mr. Cartwright."

Mark took back the quill and notebook. "Thank you, Lady Arabelle. Just a few more questions."

"You're doing splendidly, dear," Lady Harriet said, as if she participated in investigations regularly.

Lady Arabelle nodded bravely. "Yes, go ahead."

Mark sat back down and faced the young woman. He wanted to look into her eyes when he asked this question. "When John collapsed. What happened? Who tried to save him?"

Lady Arabelle's eyes filled with tears that spilled down her pale cheeks. "I . . . did. I stood and tried to reach him but Mr. Hillenbrand and Mr. Cartwright stopped me. They said we should wait for the doctor."

"Oh, dear, how awful it must have been," Lady Harriet interjected.

"What did the others do?" Mark asked, still focused on Lady Arabelle's face.

"There wasn't much they could do." The young woman uttered a shaking sigh. "Everyone jumped from their seats and stared for the most part. Lord Anthony rushed to him and listened to see if he was breathing."

Lady Harriet dabbed at her eyes while nodding intently. "Awful, dear. Just awful."

"One more question," Mark said. "Did John say anything to you that night or just before that indicated that he'd had a falling-out with any of the other men who attended the dinner?"

Lady Arabelle sat silently for a few moments more. "No, nothing. He didn't know Mr. Cartwright well and he was fast friends with both Lord Hillenbrand and Lord Anthony."

Mark closed the notebook and stuck it back into his coat pocket. He stood again and crossed to the desk to return the quill, making a mental note to never allow Lady Harriet into another interview. "Thank you, Lady Arabelle. You've been quite helpful. That will be all."

CHAPTER THIRTY-FOUR

Nicole and Regina hovered outside the doors to the small green drawing room, their ears pressed against the wood. "Mark is in there with Lady Arabelle," Nicole reported. A zing of excitement shot through her. She loved the start of an investigation. Even one she hadn't been invited to participate in.

It was much better listening at doors than dwelling on what had happened last night between her and Mark in bed. It had been . . . amazing. Unforgettable. At the moment, she was doing her best to try and forget it. Because if she thought about it . . . considered what had happened between them last night, the intimacies they'd shared, the walls she'd spent ten years building tumbling down in a matter of a few hours, she would go mad. It was much better to focus on the investigation, at least the part she and Regina could help with. It was the only thing keeping Nicole sane at the moment. She liked nothing more than a good investigation. It was the perfect distraction.

Regina nodded. "Who should *we* start with?"

Nicole's voice remained a whisper. "They suspect Mr. Cartwright and Lord Hillenbrand. There's little chance they'll allow us to question either of them first. So I propose that we start with Miss Lester and her mother. No doubt they have the least to say, but we can begin at the bottom and work our way up."

Regina threaded her fingers together and stretched them in front of her. "Sounds like the perfect plan."

Nicole smiled at her friend. "All we have to do is mingle in the other drawing room." The ladies had already decided their informal investigation would have to take the shape of merely being hospitable to their guests and asking discreet questions over tea. Overt questioning would draw suspicion.

"Let's go." Nicole moved away from the green drawing room's door.

The two ladies made their way to the larger drawing room. Nicole paused just before they went inside. She leaned over to Regina and said, "Pay attention to the types of questions I ask. I've been trained by the best, Daffin Oakleaf."

A quick wink from Regina was her only answer before they pushed open the doors to the blue drawing room and made their way inside. After the introductions had been made, Nicole and Regina took places in chairs at right angles next to the settee upon which Miss Lester and her mother sat.

Mr. Cartwright stalked out into the corridor. Lord Hillenbrand exited too. Lady Arabelle's mother had gone to wander the corridor to wait for her daughter's return. Lord Anthony, Miss Lester, and her mother, Tabitha, were the only guests who remained.

Tea had been served and Nicole made use of it to begin her conversation with Miss Lester. Nicole studied Molly Lester. The young woman was slight and pale with nondescript brown hair and pale brown eyes, freckles on her face and a melancholy air. She looked as if she'd been kept in a sickroom most of her life and had only just come out to see the sun. She was the complete opposite of her beautiful, well-dressed friend Lady Arabelle.

"Would you care for some tea, Miss Lester?" Nicole asked.

"Yes, thank you." Miss Lester's voice was tremulous and her feet patted the floor in a nervous fashion. She wore a black gown of questionable value and Nicole doubted her pearls were real. Molly's mother stood and stared out the window across the vast lawn. Good. The better to speak with her daughter alone.

Meanwhile, Lord Anthony remained quietly in the corner looking lost in thought.

Nicole made a show of preparing Miss Lester's tea. "One sugar or two?"

"Two, please," the young woman replied softly.

Nicole handed the cup to Miss Lester and poured some tea for herself and Regina. "I'm sorry we had to meet under such trying circumstances." She kept her voice low so their conversation wouldn't be overheard by the room's other occupants.

"I agree. This is a sad occasion indeed." Miss Lester shook her head and heaved a miserable sigh.

Nicole slowly stirred the lumps of sugar into her teacup. "It must have been awfully difficult for you, witnessing such a horror."

The young lady took a shaky breath and her eyes filled with tears. She met Nicole's gaze. "Oh, it was, Mrs. Grimaldi. It was."

Regina silently sipped her tea while Nicole asked, "Can you tell me what happened?"

Miss Lester nodded slowly. "One moment we were all talking and laughing and the next, Lord Coleford was clutching his throat and choking." Her eyes widened in fear. "He fell to the floor and his wineglass spilled everywhere. We called for the doctor, but by the time the man arrived, it was too late." The last word was barely a whisper. Tears slipped down Miss Lester's cheeks.

Nicole reached out and squeezed the younger woman's wrist. "Did anyone try to help him?"

Regina leaned forward in her seat, but kept her silence, her astute blue eyes assessing everything.

Miss Lester pressed a pale hand to her cheek. "Lady Arabelle tried to go to him but Mr. Cartwright and Lord Hillenbrand held her back. They didn't want her exposed to such awfulness. They may have saved her life. If she'd put her lips to his, she might have been poisoned too."

"Poisoned?" Nicole's teacup nearly toppled from her hand. She righted it and cleared her throat. "Who told you Lord Coleford was poisoned?"

"Wasn't he?" Miss Lester asked timidly, her eyes darting back and forth between Nicole and Regina's faces. "Lord Hillenbrand told me that's what everyone was saying. Your husband and Mr. Oakleaf are here because they suspect Lord Coleford was murdered, aren't they? The rumor about the poison is true."

"My husband was merely asked to investigate," Nicole assured her. She made a mental note to ask Lord Hillenbrand where he'd heard that news.

"Oh, Mrs. Grimaldi, Lady Regina." Miss Lester turned to look at both women, one after the other. "Who would do such a hideous thing? And to poor Lord Coleford? He was a terribly nice man." She shook her head piteously and took a sip of tea.

"Did you know him well?" Regina interjected, her voice kind and patient.

Another head shake from Miss Lester. "Not well, no. At the start of the Season I danced with him a few times at a ball here and there. That was before Arabelle captured his fancy."

"You're friendly with Lady Arabelle?" Nicole asked.

"Oh, yes, we've been friends for years. We're the same age, Arabelle and I. Made our debut together this year. Of course Arabelle is the beauty. She has all the admirers. I cannot blame them."

"Did you know any of the other people at the dinner?" Nicole asked next, studying the minute frown that had crept upon the other woman's features.

The girl blushed slightly and turned her head away. "Mr. Cartwright was quite charming. I was immediately taken with him."

Nicole and Regina exchanged a glance.

"Had you met Mr. Cartwright before?" Nicole asked Miss Lester.

"Just once. At another party. He was ever so nice to me. He treated me so kindly."

"You didn't know the others?" Nicole prodded.

"I'd never met Lord Anthony before," Miss Lester said. "I'd met Lord Hillenbrand a time or two. He proposed to Arabelle earlier in the Season, you know?"

"Yes, I'd heard." Nicole thought for a moment. "He didn't seem to harbor ill will over the fact that she turned him down?"

"No . . ." The young woman glanced toward her mother. "At least I didn't think so."

Nicole furrowed her brow. "What do you mean?"

Miss Lester took a tentative sip of tea. "I mean he seemed fine until . . ."

"Until when?" Nicole prodded, leaning forward, her heart beating faster.

"Until the night of the dinner party." Miss Lester leaned forward and lowered her voice. "That night I saw him do something quite peculiar."

CHAPTER THIRTY-FIVE

"Grimaldi, there you are, good to see you." Lord Tottenham's voice boomed through the corridor outside the duke's study. "How's the investigation coming?"

Mark opened the door to usher the man inside. "I've just come from speaking to Lady Arabelle and intend to speak to Mr. Cartwright next. How was your journey here?"

"As good as can be expected," the older man thundered. "With my gout, no long ride in a coach is ever pleasant." He laughed heartily at his own words.

"I suppose not." Mark gestured for him to take a seat. "Care for a drink?"

"I always care for a drink," Tottenham replied with another loud laugh.

Mark crossed to the sideboard near the windows and poured two glasses of brandy. When he returned to hand a snifter to Tottenham, the large man had fit his girth into one of the oversized dark leather club chairs arranged in front of the duke's desk.

"The memorial is in the morning?" Tottenham asked, taking a swig from his glass.

"It is." Mark nodded. He eyed the older man carefully. Was his promotion riding on whether he uncovered the culprit quickly? He could only assume it was.

"Do you hope to have your suspect by then?"

"Oakleaf is speaking to Lord Anthony now. We don't suspect him, but he could have some information that may point us in the correct direction."

"Sounds good." Tottenham took a large swig of brandy.

Mark seated himself in the matching chair and cleared his throat. "How exactly are you related to the Colchester family?" He'd never heard that Lord Tottenham was related, but then most of the aristocracy was related somehow. Inbred group of people that they were.

"Oh, I'm only a distant cousin. Quite distant, by marriage. More distant than Mr. Cartwright even." Tottenham laughed even louder and took another swig of brandy.

Mark studied the man's face. He'd been worried that Lord Tottenham may have already learned that he was the duke's nephew, but watching him now he was certain that wasn't the case. Regardless, the longer this conversation lasted, the sooner Mark would be forced to admit to his relationship to the duke. He needed to turn their conversation back to the investigation.

"Speaking of Mr. Cartwright, Oakleaf and I have

decided to ask the duke to tell Mr. Cartwright privately that he's not the heir."

Tottenham's bushy gray eyebrows shot up. "I didn't know he wasn't."

"Yes, well, the duke told us that much . . . in order to help with the investigation." Mark cleared his throat again. Damn. This was hardly moving away from the awkward bit.

Tottenham's brow furrowed. "What purpose do you hope telling Mr. Cartwright ahead of time will serve?"

Mark turned his untouched brandy glass in his hand. "We want to gauge his reaction to the news . . . privately."

"Ah, I see. That may well be the best course. Can't wait to hear what the man says. Though it can't be easy learning you're not a future duke." Tottenham laughed again and his belly shook.

"Agreed." Mark hesitated. Now would be the perfect time to admit to Tottenham that *he* was related to the family, but his pride kept his mouth closed. He refused to tell him before the man had made a decision about the Home Secretary position.

"Any decision yet as to who will be the next Home Secretary?" he asked instead. Might as well get right to it.

Tottenham nearly drained his glass. His belly wobbled more as he turned in his seat. "Ah, always thinking about business, aren't you, Grimaldi? That's why they call you the stone man, isn't it?" He chuckled more. "I tell you what, find out who Coleford's killer is before the naming of the heir and the position is yours."

Mark blinked. "Truly?" It couldn't be that easy, could it? Find the killer and receive the position? How many brandies had Lord Tottenham had today? Never mind. It didn't matter. The man had said it and Mark intended to hold him to it. He needed to wrap up this investigation as quickly as possible. If he could identify the killer before the heir announcement, he'd be able to tell Tottenham ahead of time and get his promotion before the news of his impending title was revealed. That would be ideal as long as Tottenham didn't become angry with him for keeping his relationship with the duke a secret. But Mark would worry about that when the time came. First thing was first. He needed to finish this investigation.

"Truly," Tottenham replied, lifting his glass in the air. "Now get me some more brandy. This glass feels a bit light."

Two hours later, Mark entered his uncle's study again. His uncle had just left and Mr. Cartwright remained in the room alone. The younger man's back was turned. He stared out the window at the meadow.

"I've spoken to the duke," Mr. Cartwright said quietly, apparently sensing Mark's presence.

"I see," Mark replied. He couldn't tell by Cartwright's voice if he was angry. He sounded more resigned than anything.

Cartwright blew out a breath. "He wanted me to know before the announcement. He showed me the codicil. I'll not take his place."

"He's quite sick," Mark replied. "This has been difficult for him."

"I know." Cartwright turned slightly to look at Mark, who came to stand near the desk, closer to him. "Congratulations are in order for you, I suppose."

Mark folded his arms behind his back and shook his head. "No. I wish my uncle no ill will and I certainly don't want the title."

"I find that difficult to believe." Cartwright's voice held a definite edge.

"I don't expect you to understand." Mark leaned a hip against the desk. "However, I do hope I can count on your discretion. We don't want the truth spread about until the announcement on Wednesday."

"You can count on my discretion," Cartwright replied, his mouth setting in a resigned line.

"Thank you." Mark mustered a perfunctory smile. "Now tell me. What do you remember about the night John died?"

Cartwright expelled another long breath. "Questioning me too?"

Mark crossed his arms over his chest and narrowed his eyes on the younger man. "We're questioning everyone."

Cartwright scrubbed a hand across his face. The lines near his eyes told the story of how weary he was. "Fine." He moved away from the window and took a seat in one of the leather chairs in front of the desk. "To be honest, I thought the invitation odd. John and I were not close. In his note he explained that Lady Arabelle wanted to meet me."

Mark furrowed his brow. That *was* odd. "Lady Arabelle? Did he say why?"

"No. He gave no details, but I decided I should go and

play the part of the doting spare. Besides, I've alway been curious to see the marquess's town house."

Mark inclined his head to the side. "And did you find it . . . to your liking?"

"Looked just like every other aristocrat's lair," Cart wright replied with a wry smile.

"Yet, you aspired to be one of them." Mark studied the man's face. Cartwright was gentry, but he was hardly aristocratic. Becoming a marquess would have been a huge step up in life for the man. Was he in the same room with a killer?

"One cannot help but dream," Cartwright replied with yet another long sigh. He turned to face Mark head on and looked him in the eye. "You think I killed him don't you? To gain the title? Seems a bit much, don't you think?"

Mark held his gaze. "Who said he was murdered?"

"Don't play dumb with me. The rumor is rampant among all of us and Bow Street wouldn't be investigat ing if there was nothing to investigate."

"Fine." Mark kept his tone calm and steady. "If not you, who do you think killed him?"

The other man scowled. "If I were you, I'd be ques tioning Lord Hillenbrand. He wanted Lady Arabelle, and from what I've been told, was jealous as a cuckqueaned fishwife over losing her."

CHAPTER THIRTY-SIX

The minute Nicole walked into the bedchamber before dinner that night, Mark pulled her into his arms and gently pushed her up against the wall next to the door, kissing her neck, her ear, her eyelid. He kicked the door shut, then grabbed her skirts and shoved them up with both hands before fumbling with the fall to his breeches, freeing himself.

Nicole eagerly helped him. This was how she liked best, she decided. When he seemed as if he couldn't keep his hands off her, so mad with lust that he had her up against the wall. This was definitely one of her favorite positions.

"I've been thinking about this all day," he breathed as he lifted her and slid into her already wet warmth.

"Me too." She crooned, pressing her head back against the wall, exposing the column of her neck to him. He nibbled down its length, the whole time clutching he hips to guide himself inside her again and again.

"Have you?" he teased, rubbing her nipple with hi thumb through the layers of her gown and shift.

"Uh-huh." She could barely talk. His hips worke against her, grinding into her, making her light-headed

"What, specifically, were you thinking about?" Hi voice came in hard pants.

"I was thinking about—" She stopped to moan an he covered her mouth with his.

After the kiss ended he said, "You were saying?"

"I was thinking about your head between my legs, she admitted, wrapping her arms around his shoulder as he held her with both hands under her thighs. Sh folded her legs around his hips.

"Want to repeat that, do you?" he growled against th side of her mouth.

"Yes," she hissed.

"Your wish is my command, my lady."

He walked with her still straddling him over to th bed and laid her down. Then he kneeled in front o the bed and pulled her hips to him. He gave her his mos wicked grin before pushing her skirts high enough t expose her and lowering his mouth between her thighs

Nicole arched up and braced herself on her palms, he fingertips digging into the bedding behind her. Oh, Goc the man was good with his mouth. Too good.

He laved at her, licking in precisely the right spot ove and over until she fell back on the bed and cried out hi name.

He moved up over her then and pushed into her in on slick smooth slide, pausing only to kiss her forehead, he

heeks, her lips. Then he braced his hands on either side
of her head and slid in and out of her again and again,
his hips keeping up the gentle torture as she moaned for
him.

"Wh . . . what were you thinking about all day?" she
asked, sliding her hands up over his muscled shoulders
and into his soft, thick hair.

"This." He slid into her again. "And the maddening
sounds you make while I'm doing it."

She groaned again. She couldn't help herself.

"I've dreamed about the sounds you make when we
make love," he said, changing the angle of his thrusts
just enough to send pleasure rolling through her anew.

Nicole caught her breath. Did he have any idea what
he'd just said? Had he meant it? He'd dreamed about the
sounds she made? Meaning over the *years* he'd dreamed
about it?

"Which sounds?" she asked, not trusting herself to
ask more than that.

He slid out of her slowly, and paused there, hovering
above her.

"No," she groaned, pulling at his hips, wanting him
back.

"That's one," he said with a wicked grin.

He slid back inside her, giving them both what they
wanted.

"What else?" she managed to breathe.

He pulled her bodice and shift down over her breasts
and sucked on one of her nipples until it made a hard
point. "Ooh," she called out, cradling his head against
her.

"That's another one," he said, his thrusts rhythmic,

slow. His panting breaths kept pace with the dance of their bodies, his hands anchored on either side of her head.

"Any others?" she somehow managed as her hips writhed beneath him.

"My favorite." His hand slipped down between their bodies, to the place where she was aching with pleasure and slick with need. She caught her breath, every muscle tightening in anticipation of his touch against the most sensitive part of her . . . and it came, intent, unerring, torturously slow. He gently explored her folds and found what would make her gasp and jerk, and then he didn't stop, even when she was all but begging for more. He rubbed her in tiny, maddening circles, too tiny, too slow, but oh, so sweet, over and over, until her skin was damp with the exertion of chasing her climax, her hair tangled on the pillow and clinging to her temples. When she actually did beg, when she lifted her lashes to find him grinning just a little, he quickened his caress at last and thrust firmly inside her at the same time. Once, twice, giving her all she wanted and more, until she cried out his name loud enough that he cupped a hand over her mouth and leaned down to whisper wickedly in her ear, "That one."

While her body still thrashed beneath him in ecstasy, he rose up and drove into her, his grin fading into fierce determination as he raced to meet her climax with his own.

"Nicole—" he cried, and with one last thrust, spilled himself inside her, while his body quaked against her, beautifully helpless in ecstasy.

* * *

Moments passed in the quiet darkness before Nicole ventured to move. Her body was thoroughly exhausted and she was blissful. She stretched her arms above her head and turned on her side to face him. She couldn't help but repeat in her mind the words he'd said. "I've dreamed about the sounds you make while we're making love." Did he mean it? Or had he merely spoken in the heat of the moment? She couldn't ask him. It would open wounds she wanted to pretend she could keep healed. Better if they kept their time in bed separate from everything else.

"Did you ever think about me? Over the last ten years?" His voice held a note of vulnerability that both thrilled and frightened her. *He* was going to ask the difficult questions apparently.

She swallowed. "Yes," she answered honestly. "From time to time." Every day. "Did you think about me?" God help her, she couldn't keep the question in.

"I did," he answered simply. "Yes, I did." Mark's fingers filtered through her hair and he hugged her tightly against him.

The harsh crack of the whip against his back would have sent him to his knees had Mark not been strung up between two poles, thick ropes eating into his wrists and causing sores upon the sores that were already there from his last beating.

"Where are your compatriots?" the French commandant asked in his native language before he drew back his arm to send the whip flying toward Mark's already scarred back again.

"What compatriots?" Mark replied in fluent French.

He knew it bothered the commandant to hear an Englishman speak his language. It bothered him even more to know Mark had no accent.

The whip slashed through the air and seared Mark's back again, making his vision go dark, the pain nearly unbearable. It usually ended when he passed out. Or at least he assumed it ended then.

"I grow tired of your games, Lieutenant. Tell me where they are camped or I shall kill you."

Mark clenched his jaw. "You have it wrong, *mon ami*. I am a lieutenant general, not merely a lieutenant."

The whip sliced through the air again and Mark's sharp groan cut through the silence.

"I do not care if you're a field marshal! You can be sure your dead body will be stripped of rank," the Frenchman gritted out, his voice growing angrier with each word.

"Go to hell," Mark managed through clenched teeth, bracing himself for the amount of pain that would surely bring darkness.

The whip cracked again and again, the Frenchman taking out his pent-up rage on Mark's back. Three, four, five more cracks. Blood dripped down his back and pooled near his dirty bare feet. Mark counted ten before his vision blurred and for only a moment the image of a gorgeous face framed with fiery red hair floated in his mind's eye, then the world went black.

He awoke in his dirty cramped cell, the pain in his back so intense he couldn't move. His dry, cracked lips opened, his breathing labored and hoarse. They would eventually toss in a crust of stale bread and a filthy cup half-full of water. It might already be near the door, but he'd have to be able to crawl over and get it. At the moment he couldn't crawl.

They wanted to know the location of his camp, the one he'd shared with the elite group of spies he'd been working with in France. He'd sacrificed himself for the others, leading the French away when they'd come too close. They'd eventually captured him. Perhaps that was what Nicole had meant when she called him reckless. Well, then, he was reckless because he'd die in a heap on the vermin-infested floor before he would give away the location of his countrymen, the allies who depended on him.

Wincing and nearly passing out again from the pain, he pulled himself up on his forearms, exhausted from that effort alone. His breath came in short, hard pants. He couldn't turn his head. He focused on the facts. They served to distract him. France. He was in France and so was Nicole. But Nicole was in Paris and he was on the outskirts of the city in a camp along the river.

Would he ever see Nicole again? Or would she merely receive a note, informing her that her husband had died? She'd probably never know how he died. The fact that he was a prisoner was a secret and might remain that way. Cade would tell her. Cavendish would find her and tell her the truth. Would she even care?

Mark still loved her. He always would. He would love her until his dying day . . . which just might be today.

Nicole pulled up the sheets to cover her chest. "How is the investigation going?" she asked to change the fraught subject of whether they'd thought about each other over the last ten years. The way Mark's head jerked when she asked it made her think she'd startled him from some deep memory. She suppressed a wince at the way her cheerful, conversational tone shattered the thick intimacy that had been hanging between them. "Do you still suspect Cartwright or Hillenbrand?"

Mark shook his head and hesitated before he spoke. "Hillenbrand is beginning to look better and better."

"I spoke with Miss Lester," Nicole ventured. She might as well admit it. If he became angry with her for participating, so be it. She'd never done his bidding before, and she wasn't about to begin now.

"Miss Lester?" Mark's voice held a note of surprise. "What did she say? Seems a mousy little thing."

"She is," Nicole replied. "But she did say something interesting. Something about Lord Hillenbrand."

"Really? What?" Mark's tone was interested. He leaned up on one elbow.

"She told me Hillenbrand did something peculiar the night John died."

The outline of Mark's attentive features was illuminated in the hint of light from the adjoining room.

"She said he brought the wine and insisted they all drink it," Nicole continued. "Apparently everyone was surprised."

Mark rubbed a hand along her arm, his brow still furrowed. "Surely John had plenty of good wine."

"Precisely." Nicole's fingers crept up to trace the sharp edge of his jaw as if they had a mind of their own. "But according to Miss Lester, Hillenbrand wouldn't allow anyone to refuse the wine he'd brought with him."

"That *is* interesting," Mark replied, "and it matches what Cartwright told me."

Nicole searched Mark's face. "Which was?"

He reached up and pushed a wayward curl behind her ear. "He said Hillenbrand was more jealous than he let on about Lady Arabelle refusing him."

"Was he?" Nicole tried to ignore the tingle that shot through her at the caress.

Mark arched a brow. "Sounds like both the perfect reason and opportunity to commit murder."

"You'll need proof, of course." Nicole bit her lip. "I can help you get it. If I investigate a bit more, that is."

Mark groaned. "Oakleaf and I are perfectly capable of—"

She reached out and traced the line of his eyebrow with her fingertip. "No one said you're not capable. I merely said I can help."

"Looking to return to your old profession?" Mark asked wryly. "Perhaps hoping to spend more time with Daffin?"

"Pardon?" Nicole's brow furrowed. She snatched her hand away from his face. "Are you quite serious?"

"You said you're an admirer of his." Mark's words were light, but she sensed the edge behind them.

Her jaw dropped. "You're jealous?"

"Absolutely not." He fell back against the pillow and folded his arms beneath his head.

"Yes you are." The urge to laugh stole over her. "You're jealous of Daffin. And it's ridiculous because *I'm* not the one who fancies him."

Mark's scowl was thunderous. "What do you mean?"

"I mean Regina can't seem to keep her eyes off him, and I'm certain the attraction is mutual."

Mark turned toward Nicole again and pushed himself up on his elbow. "No. Truly?"

"Yes, truly. I'm surprised you haven't noticed it yourself. You pride yourself on recording details and nuances between people. Where is your famed eye now, General?"

"Sitting in a cupful of jealousy, apparently," Mark replied, groaning.

This time Nicole rose up to look at him, clutching the sheet to her breasts. "You admit it?"

"Damn it," he muttered.

To her utter astonishment, faint color warmed the ridges of his cheekbones. It was the first time she'd ever seen him blush.

"Hearing you and Oakleaf express your mutual admiration for each other this week has done little to keep my jealousy at bay." He waved a fist in the air in mock ferocity. "He'd better have honorable intentions toward Regina or I might have to call him out."

Nicole laughed and fell back against the pillows. "I don't think it's Daffin you need to worry about. I get the distinct impression Regina's intentions toward *him* are not honorable in the least."

Mark grinned and rolled atop her. "Just like my intentions toward you." He took her smiling mouth in another long, drugging kiss.

An hour later, after having been thoroughly made love to again, Nicole watched as Mark slipped out of bed, whistling, and made his way into the adjoining room to prepare for dinner. Nicole snuggled into the deep, soft mattress and pulled a pillow over her head, splaying both arms wide. The man was ungodly good in bed, handsome, and charming. The last couple of nights with him had been amazing, but she shouldn't allow herself to enjoy it as much as she had. She must not lose her heart to him, no matter how much pleasure he gave her, and her heart was already slowly but surely slipping into the fray. Which could only mean one thing. One bad thing. She bit her lip. She was headed down the path of her own destruction.

CHAPTER THIRTY-SEVEN

The next morning the entire household, including many of the servants, stood somberly on the small grassy area next to the family cemetery at Colchester Manor. Two strapping footmen had carried out the duke's chair and set it up next to the grave. The two young men had returned to the house to assist the old man in his long walk to the spot. The entire assembly waited for him.

The vicar from the church in the nearby village was there. John's coffin had already been placed in the ground overnight. The duke said a few words and Lord Anthony gave a small speech as well. The vicar blessed the grave and spoke of John's childhood and what a good man he'd been. When it was over, there was hardly a dry eye among the crowd.

Mark couldn't bring himself to cry. He was there to do a job. He couldn't allow emotions to get in the way. He and Oakleaf, along with Cartwright and Hillenbrand, were the only ones who weren't crying. Besides, he was the stone man, wasn't he? He couldn't help wondering, if he'd grown up knowing his cousin, would things be different now? Would he be devastated? Upset at least? Instead, he felt like an intruder on this family's misery. He shook his head. It was too late for regrets. He had a job to do.

He surreptitiously watched each of the guests as they listened to the eulogy. Specifically, he kept an eye on Hillenbrand and Cartwright. Both men wore solemn expressions. Hillenbrand's was more resigned, while Cartwright's seemed angry. Lady Arabelle appeared overcome with grief, as did her mother, while Miss Lester and her mother periodically dabbed at their eyes with their black handkerchiefs.

When the ceremony was over, Regina and Lady Harriet each placed a white lily on the gravesite and the duke stooped down and placed his hand on the mound of dirt that covered the body of his only son. Mark swallowed.

It wasn't until the duke was being helped back to the house and all the others, save Oakleaf, had turned to make their way back as well, that Mark stopped the next person he meant to question.

"Lord Hillenbrand," he called. "May I have a word?"

Hillenbrand turned and narrowed his eyes on Mark. "I was wondering when you'd come for me," he said in an impatient voice. "Let's get this over with."

The others slowly walked toward the house in a group. Oakleaf wandered not far away to a small flower bed on the far side of the graves, while Mark remained next to the cemetery gate. He intended for his conversation with Hillenbrand to be private. "It shouldn't take long. I have a few simple questions."

Hillenbrand glared at him, a fist on his hip. "You want to know if I killed him."

Mark eyed him carefully. "Did you?"

"Of course not." Hillenbrand slashed an arm through the air. "Don't be ridiculous."

Mark studied the nobleman. His instincts told him that with this particular man, being direct would be the best tactic. "I'll be honest with you." Mark strolled a few paces away and casually brushed away debris from a high, mossy obelisk. "John's wine was poisoned and I hear you brought the wine that night." He stole a calculating look at the other man.

Hillenbrand's face turned bright red. "I . . . I . . . yes, I brought the wine, but that doesn't mean I *poisoned* it. We all drank from the same bottles. I drank it myself."

Mark narrowed his eyes on the slightly shorter man. "Why were you so hell-bent on providing the wine?"

Hillenbrand clenched his jaw. "I'd just received a shipment. A new case from France. It was a lovely Burgundy. I wanted to share it with my friends. By God, man, you can't think that alone makes me guilty of *murder*."

Mark contemplated him. Hillenbrand was right. The simple act of bringing wine didn't prove anything. French wine had become increasingly prized since the wars had ended and the English were allowed to freely order it again. It was still suspect, however, that Hillenbrand had brought the wine that was later found to be poisoned, and according to Cartwright, Hillenbrand had a reason to be angry with John.

"What about Lady Arabelle?" Mark prodded. "Weren't you jealous because she accepted John's suit and rejected yours?"

Lord Hillenbrand snorted. "I was peeved at first, but I hardly spent time stewing on it. There are plenty of lovely young women in London."

"Like Molly Lester?" Mark countered.

Hillenbrand tugged at his lapels, looking a bit uncomfortable. "Uh . . . no. She's not precisely my sort."

Mark nodded. Something told him Hillenbrand was telling the truth. "One more thing. Did you see anyone else with the wine? Or anything else questionable that night?"

The man hesitated. Mark got the impression he was about to say that he had. But then, "No. I . . . I saw nothing."

Mark narrowed his eyes. "If you remember something, I do hope you'll bring it to my attention immediately."

"Of course." Hillenbrand nodded. "May I go now?"

Mark nodded toward the slowly moving crowd. "Yes, you're free to leave."

After Hillenbrand stalked away to catch up to the others, Oakleaf strolled over to meet Mark at his spot next to the gate. "What did he say?"

"He denied it, the poisoning, that is. He admitted bringing the wine, however."

Oakleaf arched a brow. "What do you think?"

"I don't know." Mark expelled his breath. "All signs point to Hillenbrand, but there's something about it that's not sitting right."

"Agreed," Oakleaf replied with a firm nod.

"What about you? Any luck questioning the others?" Mark asked.

Oakleaf gave a humorless smile. "Lord Anthony was so overcome with grief he wasn't particularly helpful, and Lady Arabelle's mother was only concerned for her daughter. Neither of them remembered anything odd about the evening. I don't have much to report, I'm afraid."

Mark elbowed Oakleaf in the ribs. "Perhaps you should ask my cousin Regina to help you?"

Oakleaf's eyes widened, then his expression settled into a smirk. "Careful there, I just might."

Mark opened his mouth to argue, but Oakleaf interrupted. "Speaking of ladies, how are things with Nicole these days? Have you two kissed and made up?" He waggled his eyebrows.

Mark scrubbed a hand across his face. "Why in the devil's name would you think I'd tell you?" Not only had he and Nicole "kissed and made up," they were having a hell of a time in bed. Mark couldn't stop thinking about her. He found it deuced difficult to concentrate on the case, actually. Falling back into bed with Nicole, being part of her life again, had been surprisingly simple and it made him uneasy because he suspected falling in love with her again could be just as simple.

Oakleaf shrugged. "Well, you're a fool if you don't clear up the nonsense between you."

Mark growled under his breath. Oakleaf's words were too much along the same bent as Mark's thoughts. Had he been crazy all those years ago to give her up?

"I knew Nicole was special from the moment she walked into my offices at Bow Street demanding to work there," Oakleaf continued.

Finally something he could argue. "Yes, well, she failed to tell her husband she had that position." Mark had wanted to kill Oakleaf last night. Today he'd been feeling more kindly toward the runner, but bringing up Nicole's past with him wasn't helping.

"Perhaps she assumed her husband would be *proud* of her," Oakleaf said, watching him from the corners of his eyes.

Mark wasn't about to explain to Daffin Oakleaf, of all bloody people, his fear of Nicole being killed. The man had never been in love. He couldn't understand. "Damn it, Oakleaf, let's get back to the house." He turned on his heel and stalked toward the estate. "We have a murderer to catch."

CHAPTER THIRTY-EIGHT

"That's Aunt Mary." Regina pointed up at a large oil painting of a beautiful woman who looked ever so much like Regina herself. She and Nicole stood in the corridor of the east wing of the manor house. Regina had brought Nicole here specifically to see her mother-in-law.

Nicole stared up at the painting with reverence, her hands folded in front of her. She could pick out small resemblances to Mark in his mother's face. Her nose was the same as Mark's had been once. The lines around her mouth were similar. And the smile in her eyes. Those were also her son's.

"She's beautiful," Nicole murmured.

"She was also as defiant as the two of us," Regina added with a grin. "I only wish I'd got to know her better."

Nicole smiled and nodded. "The duke said she was a woman who knew her own mind."

Regina glanced at her companion and rolled her eyes. "I hate it when men say that. Knew her own mind. Everyone knows their own mind, it doesn't matter if they're female or not. I certainly know my own mind."

Nicole laughed. "That you do, my friend." She wrapped her arm around Regina's. "And does your mind fancy Daffin Oakleaf?"

Regina shot her a sideways wicked grin. "First, I am in mourning and that is an entirely inappropriate question."

"I beg your pard—"

"And second, who *wouldn't* fancy that man?" Regina's grin widened. "He looks like he stepped out of the pages of a novel about the Greek gods." She fanned herself with her hand.

Nicole returned her grin. "He's quite handsome, I'll give you that."

"And he carries a truncheon and handcuffs," Regina added, clapping a melodramatic hand to her breast as though to still a rampaging heart.

"He has a pistol too," Nicole said with a wink.

Regina shivered. "I'll wager he does."

Nicole's crack of laughter echoed across the corridor. "That's why I love you, Regina. You're positively irreverent."

"What do I have to be reverent about, I ask you?" Regina sighed. "I'm absolutely sick over John's death, but honestly it's truly made me consider things . . ."

All the mirth faded from Nicole's expression. "Such as?"

"Such as how terribly short life can be. I need to change. I must pursue the things I want."

"Which are . . . ?"

"Precisely what I need to decide," Regina said with another sigh. She shook her head. "You never told me . . . what happened between you and Mark . . . to make you leave for so long?"

Nicole stared up at the gorgeous painting of the mother-in-law she'd never met. Memories overtook her.

It hadn't been until that fateful night three months after they'd married, that all hell broke loose.

Nicole had come home from a meeting with Daffin and Mark had been there, a grim look on his face. An open letter sat on the table in front of him, a bouquet of white roses tossed haphazardly on the tabletop.

"What's wrong?" she asked, her brow knitted in confusion.

He pointed to the letter. "This."

She slid the letter off the table. It was written in her mother's hand. She looked up at Mark. "You read a letter from my mother to me?"

She hadn't been alarmed. Usually her mother's letters were filled with inane bits of gossip or boring news about the servants at the country estate. What did it matter if Mark read it?

"It was addressed to both of us," he intoned.

She flipped the letter over to see the front. He was right. It was addressed to *My darlings, Nicole and Mark.*

"So." Alarm crept up Nicole's back. "What did she say?"

He crossed his arms over his chest and glared at her. "Read it yourself."

She scanned the words. The first page was a lot of inane drivel as usual, but as she turned the page, her breath caught in her throat as she saw the words that would forever haunt her. *"I do hope you reconcile with your family, dear Mark. We'd love to have the duke and duchess for Christmas dinner in Sussex."*

She glanced up at Mark, her heart racing.

His voice was calm, measured, but there was no mistaking the anger there. "You know?"

"Know what?" Her heart thumped in her chest. Her grasp had gone moist and trembling on the pages of the letter.

"Nicole, I swear, if you lie to me . . ." A muscle leaped in his jaw. He closed his eyes. "You know who my family is?"

She couldn't tell him Daffin had told her. She'd promised Daffin. She sat down across from Mark, reaching for words of reassurance. "I do, but I didn't find out until—"

His voice rose. "You knew? Before we married, you knew?"

She took a deep breath. She had to be honest with him. "Yes, I knew. But I don't see what—"

"And your mother and grandmother knew too?"

He had to listen to her. She had to explain. "Yes, but—"

He shot to his feet. "Why didn't you tell me you knew?" Each harsh word sounded like a crack from a pistol.

Her anger ignited then, and she rose from her chair, lifting her chin to meet his angry gaze head-on. "Why didn't you tell *me*? You should have!"

"I have never publicly acknowledged my family and I never intend to," he snapped. "As far as I'm concerned, they don't exist. That's why I never told you."

"Why didn't you tell me *that* then?" she demanded, her voice rising to match his. "Why would you keep it from me?"

He slammed the palm of his hand on the tabletop, making her jump. "Why didn't you ask me about it when you found out, instead of sneaking around feigning ignorance?"

She pressed her fists against her hips, arms akimbo. "I wanted *you* to tell me!"

He sucked air through his closed teeth. "Is there anything else you need to tell me?"

"Yes." Nicole straightened her shoulders and met his gaze squarely. She cringed now when she thought about how cavalier she'd been with words back then. "While we're on the subject. You should probably know that I'm an unofficial member of the Bow Street Runners. I work with them for bounties whenever the mood strikes."

He stepped closer to her, too close, so close that she felt the heat of his body, of his words, of his rage burning her. "I already know that."

"What?" she gasped, her heart beating so hard in her chest that it ached.

"I'm training to become a spy. Do you think I wouldn't have concluded where my own wife goes when she's out?"

"You spied on *me*?" Betrayal ripped at her insides. He'd led her into a trap and sprung it on her.

"You failed to tell me," he countered.

Her fists remained clenched at her sides. She wanted

to lash out at him. Wanted to hurt him. "Does that bother you too?" She folded her arms across her breasts to protect her heart, even as she refused to step back from his hulking proximity. "Do you not want your wife doing something other than being a quiet little mouse? Because that's *not* who you married."

Anger transformed the face she so loved, rendering it a stranger's. "I'm beginning to think I have no idea who I married."

"You're right. You don't know me at all," Nicole retorted, looking away from his stony face. Tears burned the backs of her eyes, but she refused to let them fall. She refused to show him her weakness.

"I know you're a liar and a schemer." He spoke the words softly, but they slashed into her heart as if he'd run her through with a blade. "What else don't I know, my darling wife?"

She whirled on him and swiped the pages of the letter and the flowers off the tabletop with one swift movement. "You should also know I'm not about to stay here with you and listen to your insults."

"Fine. Leave then." He stalked to the door and threw it open for her so hard it banged into the wall, sending powdered plaster floating into the air. "Run back to your aristocratic life and live in the lap of luxury. You're obviously so enamored of the peerage, you belong with them. With all the others of your set; spoiled, overindulged, flighty, vapid little things. Be as useless as the rest of them. If you were expecting me to take up as the grandson of a duke one day, I regret to inform you, you couldn't have been more wrong. I'd *never* lower myself to the peerage."

The tears blurring her eyes overflowed at last and slid hotly down her cheeks, but she didn't stay to let him see how he'd crushed her. She'd fled the flat, run to the nearest corner and hired a hackney to take her to her grandmother's house. She'd cried a thousand tears that night. That's what Mark thought of her? That she was so obsessed with titles and money and the *ton* that she'd pretended not to know he was the grandson of a duke in order to be related to the prestigious Colchester family? If that's what he truly thought, he *didn't* know her at all.

Her mother had attempted to comfort her. Her grandmother had tried to talk her into returning to him and begging his forgiveness. If they thought she would crawl back to that man, they didn't know her either. None of them did.

Days later, she talked to Daffin. He'd already mentioned to her that his contacts in the War Office had been looking for a female spy. They needed someone in France who could operate at the highest levels of Society in Paris. He'd recommended her for the position. She'd turned it down because she wanted to stay with Mark. Daffin assured her the position was still hers if she wanted it, though he was baffled as to why she was so hell-bent to leave the country of a sudden.

Nicole never shared anything about her falling-out with Mark. Instead she spent the next fortnight securing the position at the War Office and preparing to leave for France. The entire time, she'd prayed Mark would come for her, send her a letter apologizing, something. He never did. She had left so he'd never think she'd wanted to stay in London and be a part of the *ton* there.

He'd believed that about her and he'd been completely wrong.

The only truth that had come out of that hideous night was the fact that they hadn't ever truly known each other. He was right. They'd married in haste. They were incompatible. They were never meant to be together.

"I'm sorry." Regina's voice pulled Nicole from her distressed thoughts. "I shouldn't have pried."

"No. No. It's all right." Nicole sighed and rubbed her forehead where a headache was forming. "It's a long, complicated story. I'll tell you about it . . . one day." One day when it was no longer painful. Would that day ever come?

"Of course," Regina said with a sympathetic smile. "In the meantime, back to our case. What did you think about what Lady Arabelle said?" They'd spoken to the grieving young woman directly after the memorial service.

Nicole and Regina continued their stroll down the long portrait gallery.

Nicole lifted one shoulder. "She certainly had some interesting things to say."

Regina nodded sagely. "Like she was the one who asked John to invite Mr. Cartwright, at Molly's request."

"Seems our Miss Lester had her sights set on the next Colchester heir," Nicole replied, lifting both brows.

"What did you think of what Miss Lester said?" Regina asked.

"I thought it was terribly interesting that John apparently had seemed to court her before he courted Arabelle."

"I was thinking the same thing." Regina stopped in front of a large portrait of the former duke. "Who do you think we should speak with next?"

Nicole arched a brow. "Mrs. Lester."

"My thoughts exactly."

Not an hour later, the two ladies were sitting in the blue drawing room alone with Mrs. Lester. The woman was as large as her daughter was slight, and she talked incessantly.

"Why, I didn't know what to do with myself that night," Tabitha Lester said, pulling a dark handkerchief from her sleeve and dotting her sweating forehead with it. "The moment Lord Coleford fell to the floor, I realized it was ever so serious."

"Did you see anything unusual that night?" Regina asked.

"No. No," Mrs. Lester declared. "Only Lord Hillenbrand insisting we all drink his wine. He made certain he poured it too. Waited until the footman left. Did Molly tell you that?" The woman plunked her hands on her wide hips and shook her head, righteously indignant.

"Yes, Molly mentioned it," Nicole replied, sharing a glance with Regina.

"Did you and Molly expect a proposal from Lord Coleford?" Regina asked. "Before he proposed to Lady Arabelle, I mean?"

Mrs. Lester's features hardened. "Lord Coleford never offered for my Molly." Her voice dripped with indignation.

"Yes, but did you expect him to?" Nicole prodded, studying the woman's face.

"No," Mrs. Lester snapped, turning away as if in disgust. "In fact, Arabelle told Molly later that he'd only asked Molly to dance in order to ask her about Arabelle."

"That doesn't sound particularly kind of Arabelle," Regina pointed out.

"No matter." Mrs. Lester stuck her nose in the air. "Mr. Cartwright has been paying Molly a great deal of attention. We expect an offer from him any day now. If only this unfortunate event with Lord Coleford hadn't happened, no doubt he would have proposed already." She gave both women a smug look as if they should be impressed with her for that news.

"Is Mr. Cartwright officially courting Molly then?" Nicole asked with wide eyes. This was the first she'd heard of a potential match between the two.

"Perhaps not *officially*," Mrs. Lester said, drawing up her shoulders. "But he's clearly smitten." She kept her nose stuck in the air while tucking her handkerchief back into her sleeve.

Nicole and Regina exchanged another glance.

"Will Molly accept if he proposes?" Regina asked, leaning toward Mrs. Lester.

Mrs. Lester gave them a look that indicated she thought them both quite dull. "Of course she will. She'd be a fool not to. Mr. Cartwright is the duke's heir, you know."

Nicole stood abruptly to put an end to the conversation. She'd had her fill of Mrs. Lester and her pretentiousness. "Thank you, Mrs. Lester. You've been quite helpful."

As Mrs. Lester quit the room, Daffin passed her on

his way in. The large woman pushed past him, forcing him to step aside.

Daffin came to stand in front of Regina, who was still sitting on the settee, while Nicole stood next to her. He crossed his arms over his chest and grinned at both of them. "What was that all about? She seemed in a hurry to leave."

"She was," Nicole replied, waving a hand in the air to dismiss the unpleasant encounter.

"Why?" Daffin asked.

"I don't think she liked the questions we asked." Regina offered Daffin a small smile that grew as she locked eyes with him.

Daffin slid onto the settee next to Regina. "What did you ask her?"

"We asked if her daughter was unhappy to be tossed over for Lady Arabelle," Regina replied.

"You didn't," Daffin said, the grin still sitting on his handsome face.

"Oh, yes, we did," Regina replied with a laugh.

"And?" Daffin lifted his brows.

Regina shrugged one shoulder and sighed. "And she looked as if she wanted to slap both of us."

"I'd have come to your aid if she had, my lady," Daffin replied, in his most charming voice.

Regina met his gaze. "I can handle myself, Mr. Oakleaf."

"No doubt, Lady Regina," the runner replied.

Nicole felt like an intruder. She quietly started for the door, but Mark briskly entered the room, saving her. He gave her a half-cocked smile, and an unexpected jolt of lust shot through her. Blast. She was in far more trouble than she'd even guessed. She was already remembering him with his clothes off and his mouth—

No. Not helpful.

She cleared her throat. "There you are, Mark. What did Lord Hillenbrand say? Did he admit to bringing the wine?"

"He admitted it," Mark replied, giving Nicole another smoldering private look before coming to stand next to the settee where Daffin and Regina remained seated. "But he insisted they all drank from the same bottles and said it doesn't make him a murderer."

"What about his pursuit of Lady Arabelle?" Nicole asked, steadfastly refusing to meet his gaze. Instead, she stared purposely over his wide shoulder.

Mark shrugged. "He said there were many other women to be had. No use crying over just one of them."

"And you believe him?" Regina asked, tearing her gaze away from Oakleaf.

"I do," Mark said with a nod.

Nicole tapped her slipper along the rug. She supposed Hillenbrand's excuses rang true. "What about Mr. Cartwright?"

"He's an odd case," Mark replied. "Definitely angry over losing the title."

"But usually if someone has something to hide, they act as if they're *not* angry," Daffin pointed out.

"Unless they simply cannot help themselves," Nicole replied. "Remember Lord Hartwell?"

"Ah, yes," Daffin replied. "You're right."

"A case you two worked together, I presume," Mark said, a combination of sarcasm and a hint of jealousy in his tone.

"Ooh, I want to hear all about it." Regina folded her hands in her lap and leaned closer to Daffin.

"It's a hideous tale, actually," Nicole began. "Lord Hartwell had choked his wife to death. But he acted the doting husband until we asked him some specific questions about his wife's activities. He couldn't control himself. He was so angry he nearly had an apoplectic fit."

"Admitted to everything in the end," Daffin finished, shaking his head.

"That's the thing about crimes involving humanity's baser passions," Mark added. "It's difficult to keep that amount of emotion hidden." He exchanged a look with Nicole.

She sucked in her breath. Passions? Emotions? He was talking about the two of them. After what he'd said last night about dreaming about her, she didn't know how to feel. They both knew their time together was limited. They both knew they were having sex to fulfill her condition, but could there be something more? Had either of them changed enough?

Nicole's thoughts were interrupted when Aunt Harriet wandered into the room, unaware of the tension bouncing among its occupants. Her batlike handkerchief fluttered in her hand. "It was a lovely memorial, wasn't it, dears?" she said with a long, drawn-out sigh.

They all nodded and murmured in unison.

Lady Harriet shook her head sadly. "Edward has taken to his bed. It was difficult for him to bury his only son. Poor, dear man."

"Yes," Mark replied, his voice clipped. "I can only imagine."

Aunt Harriet continued to wave the handkerchief in

the air. She turned to Mark and Daffin. "At least we have the naming of the heir tomorrow to look forward to. What's next for the investigation?"

Nicole exchanged a knowing look with Regina.

Nicole took a deep breath. "We have one more important question to ask someone."

CHAPTER THIRTY-NINE

Mark sat in the study again the next morning, Oakleaf to his right. His uncle sat behind the desk. Mark was supposed to be focused on the conversation about how they intended to announce the heir later that afternoon, but his mind kept drifting to Nicole.

They had spent another passionate night together. He was getting little sleep, but that was fine with him. It was odd, however, how they spent hours in rapture together in bed, but during the days spoke to each other as if they were barely more than acquaintances. If it weren't for the heated glances they'd shared, he'd wonder if their nights together weren't figments of his imagination. Nicole actually seemed standoffish. He'd try to catch her eye and she'd glance away. He'd try to move closer to her and she'd drift away. But her reaction to his touch in bed was real. He could feel it. He could tell. She was enjoying herself and so was he. So what was the problem?

Even as he asked himself the question, he answered it. The problem was and always would stem from the night they'd broken their marriage apart.

He'd come home whistling, flowers in his hand, purchased from a street vendor near the circus. Nicole wasn't home. Was she at the runners' office again? Early in their courtship he'd begun to suspect there was some pastime she engaged in that he knew nothing about. It was easy to follow her, to figure it out. He trusted her but he had to ensure she was safe. The moment he realized she was working with the runners, a fear like none he'd ever known had gripped him. It stayed with him day and night. He would have to bring it up eventually if she didn't, but he hoped she would tell him first. She needed to trust him enough to share her secret. If it meant that much to her, he would allow her to continue her work, but he'd never lose the fear that gripped him when he thought of her putting her life in danger.

He was about to climb the stairs to their flat when Mrs. Allworthy, the woman who owned the building, called to him from behind her shop's closed door.

"Some letters arrived for you, Corporal," the older lady called out in a singsong voice.

Mark stopped on the first step, smiled to himself, and turned back to wait for Mrs. Allworthy's door to open. When it did, she handed him a small stack of correspondence and crossed her arms over her chest. "I suppose those are for your lovely wife." Mrs. Allworthy nodded to the flowers.

"They are," Mark replied with a wide grin. "White roses are her favorite."

Mrs. Allworthy sighed. "I wish my husband was that thoughtful."

Mark pulled a rose from the bouquet and presented it to the landlady with a bow. "For you, my lady."

"Thank you, Corporal," the woman replied, taking the rose from him and smiling from ear to ear.

Whistling again, Mark made his way up the stairs.

He entered the flat and tossed the flowers and the correspondence on the small table that sat in the corner of the tiny kitchen. He turned in a wide circle to find a vase or some other contraption to hold the flowers when one of the letters caught his eye. *To my darlings, Nicole and Mark.* He picked up the letter and turned it over in his hands. The Whitby stamp covered the back. Lady Whitby didn't usually address her letters to both of them. She'd just recently left for her country house in Sussex. Letters had only just begun to arrive for Nicole from her mother. He smiled to himself. He was already settling into his new family. Even though he didn't like to admit it, it felt good to no longer be alone in the world. When was the last time he'd received a letter that wasn't about work?

He wiped his hands on his breeches and ripped open the correspondence with one finger. The first page was a lot of womanish gossip and dull details about how the servants had aired out the country house. On the next page, however, he stopped. He had to read one line again.

"I do hope you reconcile with your family, dear Mark. We'd love to have the duke and duchess for Christmas dinner in Sussex."

He'd read it three times before the import of the

words sank in. Lady Whitby knew who his uncle was. Knew it and mentioned it casually in a letter as if she and Nicole had discussed it before. They must have. Which meant . . .

Nicole knew too.

All the breath left his lungs as if someone had jabbed a fist through his middle. Suddenly it made sense to him, why a countess had agreed for her only daughter to marry a seeming no one in the army. The dowager countess had assured him they expected him to do great things one day, but it hadn't been that at all. They hadn't had faith in him. They'd looked at him like the grandson of a duke. They'd approved of him because he was a member of the illustrious Colchester family. And Nicole had known too. Known and kept it from him.

He sank onto the chair next to the table and pressed a hand over his eyes. She was just like his grandfather and everyone else on his mother's side of the family. Nicole had pretended not to care about family ties or the *ton*. She'd even agreed with him when he'd made the case that they didn't need any of the expensive wedding gifts they'd received from her family.

Light footsteps on the stairs told him Nicole was on her way up. He forced himself to release the tension in his muscles and breathe. He would not jump to conclusions. He would ask her first. Perhaps she had some explanation. Perhaps her mother had known and merely assumed he and Nicole had discussed it. A shred of hope planted itself in his mind.

But she hadn't denied it. Not only had she admitted to it, she'd tried to blame *him* as if he had some obligation to claim a family he'd purposely disowned. She'd gone on to admit she'd been keeping *another* secret from him. The one where she was regularly risking her life by working with the Bow Street Runners. When he considered the two secrets together, he realized what a sneak she was. Why the hell *had* she failed to mention that important piece of news to him?

In those moments, Mark had realized he had no idea whom he'd married. He had allowed his overwhelming attraction to Nicole Huntington to blind him to all the reasons they were not a good match. He'd been a damn fool, consumed with lust. Not love. How could he love someone who wasn't honest with him? How could he love someone he didn't even know?

The next weeks had been torture. He'd wanted to go to her a hundred times. He'd wanted to ask her to—beg her—to give him some reason, some explanation that would make it all right. But his damned pride kept him from it, and by the time he'd determined to go to her grandmother's house and ask where the hell his wife was, Nicole had left for France of all deuced places. She'd left for France to become a *spy*. The irony nearly sent him to his knees.

He spent the next ten years trying to forget her. Pretending as if the months spent with her had never happened. As if he'd never even met her. Aside from the nightmare of his incarceration in a French prison camp, he'd been moderately successful at it too . . . until his need for his blasted promotion had brought him to her door.

The promotion. Mark swallowed to ease a throat that had gone dry at the torturous recollections. There would be time later to worry about his complicated relationship with Nicole. He needed to concentrate on solving his cousin's murder. The naming of the heir was only a few hours away. Things were about to get exceedingly complicated.

"If we cannot prove Hillenbrand is the killer before the heir is named this afternoon," Mark said to the others, "I shall be forced to have an extremely awkward conversation with Lord Tottenham."

"You think it's Hillenbrand, not Cartwright?" the duke asked, struggling to remain upright in his chair.

"We're not entirely certain," Mark replied, scrubbing a hand through his hair. "I intend to question Cartwright again. Neither man has admitted to anything that would incriminate him."

Oakleaf shifted in his seat and cast Mark a hard look. "Time is of the essence. We'll have to question them more directly. No more playing nice."

A swirl of color near the door caught Mark's attention. He turned to see Nicole and Regina standing at the threshold. Regina was dressed in black again, while Nicole wore a pretty dark green day dress. Her hair was piled high atop her head and she had a mischievous grin on her face. Despite the memories he'd recently sorted through, a pang of lust shot through him.

"Yes, ladies, what is it?" the duke asked, coughing quietly into his handkerchief.

Nicole and Regina made their way into the room, their arms crossed over their chests, smug smiles on their faces. "We think we know who poisoned the wine, and we need your help to prove it," Nicole announced, her gaze directed at Mark.

Mark shot to his feet. "What? Who?"

"We have a plan," Nicole said. "You must ask Lord Hillenbrand again if he insisted upon pouring the wine."

"Hillenbrand did it?" the duke rasped, his cloudy eyes darting back and forth between Nicole and Mark.

"We just need to know the answer to the question about him pouring the wine," Nicole replied.

"Why?" Daffin asked, his green eyes narrowed on the women.

"Because that's what Molly Lester told us," Regina said.

Nicole nodded. "Yes, and either Lord Hillenbrand is lying . . . or Molly Lester is."

Ten minutes later, Mark and Daffin stood alone with Hillenbrand in the study.

"So you're telling us you were never alone with the wine that night?" Mark asked, his eyes trained on the younger man's face.

"I had it in my coach with me, if that's what you mean," Hillenbrand said, his face growing more mottled with each moment. "The butler brought it in."

"Did he open it?" Daffin asked. The runner's arms were casually folded behind his back.

Lord Hillenbrand ground his teeth, his fingers clenched and unclenched into fists. "No. I did. Look here, man, we've already been over this."

"What if we told you that Miss Lester said you were alone with the wine and acting peculiar?" Daffin offered, leaning one hip against the desk as he studied Hillenbrand.

"What!" Hillenbrand's face clouded with rage. A vein bulged in his neck.

"She told us you poured the glasses yourself," Mark said, pacing thoughtfully toward the window. "That you insisted upon it."

"That little liar. She's the one who insisted upon pouring it!"

CHAPTER FORTY

Nicole peered into the drawing room. All the guests were gathered, waiting for the duke to arrive to announce the heir. As predicted, Molly was perched next to Mr. Cartwright, cooing into his ear.

Nicole and Regina had come to the conclusion that Molly was the killer. They simply had to find a way to make her admit it. They sent a footman to ask Mr. Cartwright to step into the next room, where they waited in the green salon.

When he arrived, the man had a puzzled look on his face. "Mrs. Grimaldi? Lady Regina? You wanted to see me?"

Nicole crossed the room to meet him. "Yes, Mr. Cartwright, we did. We, ah, need your help."

Nicole and Regina each took an arm and gently led him into the room.

The frown remained on his face. "What's that?"

"We need you to tell Miss Lester ahead of time that you're not the heir," Regina explained with a pleasant smile.

Mr. Cartwright shook his head. "The duke and General Grimaldi asked me to keep it a secret until the duke makes his announcement."

"Yes, we know that," Nicole said hurriedly. "But we need you to tell Miss Lester and only Miss Lester. We'll be watching through the keyhole. The duke and my husband both know about this."

Mr. Cartwright's eyes widened. "You don't suspect Miss Lester—"

"Please, Mr. Cartwright. We'll have a footman bring her and her mother here. All you need do is tell her what the duke told you." Nicole kept her voice even and calm.

"Very well." Mr. Cartwright's tone was clipped. He didn't seem convinced, but as long as he was willing to do as asked, Nicole would not spend precious time trying to explain to him.

Satisfied, Nicole and Regina slipped from the room. A few minutes later, a footman escorted Molly and her mother inside to join Mr. Cartwright. Nicole and Regina crouched near the double doors where Mark and Daffin joined them.

"Now listen," Nicole said, trying to ignore the rush of heat through her body with Mark so close to her.

The two men pressed their ears to the doors as Molly began speaking while Nicole and Regina took turns watching through the keyhole.

"Mr. Cartwright." Molly rushed to the settee to sit next to him. Her mother remained standing near the door. "What is it?"

"I have something to tell you, Molly." To Nicole's surprised delight, Mr. Cartwright played the role perfectly. "I have to tell someone. It's killing me."

"What?" Molly searched his face. She leaned toward him. "You can tell me."

Mr. Cartwright tugged at his cravat. "The duke." Cartwright cleared his throat. "He called me into his study earlier to tell me . . ."

"Yes?" Molly prodded, still searching his face.

Mr. Cartwright glanced away. "To tell me I'm not his heir."

"What?" Molly's face turned bright red. Her eyes widened with panic. "There must be some mistake. Of course you're the heir."

"That cannot possibly be true," Mrs. Lester added, hurrying toward the settee to join them.

Cartwright stole a glance at the door. "I'm afraid it is true. I'm not the heir. Turns out General Grimaldi is the heir. He's the duke's nephew on his mother's side."

Molly's face was mottled. "General Grimaldi? You must be jesting. He's no more related to the Colchester family than I am."

"General Grimaldi, indeed," Mrs. Lester snapped, spittle flying from her lips.

"I'm not jesting," Mr. Cartwright continued, impressively convincing in his earnest delivery. "Grimaldi is related to them. It was a surprise to everyone, apparently, even the general. The part about him being the heir, I mean."

"No," Molly muttered. "No, this cannot be happening." She stared unseeing at the rug.

Out in the corridor, Nicole straightened. "Now. Give

me five minutes." She turned to face Mark. "Your uncle knows what to do, correct?"

Mark nodded.

Nicole pushed open the door to the salon while the others hid against the nearby wall so they wouldn't be seen. "Oh, my. Miss Lester, Mrs. Lester, Mr. Cartwright. I didn't know you were here." Nicole closed the door behind her.

"It's all right, Mrs. Grimaldi," Cartwright said, obviously relieved to see her. "I was just telling Miss Lester and her mother that I am not the duke's heir. A fact I believe you're already aware of."

Nicole bowed her head. "Yes, I know. It turns out Mark is the true heir. None of us knew."

"What are you both prattling on about?" Molly's voice was high-pitched and filled with disbelief. She shot to her feet. "You're both mistaken. You're both mad."

Mrs. Lester pulled out her handkerchief and fanned herself rapidly. "No. No. No," she mumbled, shaking her head.

"I'm afraid I'm not mistaken." Nicole sighed and blinked innocently at Miss Lester. "The duke told Mark and me the night John died. I saw the paperwork myself. A unique codicil in the will. It was as much a surprise to Mark and me as—"

"Stop it!" Molly clapped her hands over her ears. "I won't listen to a moment more of this insane drivel. Mr. Cartwright is the heir. Everyone knows it. Even Lord Coleford did."

"No," Nicole said calmly. "John didn't know Mark was the heir. His father never saw a reason to explain it to him. Mark hadn't wanted his family connection to be revealed. He's never publicly acknowledged them, nor they him."

"That's madness. It makes no sense," Molly gasped. "Who wouldn't claim a connection to a duke?"

"If you knew my husband, you'd know why it makes perfect sense," Nicole replied, glancing at the door.

"You're lying," Molly insisted, narrowing her eyes on Nicole.

Nicole met the younger woman's stare. "What possible reason would I have to lie about such a thing?"

Molly turned on Mr. Cartwright, her face a mask of outrage. "How long have you known about this?"

"Since yesterday," Mr. Cartwright admitted, glancing uneasily at Nicole.

"You've known you weren't the heir since *yesterday* and you've allowed me to continue traipsing after you like a lovesick fool?"

"Careful, Miss Lester," Nicole warned. "You sound as if you may only have been interested in Mr. Cartwright while he was the presumed heir."

"Of course she was only interested in him if he was the heir," Mrs. Lester barked. "Why would she give a toss about a nearly penniless mister?"

Mr. Cartwright's face hardened.

Molly opened her mouth to retort, but a knock on the door stopped her.

Mark pushed open the door and cleared his throat. "The duke asks for everyone's presence in the drawing room. It's time for the announcement."

Molly and her mother exchanged uneasy glances before stomping out of the room together, hurrying away from Mr. Cartwright. Nicole and Mr. Cartwright followed slowly behind them. Once in the corridor, Mr. Cartwright paused to give Nicole and Mark a wry smile. "Seems you may have been right about her after all."

Nicole, Regina, Daffin, and Mark exchanged hopeful glances.

"Just one more part," Nicole said, nodding to the room where the others waited. "Let's get this over with."

They all made their way into the blue drawing room. The duke sat in his wheeled chair at the front of the room. All the other guests, including Lord Tottenham and Lady Harriet, were gathered there. The will lay on a side table next to the duke's chair. As soon as everyone entered the room and Mark closed the door, the duke cleared his throat and regarded the room full of people. Some were standing and others were sitting, but everyone stared intently at the duke.

"We've gathered here this afternoon for the reading of John's will, which I shall allow my solicitor, Mr. Brooks, to handle." A small bespectacled man at the front of the room nodded to everyone. "But first I want to get on with the other part I'm certain you're all waiting for. The naming of the heir."

Silence filled the room as if the assembly drew a deep breath.

"I know many of you thought the heir was Mr. Cartwright . . ."

Nicole watched as Molly's face scrunched into a hateful knot.

"And you're right," the duke continued. "Mr. Cartwright, is, in fact, the heir."

"What?" Molly leaped from her seat and stamped her

foot. Her hands were clutched in fists and her face was a splotchy red color. "He just told me he wasn't the heir."

"What's going on here?" Mrs. Lester glanced around the room, her eyes narrowed in suspicion.

Molly rushed over to Mr. Cartwright. "Is it true? Are you the heir?"

Mr. Cartwright swiveled to look at the duke. "Am I?"

"Indeed," the duke replied with a nod.

Molly fell to her knees in front of Mr. Cartwright's seat. "Oh, Mr. Cartwright, I'm so sorry. I'm so, so sorry I was rude to you earlier. I was just surprised and I—"

Mr. Cartwright's face was a mask of stone. "I believe your mother said it all."

"No. No. No. She didn't mean it," Molly insisted. "Did you, Mother?" She turned ferociously on her mother. "Tell him you didn't mean it!"

"Of course not," Mrs. Lester said, moving as quickly as her short fat legs could carry her to Mr. Cartwright's side. "I meant nothing of the sort."

Nicole cleared her throat and stepped forward. "Did you mean what you said about Lord Hillenbrand then?" she asked Molly.

Molly turned to look at Nicole, confusion sweeping across her face. "What do you mean?"

"You told me and Regina that Lord Hillenbrand insisted upon pouring the wine the night John died."

Lord Hillenbrand surged to his feet. "Yes, I heard as much, and we both know that's an outright lie." He pointed at Molly. "You were the one who insisted on pouring the wine at the side table that night, Miss Lester."

Molly's eyes widened in fear and she glanced around

at the sea of confused faces. "No, that's not true. That's not—"

"It is true," Mr. Cartwright intoned. "Now that I think about it. I remember you pouring the wine in the corner of the room. Your mother was with you. You waited until the servants had left."

Molly sank to the floor, her face pale, her dreams clearly slipping through her fingers.

"Molly." Lady Arabelle stood, her voice filled with distress. "Tell me this isn't true. You were pouring the wine that night, I remember, but . . . oh, no, no, Molly, you couldn't have." Lady Arabelle collapsed into her seat in tears. Her mother rushed to her side to comfort her.

"Oh, shut up, Arabelle," Molly said viciously, grabbing the arm of a nearby chair and stumbling to her feet. "You don't understand anything. You've always got whatever you wanted with barely having to crook your little finger. I'm the one who has had to accept second best my entire life."

"What are you saying?" Arabelle sobbed, her blue eyes bright with tears.

"I'm saying, I wasn't about to stand by and let you become a marchioness and a duchess while I married a nobody. Mr. Cartwright was the next in line and I intended to finally be one step ahead of you."

Arabelle shook her head. "You would murder an innocent person in your quest to become a marchioness?"

"I wouldn't have had to murder *anyone* if it wasn't for you," Molly screamed. "If you hadn't horned in on Lord Coleford when he was clearly interested in *me,* none of this would have happened."

Molly's eyes were wild as she swung her gaze about the room, lighting on each pale, pitying face. She scratched at her arms and turned in a wide circle. "I've always been overlooked. No one cared about me. No one looked twice at me. Lord Coleford barely noticed me. He asked about Arabelle when we danced. But when Mr. Cartwright was so kind and sweet and looked at me as if I were a person . . ." Her face went soft for a moment. "I thought I'd found someone who truly liked me. And . . . he was so close to becoming a marquess. So very close. I knew I couldn't allow Lord Coleford to marry Arabelle and possibly produce an heir. That would complicate everything."

"Yes, must do away with him before he produces an heir," Mrs. Lester agreed, nodding, her eyes unfocused. She looked small and sunken into the chair she'd collapsed into, even as her daughter's sanity crumbled to dust.

Molly lifted her chin and glanced around the room. "I know I was wrong, but they were wrong too."

"Who?" Daffin asked, carefully.

"All the people who ever overlooked me," Molly replied in a voice that had gone high, little-girl-like. "Everyone who ever treated me unkindly. Mr. Cartwright was kind to me. Mr. Cartwright saw me for who I truly am."

Mr. Cartwright had a horrified expression on his face. He took a step away from her. "No, Molly, that's not true. I *failed* to see you for who you truly are, a scheming murderess. I thought you were a sweet, quiet young woman who was looking for someone to share the rest of her life with and who didn't mind that I didn't have a title. I'd no idea the lengths you'd go to in order to get one."

Molly stared up at Mr. Cartwright, aghast. "You're going to denounce me too?"

Mr. Cartwright shook his head in disgust. "You killed Lord Coleford. Of course I denounce you."

Molly let out an ungodly scream and threw herself toward Cartwright, stabbing at his eyes as if to scratch them out, but Daffin Oakleaf stepped in the way, blocking her path. He grabbed her wrists in one large hand and spun her around, wrestling her into the pair of darby handcuffs he'd pulled from his jacket pocket.

Molly tried to struggle out of Daffin's hold.

"Careful," he said against her ear. "Don't make me use my truncheon on you."

From her position near the doorway, Regina gave Nicole a little smile.

Daffin carted both Molly and her mother out of the room while everyone else stared at one another aghast.

"My apologies," the duke said, clearing his throat and addressing the room at large. "I had to tell a bit of a fib there in order to get Miss Lester to confess. I'm exceedingly grateful it worked."

"A fib?" Lord Anthony echoed.

"Yes," the duke replied with a faint smile. "The truth is that Mr. Cartwright is not the heir, as he's already been told. Thank you for your help, Mr. Cartwright."

Mr. Cartwright gave a grave nod. "I'm only glad we've found the culprit. Shocking as it is."

In the back of the room, Lord Tottenham cleared his throat. "Then who is the heir?"

CHAPTER FORTY-ONE

Mark swiveled on his heel. It was time. He had to tell the truth. "Lord Tottenham," he intoned. "Before His Grace makes the announcement, may I have a word with you . . . alone?"

Tottenham's face wrinkled into a confused frown, but he nodded and followed Mark to the door.

"We won't be long," Mark informed the occupants of the room. On his way out, he whispered to Nicole, "Please join us."

"Me?" Nicole pointed to herself.

Mark grinned at her and nodded.

Regina pushed Nicole toward the door. "Go," she mouthed.

Nicole followed the two men from the room. The three of them entered the green salon next door.

As soon as the door shut behind them, Tottenham turned to Mark, tugging at his waistcoat that bulged over his belly. "I know what this is about, Grimaldi. I promised you your promotion if you solved the case. Not to worry, I'm a man of my word and you shall have it. I hardly think we needed to delay the announcement because of it, however. I, for one, am on tenterhooks to hear the news, especially since I learned the heir is not Cartwright."

Mark folded his arms behind his back and braced his feet apart. He faced Tottenham head-on. "I believe once you know what I have to say, you'll agree this meeting was necessary, my lord."

"Eh?" Tottenham's face puckered into another frown. "Very well, then. Proceed." He crossed his arms over his girth and waited for Mark to speak.

"First," Mark began, pacing toward the windows. "I could not have solved the case without my wife." He smiled at Nicole, who returned his smile. She'd never looked more beautiful. "I was convinced the killer was either Lord Hillenbrand or Mr. Cartwright. It was Nicole who spoke to Miss Lester and realized she was hiding something."

"Perhaps I should make your wife the Home Secretary, then," Tottenham replied with a hearty laugh.

"She would be a fine choice, my lord," Mark replied humbly. He looked at Nicole and felt something that went beyond pride, something that sent warmth through him and put a knot in his throat.

"I, however, don't aspire to be the Home Secretary," Nicole replied, crossing to her husband and twining her arm through his. She gently tugged him back toward Tottenham. "But my husband does and he will gladly accept your offer, my lord."

"Excellent," Tottenham replied, lifting his fleshy chin.

Mark winced and rubbed the back of his neck with his free hand. "First I must tell you something. Something that is certain to come as a surprise."

"What's that, Grimaldi?" Tottenham's craggy brows dropped lower over his eyes.

Mark took a deep breath. This was it. If he said the words that hovered on his lips, there would be no turning back. "When the duke makes the announcement, he'll be naming me as the heir to the Duchy of Colchester." He hung his head.

Nicole squeezed Mark's hand. Mark glanced back up. His entire future hung in the next few moments.

"The devil you say?" Tottenham's eyes were wide as carriage wheels. "What are you talking about?"

Mark straightened his shoulders. "I am the son of Mary Grimaldi, the duke's sister. The will contains a codicil naming the next male in the direct family as heir. That is me."

Tottenham's eyes instantly filled with what could only be described as joy. "By God, man, are you telling me my new Home Secretary is also a marquess?"

"I'm afraid I am, my lord." Mark swallowed the lump that had been lodged in his throat since he'd asked to speak with Tottenham alone.

Tottenham clapped his hands. "Are you quite serious? It couldn't have turned out better if I'd planned it."

Mark stared at him as if he'd taken leave of his senses. This was hardly the reaction he expected. "It's not a role I aspired to, my lord, that of marquess, I mean."

Tottenham tugged at the lapels of his coat. "Are you

mad? Do you realize the type of influence you can bring to the position as a marquess?"

"That's what I've been trying to tell him," Nicole added, a wide smile on her face.

"I hadn't thought of it that way," Mark replied. He covered Nicole's hand with his own and smiled at her warmly.

"Well, start thinking of it that way, Coleford. You're bound to be able to pass any reforms you want with the Colchester name behind you."

Mark stood there, dumbfounded. Could he really do more good as an aristocrat? The role he'd rejected his entire life. Damn. He'd been a fool and an arse for not recognizing it sooner.

"I won't let you down, my lord," Mark promised. He let go of Nicole's arm and bowed to the older man.

Tottenham stepped forward and clapped Mark on the shoulder. "I know you won't, Grimaldi. I know you won't."

"Shall we get back?" Nicole said, her eyes suspiciously bright. "I presume the rest of the drawing room is eager to hear the news."

"By all means," Lord Tottenham replied, gesturing for Nicole to precede them to the door.

The three of them filed back into the other room, where Mark nodded at the duke.

The duke smiled and returned Mark's nod, then turned to the room at large whose occupants had fallen utterly silent. The atmosphere grew instantly thick with anticipation. "Everyone, it's time for me to introduce you to the heir to the Duchy of Colchester, my nephew, Mark Grimaldi."

A gasp went up around the room and the duke grinned proudly as Mark explained to everyone how he was related to the family and why he'd inherited the title.

Lady Harriet and Regina beamed. The rest of the group offered Mark their congratulations. Even Mr. Cartwright looked pleased for him.

"Remember, this means you must get to work on an heir right away!" Lady Harriet declared, nudging Mark in the side.

Mark and Nicole exchanged a glance. Her hand stole into his and his fingers closed around hers, anchoring her to his side.

Two hours later, they gathered with Regina in the grand foyer to bid farewell to Daffin, who was on his way back to London.

"I'm pleased that our little team was able to find the truth," Daffin said, a broad grin on his face. "Mrs. Lester and Molly are already on their way back to London to face the magistrate."

"Thanks to Nicole." Mark gave his wife a fond, tender smile.

"Oh, no," Nicole replied. "Not just me. I couldn't have done it without my steadfast assistant, Regina. I daresay she'll make a fine investigator one day."

Regina bumped her shoulder against Nicole's. "I daresay we make a fine team. Two female minds are better than one."

Daffin narrowed his eyes on the ladies. "Why did you two suspect Molly in the first place?"

"Honestly, we questioned her first only because she was there," Nicole admitted. "But once we listened to her story, we were able to see through her because we know what it's like to be that age and looking for a match."

"Something Oakleaf and I know nothing about." Mark shook his head.

"You're willing to admit that ladies make good investigators?" Nicole asked him with a pointed look.

Mark laughed. "I'm even willing to admit that at times they make *superior* investigators."

"I've known that since I last worked with you, Nic," Daffin said, placing his hat on his head. He bowed to Nicole. "Job well done, my lady." He turned to Mark. "I'll see you back in London, Grim."

Mark clapped the runner on the shoulder. "Yes. You'll have to come for dinner one night soon, Oakleaf."

"I'd like that," Daffin replied. He turned to Regina and his smile grew warmer. "Will you be there too, Lady Regina?"

"I might be persuaded to join you," Regina said. "Though I'll still be in mourning for the next three weeks."

"Of course." Daffin ran a finger along the brim of his hat and nodding. "Until we meet again then, my lady."

The runner strode out the door, down the steps, and pulled himself up into the waiting carriage. Regina watched him go and sighed.

Mark shut the door to the study behind him and faced his uncle, who sat behind the large desk. "You wanted to speak with me?" He cleared his throat. "Privately."

"Yes." The duke nodded.

"At your service." Mark folded his arms behind his back and braced his feet apart.

His uncle eyed him carefully. "Thank you for finding the people who killed John."

Mark swallowed. "It was the least I could do, Your Grace."

"You still refuse to call me 'Uncle'?"

"No, I—"

"Are you going to take it, Mark? The duchy, I mean."

Mark hung his head and scrubbed his hand across the back of his neck. He'd known this moment would come and was prepared for it. He'd had time to fully digest the import of his mother's letter. "Yes," he breathed. "I will take it when the time comes."

"I am quite sick. The time will be upon us soon. There is much I must tell you, Mark. Things you must learn."

Mark gave his uncle a solemn nod. "I understand."

"I suggest you begin coming to my house in London, say, twice a week. We can discuss the estates and books and the tenants."

"As you wish. I will speak to my solicitor. He'll come too."

"A fine idea."

Mark turned toward the door to leave.

"Wait." His uncle's voice stopped him.

"Yes?"

"What about Nicole? Are you and she reunited . . . truly, for good? Will she serve as your duchess?"

Apparently, they hadn't done as good an acting job as Mark had believed. He refused to lie to the old man. "No. We're not. She returned to help me. She's been doing me a favor all this time."

His uncle's brows dropped. "For what in return?"

Mark shifted on both feet. "Suffice it to say, we both got something we wanted out of it, but she will be returning to France eventually."

"Do you love her?"

Mark steeled his jaw against the unexpected question. He only needed to repeat what he'd been telling himself every day since she'd come back into his life. If he said it often enough, he might even begin to believe it. "I never even knew her, Uncle. Nicole and I never should have married in the first place."

The duke arched a gray brow. "You won't be sorry to see her go?"

He'd be sorry to see her go all right, but what did that have to do with anything? "We're two different people, Nicole and I."

"That's not what I asked. Will you be sorry to see her go?"

Mark straightened and stared out the window. This was more difficult than he thought. The sooner this conversation ended, the better. He ground out the words between clenched teeth. "It's best for both of us if we return to our normal lives as soon as possible."

CHAPTER FORTY-TWO

Nicole stared at the blank piece of vellum again. She'd put it off long enough. She must write her mother. No doubt Mother's letters to her had been stacking up in France. The woman was probably worried about her. Why was it so difficult to scribble the words to tell her mother she was living under the same roof as her husband again? Perhaps because a letter had started all the trouble to begin with. Nicole tossed down the quill and let her head drop in exasperation.

She and Mark had been back in London for two days. Mark hadn't touched her. She'd slept in her bedchamber, next door to his, wondering if he would come. But he hadn't. She doubted he'd come tonight, either, and after what she'd overheard him say to his uncle in his study in Surrey, she doubted he'd ever return to her bed.

"It's best for both of us if we return to our normal lives as soon as possible." Those words slashed through her heart each time she remembered them. She hadn't meant to eavesdrop. She'd merely been seeking Mark, to ask him about their plans to return to London. She'd heard his deep voice coming from his uncle's study and made her way down the corridor to the room. She'd raised her fist to knock when she'd heard the duke ask, "Do you love her?"

Her heart had stopped beating. Her breath caught in her throat. God help her, she'd stood in stone silence waiting with bated breath for Mark's reply. "I never even knew her," he said. She closed her eyes, letting the pain wash over her. Of course she'd read too much into their nights together. While she'd been falling in love with him again, he'd merely been fulfilling his side of the bargain.

She pressed the heel of her hand against her eye. A dark thought had crept through her mind after Mark had received his promotion. He didn't need her any longer. He'd got everything he wanted. And then some. The Duchy of Colchester would be his eventually in addition to the position as Secretary of the Home Office. She was unnecessary, unneeded. His own words confirmed it. He wanted to return to his normal routine as soon as possible.

She pinched the bridge of her nose to disperse the sting from the threat of tears. That was it. She'd made her decisions. Both of them. First, she dropped the scribbled upon vellum in the rubbish bin beside the desk. She wouldn't write to her mother from London. She could write to her from France. Second, she was going back. As soon as possible. She'd done what Mark had asked of her. She refused to overstay her welcome. It had been foolish to want a baby with him. Foolish and self-ish of her. The whole idea had been ridiculous, but even if she wanted to stay, she couldn't. It was torture. The nights with him in Surrey had been magnificent, but they'd come with strings attached. Long, tangled strings.

She impatiently dashed away tears that formed as quickly as the realization. She'd known from the beginning that she couldn't just sink back into bed with him and feel nothing. She'd known when he touched her body and made her feel like he was a virtuoso playing a violin that she wouldn't be able to keep her emotions from becoming involved. And they were. She'd fallen in love with him again. She loved him and he still blamed her for the same thing he'd blamed her for ten years ago. Nothing could change that.

Staying with a man who didn't love her was impossible. It would kill her. There was no telling how long it would take to get with child. What if she couldn't conceive? They could potentially stay together for months, years. She'd be breaking her heart open again. She had to leave. As soon as possible. The longer she stayed with him, the more entrenched her heart would become. She swallowed hard, tucked her chair beneath the desk, and turned to face the door. There was only one way she knew to convince him to let her go with few questions asked. The thought of leaving made her heart ache, but the thought of staying made her miserable.

She straightened her spine and ran both hands over her damp cheeks. This weeping would not do. When had she become such a crier? Good heavens. She must pull herself together.

A soft knock at the door that separated her bedchamber from Mark's made her jump. "Come in," she forced herself to say in a false-bright voice.

Mark entered the room. He wore his breeches, a shirt opened to reveal his muscled chest, and little else she surmised from a quick, enlivening glance down to his beautiful bare feet. Had he come to make love to her again? She wanted him to. Oh, how desperately she wanted him to.

"Are you recovered from the journey from Surrey?" he asked, coming to stand near the bed, only a few paces from her.

"Y-yes. Are you?" She couldn't meet his gaze for fear she would weep again.

"I think so."

She wrapped her arms around herself tightly. It was cold in the room of a sudden. "You got everything you wanted, didn't you?" she murmured.

"I got the *one* thing I wanted. I never wanted the duchy."

"Ah, of course." She moved toward him and hesitated, then reached to place a hand on his elbow. "Mark, I don't think you should take the duchy if you truly don't want it."

He searched her face, confusion written across his expression. "What?"

"It's not worth it. Your uncle will manage it. There will be someone else to take it. There always is."

He bit his bottom lip as if considering her words, then he said slowly, "I'm surprised to hear you say that. Don't you want the duchy . . . for our child?"

She couldn't talk to him about their child. Their non-existent child. The lump in her throat blocked any words on the subject from coming out. Instead, she said, "I never expected to be a duchess or the mother of a future duke."

Those words emerged more poignant than she'd meant them to be. They both remained silent for several moments. Mark's dark gaze was relentless on her, while hers darted about, for if it were to land on his beloved face, the tears would start again.

He gave a small shake of his head and wandered away, toward the window, where he pushed aside the curtain to stare out into the inky night sky. "And did you get what you wanted, Nicole?" Was it her imagination or was there a slight tremor to his voice?

Nicole's hand went to her belly. This was it. The moment to secure her freedom from this mad bargain she never should have made. "Yes," she forced herself to say. "I believe I have."

His shoulders dropped slightly. He let the curtains close and turned back to face her. "Are you certain?"

"Relatively certain." Her voice quavered. God strike her down for lying, but it was the only way she would be able to refuse him her bed. The only way he would understand why she was leaving. She'd worry about the consequences later. She could always inform him by letter that she'd been mistaken or that she'd lost the babe.

"So, that means . . ." His words trailed off.

She cleared her throat. "I'd like to return to France. Until after the baby is born. If that's all right with you."

"Is that what you want?" His eyes searched her face.

She turned her gaze to stare at the wall and bit the inside of her cheek. "It's what I prefer, yes."

"Very well," came his calm, measured voice. "You know I won't force you to stay."

"Thank you." She could barely push the words past the lump in her throat as he started past her to leave the room.

"Mark?" she called.

He stopped at the door. "Yes?"

"Are you angry? That I was investigating at Colchester Manor?"

The hint of a smile tugged at the corner of his mouth when he glanced at her over his shoulder. "Of course not. You were the one on the right path all along."

She smiled too. "I must say I was surprised to hear you admit it."

He hung his head and stared at his feet. "I'm no longer the arrogant young man I used to be, Nicole. I've seen too much of life and its atrocities."

Fresh tears stung Nicole's eyes, born not of grief for her own heartache but of compassion. She never thought she'd hear him say such a thing. "I always believed you hated me for not telling you I was affiliated with Bow Street until after we married."

"No, Nicole. I didn't care that you worked with them. I cared that you kept it from me." He turned to face her and took a few tentative steps toward her. "Your work with the runners frightened me. I didn't want you to be hurt. What I blamed you for is the fact that you knew who my family was. I was convinced you'd only pretended to love me. I thought you wanted to marry a duke's grandson, not a corporal in the army."

"I never cared that you were a duke's grandson," she

said softly. "I loved the corporal. Can you believe that now, Mark?"

He searched her face, and a hint of vulnerability flashed in his eyes. "Does it make a difference?"

She had to pinch her arms to keep the tears from falling. "No," she whispered, hanging her head. "I suppose it doesn't. Not after all these years."

"Do you . . . still want to go?" he asked, the vulnerability in the question undeniable now.

It felt as if an invisible knife carved a hole in her chest. "I must."

He drew a deep breath, closed his eyes, released it, and finally gave a nod of surrender. "Very well," he said, as he slowly opened his bedchamber door. "Have the maids help you pack. I'll provide my coach for your journey to Dover."

She didn't allow herself to weep until he shut the door behind him.

CHAPTER FORTY-THREE

The Curious Goat Inn was filled with its regular midday patrons. Men drinking and laughing, the odd woman sharing a pint, and children selling papers in the street outside. Mark strode in and immediately saw his colleagues sitting at a large round table in the middle of the room. The Cavendish twins and Daffin Oakleaf looked like a trio of Nordic gods in the midst of mere mortals. Mark strolled over, grabbed a wooden chair, turned it around, and straddled it.

"If it isn't the stone man, himself," Rafe Cavendish said, clapping Mark on the shoulder.

"And if it isn't the viscount spy," Mark rejoined, folding his arms across the chair back.

"Ah, ah, ah, careful making fun of those of us who have a title, Grim. I hear you're about to become a marquess any day now," Rafe replied, a sly grin on his face.

"Is that true?" Cade Cavendish shook his head. "Can't believe it. The good general, a future duke?"

"Yes, it's true," Oakleaf replied, taking a quaff of his ale. "Now I'm the only one of the lot of you who doesn't have a title. Woe is me."

"Shut it, Oakleaf. You know we envy you for it," Cade replied, elbowing the runner in the ribs.

"Yes, enough to pretend you're me from time to time, eh, Cade?" Oakleaf, arched a brow in the privateer's direction.

Cade shrugged. His grin didn't falter. "At the time, I was *persona non grata* in London. Needed your good name to get me through the door. We look alike, or so I'm told. Though I think I'm a sight more handsome than you'll ever be."

"Then you won't mind if I pretend I'm you the next time I'm in a pinch?" Oakleaf asked Cade, blinking innocently.

Cade bristled and sucked down a healthy portion of ale. "Ugh. I suppose I do owe you one."

"Perfect," Oakleaf replied, setting down his mug with a satisfied sigh. "The next time I need to pretend I'm a pirate knight, I'll be certain to invoke your name."

All four men laughed.

"What are you doing here, Grim? Got another mission for us?" Rafe called over a barmaid and ordered himself and Mark a mug of ale.

"No," Mark replied. "I'm completely devoid of missions. Now that I'm Home Secretary, I'm working on my new plan for the police force."

Oakleaf whistled. "Yes, well, the police force sounds far less exciting than being a runner."

Mark cast him a wry look. "It might be, but I'm attempting to secure funding from the government so you and your lot won't have to rely on bounties."

"Can't say I've ever disliked relying on bounties. They've made me a wealthy man," Oakleaf replied with a grin. "I reckon if this police force business takes off, I'll go into private practice as an investigator."

"I wouldn't blame you, Oakleaf," Mark replied. "The police force won't earn the same purses you have."

The barmaid returned and plunked down an overflowing mug of ale in front of Mark.

"Where's the missus, Grim?" Cade interjected. "I was hoping you'd introduce us at long last."

"Yes, Daphne and Danielle want to have you both over for dinner sometime soon," Rafe threw in. "They nearly had fits when we told them you've been secretly married for ten years."

"It wasn't a secret," Mark said, some of his joviality slipping away. "I was merely . . . judicious about whom I informed."

"Spoken like a true spymaster," Rafe replied with a grin. "When will you come to dinner then?"

Mark shook his head. He stared down at the scarred pattern on the old tavern table, then lifted his mug and took a drink. "I'm afraid there will be no dinner."

"What?" Cade asked. "Why?"

Mark wiped a hand across the back of his mouth and set the mug on the table with a hollow thump. "Because Mrs. Grimaldi, soon to be the Marchioness of Coleford, is even now on her way back to France."

Oakleaf choked on the ale he was drinking and slammed his fist against the table. "The devil you say.

Thought the two of you had finally set things to rights."

Mark groaned and ran a hand over his face. "I rather thought the same thing, but apparently I was wrong."

"Look," Rafe said, bracing his forearm on the table and leaning across it toward Mark. "Cade and I have had issues with our wives in the past, believe me. Why don't you tell us the problem and we can help you solve it?"

Mark stared at the viscount spy as if was torn between astonishment and the urge to laugh. "You cannot be serious."

"Go ahead. We're happily married men, you know," Cade prompted.

The barmaid returned with two more mugs for the twins. Rafe spun one across the table to Cade before saying, "I know what you're thinking, Stone Man. You cannot tell your former subordinates about your private life. But we don't work for you anymore. You're the Secretary of the Home Office now, not the spymaster."

Mark eyed him carefully. Rafe made a certain amount of sense.

"Yes," Cade added. "We're your *friends* now. And friends tell each other things."

Mark glanced at Oakleaf, one brow quirked.

The runner shrugged. "Can't say I know much about how to keep a wife, being a bachelor myself, but I'm game to listen and help however I can."

Mark shook his head. This conversation was quickly making him uncomfortable. He'd never had friends— he hadn't had time. But something about their offer held a certain appeal. He took a deep breath and glanced at their somber, earnest faces. By God, they were actually waiting to help him. He couldn't believe he was even considering this. He'd run the details of his last talk with Nicole over and over through his mind for days now and was no closer to a solution. Perhaps the Cavendish brothers and Oakleaf *could* help. Stranger things had happened. Nicole was gone. Telling them about it couldn't make the situation worse. What did he have to lose?

Mark grabbed his mug, bellied up to the table, and spent the next ten minutes recounting the basics of his final conversation with Nicole.

"She's going to have a baby?" Rafe Cavendish's crystal-blue eyes were wide as saucers.

"Yes," Mark mumbled. "At least that's what she told me. I suspect she may have only said that to get away from me, however."

"What? *Why* are you letting your wife and possibly an unborn child sail off to France?" Oakleaf gave Mark a look that clearly indicated he thought he'd lost his mind.

"It's not my choice. It's hers," Mark retorted. "I'm not about to order her to stay after everything we've been through. I'm not a complete Neanderthal."

"But what if she thought you *wanted* her to stay?" Oakleaf pointed out. "You don't think she would?"

Mark scratched his head. "What do you mean?"

Oakleaf planted a fist on the table. "You fool. Did you ever *tell* her you wanted her to stay? Did you ever *ask* her to?"

Mark glowered at the runner. Oakleaf wasn't even married. Why was he the one suddenly making sense?

Mark frowned. "No."

"Why not?" Rafe asked in complete bewilderment.

"I didn't think she'd say yes," Mark bit out, his neck growing hot. He wanted to punch all three of his so-called friends in the throat at the moment.

"You mean you were too proud to tell her," Oakleaf replied.

Mark clenched his jaw. "Perhaps."

"So you don't know what she'd say?" Cade asked.

Mark tugged at his cravat. "I suppose not . . . officially."

Oakleaf slammed his mug on the table. "Well, you're officially an idiot. Go find her and ask her. Tell her you want her to stay. Tell her you cannot live without her. Tell her you want her and your baby in your life permanently."

Mark stared at them in astonishment. By God, his friends were right. He'd been a complete fool. He shoved back his chair and shot to his feet, his heart hammering a resolute rhythm in his chest. He only hoped he could find Nicole in time. Her packet to Calais was set to leave in the morning. He'd have to ride hard for Dover.

He tossed coins on the table to pay for his ale and offered his friends a vibrant smile, feeling truly alive for the first time in days . . . weeks . . . hell, years. "Wish me luck, chaps."

"Good luck, Grim," all three shouted in unison, holding up their mugs and clanking them together.

Mark turned on his heel and raced for the door.

"Would you look at that?" Cade Cavendish whistled from behind him. "Looks like the stone man ain't made of stone anymore."

CHAPTER FORTY-FOUR

Nicole and Susanna stood on the dock, waiting in a queue to board the packet to Calais. They'd traveled to Dover over the last two days, Nicole sick with unhappiness. Leaving Mark hadn't saved her heart. Her heart was long shattered, and she didn't even have a baby for her trouble. She'd been a complete idiot. She should have known from the moment he arrived in France that their bargain would end up benefiting him and hurting her. She'd spent the last ten years steeling her heart against the man, only to let all the barriers come crashing down in a matter of weeks. It was her own fault. Fool that she was.

Susanna had agreed to travel with her. The girl had never been to France and was looking forward to it. Nicole told her she could decide once there if she'd like to stay and would pay for her travel back to London if she decided not to.

Susanna's constant chatter was the only thing keeping Nicole from launching herself into the Channel. She was exceedingly grateful for the girl's cheerful company. They began the slow ascent up the gangplank. Nicole felt as if lead weighed down the bottoms of her shoes. Each step she took was more difficult than the last.

"We sure were surprised when ye arrived," Susanna said. "Louise didn't think ye'd stay. But the rest of us, we thought ye would. The general's been a sight happier to live with since ye've been there, I'll tell ye. I'll be sorry ta come back and see him sad."

"Pardon?" Nicole stopped and stared at the girl. Had Susanna just said Mark had seemed *happier* since she'd been in London? Was that possible?

The maid opened her mouth to reply when a commotion behind them in the throng of coaches and people swarming the dock caught their attention.

A young man jumped up on some barrels and waved his cap frantically in the air. "Make way! Make way! The Duke o' Colchester's coach is comin' through and it's urgent!"

"Colchester?" Nicole murmured as her pulse took flight. "Surely there's been a mistake. He couldn't have meant the Duke of Colchester." Using her gloved hand, she shielded her eyes from the morning sunlight to squint through the crowd.

"Well, I'll be," Susanna said, shielding her eyes alongside Nicole. "He was right. That is the Duke of Colchester's coach if ever I saw it."

The large black coach with the emerald-green crest made its way through a throng of vehicles that all moved to the side for it. Nicole watched in wide-eyed surprise as the vehicle progressed slowly but unerringly toward the dock and the packet she was boarding. She stood arrested, halfway up the gangplank when the coach pulled to a stop in front of it.

The moment the carriage stopped, the door flew open and Mark jumped out. His gaze met Nicole's.

"Are ye the Duke o' Colchester, sir?" a boy at the bottom of the gangplank shouted.

Mark was already racing toward the gangplank, dodging people and trunks. "I will be one day," he shouted back to the child.

Nicole's breath stopped. She clutched a gloved hand to her hammering heart. Was this truly happening?

"Gor, me lady," Susanna said, pulling on the strings to her bonnet. "I can't believe that man's running up this plank after ye. Ye'd best ready yerself. It looks as if he's about ta cause a right big scene."

Nicole's eyes filled with tears while her knees wobbled with relief. "He already has, Susanna. He already has."

"Nicole!" Mark yelled, never breaking the contact of their gaze as he dodged more people, ropes, and crates to push up the gangplank toward her.

The moment he reached her, he grabbed her and swept her off her feet into his arms. He was out of breath, his hat had fallen off, his dark hair was mussed, and he'd never looked better.

"I'm damned glad I caught you in time," he breathed, pressing his forehead to hers.

"I'll just wait on the dock, me lady." Susanna bobbed a curtsy before rushing down the gangplank and through the other travelers staring up at the couple.

"What are you doing here?" Nicole was breathless too. She pressed a hand to Mark's cheek, unable to stop herself from touching him to see if he was real.

"I don't want you to go, sweetheart." He pulled her closer. "Stay, please." His voice was hoarse with emotion.

"What? Why?" Her heart hammered in her chest so hard it hurt.

"Don't you know, Nicole? You're perfect for me. You always have been. You don't back down to me. You don't let me off the hook and you would never even *consider* kowtowing to me."

"You're right about all those things," she agreed, laughing even as tears clung to her lashes.

He pressed his lips to her cheek. "You see me for who I am. I've never asked for a thing from anyone and never taken a handout or used my family's name or wealth to further my ambitions. And you understood why."

Tears dripped down her cheeks. "Because you're proud and strong and self-made and self-reliant."

"Yes, but I was an idiot. I was so hell-bent on pushing away my family that I let it cost me my happiness. I let it cost me you. All for the sake of my damned pride." He pressed his forehead to hers again, and his voice dropped and grew shaky. "You told me once that sometimes life calls upon us to be the things we never thought we were meant to be. You were right. I'm sorry I didn't recognize that until now. I'm sorry for everything, Nicole. I can't live without you. I don't want to, at least."

Tears still clinging to her lashes, she clasped his hands and squeezed them, then brought them to her lips and kissed them reverently. "Oh, Mark, you're perfect for me too. You don't let me run roughshod over you.

You see me for who I am, not awkward and different and sticking out like a sore thumb. You understand why I like to do what I do. You're my match both mentally and physically."

"You're a diamond in a sea of rocks," he breathed, his mouth so close the accolade touched her lips like a kiss.

She swallowed and studied his face. "Remember when we traveled to London? I had one more question I never asked you."

"Yes, and the fact is that I was never with any other women. In ten years. I only ever wanted you," he declared fiercely.

"That is not what I was going to ask," she said with a laugh, swiping the tears from her cheeks with the back of one gloved hand. "But I must admit I'm glad to hear that."

He searched her face. "What were you going to ask?"

"Do you love me?" She looked into his eyes, knowing the answer would determine their future forever. Even as her heart recognized the instant softening of his features, the answering smile creeping over his lips, she had to hear the words. "Do you, Mark?"

He cupped her cheek in his large, warm hand, his gaze more tender than she'd ever seen. "Nicole. My Nicole. I love you more than anything else in this world."

"Even your work?" she countered, past the lump lodged in her throat.

He pulled her against his hard frame and hugged her fiercely. "Even my work, my darling, especially my work."

An hour later, they'd secured the trunks and Nicole and Mark had settled into the duke's coach as it rode away from the docks. Susanna had agreed to ride back alone in Mark's coach. They promised her another trip to France soon.

"Before we go any farther," Nicole said, clutching Mark's hands and facing him. "I have to tell you something. Something important."

"What is it?" Mark watched her carefully.

"It's something that may greatly influence your feelings for me."

Alarm bells sounded in his head. "What?"

"I lied to you," she said in a rush, her face flushed.

He closed his eyes and clenched his jaw. "About what?"

Her gloveless hands were squeezed together in her lap so tightly they were colorless. "I'm not actually with child. At least, I don't think I am."

Relief filled his brain. He heaved a sigh and slumped against the coach seat. "I thought you were going to say you lied about loving me."

The hint of a smile touched her lips. "Never. I love you. I just had to get away from you to protect myself . . . because I didn't think you loved me back."

He tilted his head to consider her. "What were you planning to tell me when no baby arrived?"

She cringed and bit her lip. "I'm ashamed to admit it, but I intended to write and tell you I'd been mistaken, or that I lost the baby."

He pulled her into his arms. "I want you to stay, Nicole. I want you to stay because I love you. I want you to stay because you're my wife. I want you to stay so we can create a family together. But no more lies. Agreed?"

"Agreed," she said, her cheeks still flushed. "And you're not angry . . . about this one?"

"I'm disappointed, but I'd be lying if I didn't say I guessed you may not have been telling the truth. We'd only been together a few days. I didn't see how you'd know in such a short time." He allowed a slow smile to curve his lips. "Besides, the way I see it, this means that we must try again."

She returned his smile. "Yes, we should try and try."

"Oh, what I must do for the sake of my demanding wife." He muttered into the curve of her neck, breathing in her lavender perfume. "*Such* a chore."

She slapped at him playfully.

"Can I ask you another question?" Nicole asked minutes later after she'd been thoroughly kissed.

"If I can ask you one in return," he replied, grinning.

That made her hesitate, but she soldiered on. "Very well, I'll go first. Did you have my bedchamber in London decorated specifically for me? Did you know I'd be back one day even before all of this began?"

His breath caught in his throat and he held it for a few moments. "Yes," he said quietly. "I dared to hope."

She sighed and pressed her mouth to his. "I feel as if I'll never get enough of the taste of you, the feel of you, the beating of your heart." She kissed him again and when at last she drew back, she asked, "What's your question for me?"

Mark rubbed a hand over her shoulder, tracing the delicate vein in her neck with his fingertip. "When I was at the *Duc de Frontenac*'s soiree that night, the *duchesse* told me your heart belongs to only one. At the time I assumed it was the *comte*."

"You want to know if it was you?" Nicole, leaned her head against his arm.

He'd never felt more vulnerable. "Well . . . yes."

She squeezed his upper arm with both hands. "Yes, it was you. It was always you."

He kissed the top of her head. "The feeling is entirely mutual, my love."

CHAPTER FORTY-FIVE

Three months later, the Marquess of Coleford and his marchioness entered the Baxters' ballroom together. As soon as they were announced, all the guests' heads swiveled to stare at them as they slowly descended their hosts' enormous staircase.

Mark squeezed Nicole's hand. "Would you look at that? Who would've thought one year ago that we'd be here like this now?"

"Certainly not I," Nicole responded with a slight shake of her head. "I intend to enjoy myself tonight. I won't be able to attend many more public events until after the baby comes in the spring." She patted her belly surreptitiously and smiled up at her husband.

"I want my child born here in England, of course, but after that we can travel back to France if you like." They'd already decided having one home in France and one in England would be the best way to manage their respective households. The servants were free to travel back and forth.

"I do want to bring the babe to see my friends in France, but for now I think we should remain in England. I doubt Mother would let me leave even if I wanted to. She is beside herself with glee that we're back together and that her first grandchild is on the way."

"Your mother and I are in complete agreement. No more investigations for you until after the baby arrives," Mark replied, smiling back at Nicole.

They reached the bottom of the staircase and strolled through the crowd, nodding at acquaintances as they went. Nicole twined her arm through his. "That's fine because I believe Regina has taken up the family interest in investigations."

"Has she?" Mark arched a brow.

"She told me last week that she intends to pay Daffin a visit on Bow Street."

Mark shook his head and chuckled. "I sincerely hope she realizes nothing can come of a *mésalliance* between her and Oakleaf. He's a bounty hunter for heaven's sake, and she's the niece of a duke."

Nicole lightly elbowed her husband in the side. "Fancy *you* being the one to be such an advocate for propriety between the classes."

Mark groaned. "Damn. You're right. I suppose my three months as a marquess have gone to my head."

"Besides," Nicole continued, a sly grin on her face. "I'm not entirely convinced that Regina's looking for, ahem, marriage, dear."

Mark winced and rubbed his forehead. "Surely you don't mean . . . an affair?"

Nicole shrugged one shoulder. "Why not? She's given up looking for a husband in the *ton* and Daffin is a fine-looking man."

Mark watched her from the corners of his narrowed eyes. "If you tell me Oakleaf is a fine-looking man one more time—"

Nicole laughed. "I'm simply saying if I were Regina, I *might* consider paying a visit to Daffin Oakleaf as well."

"For work you mean?" Mark grinned at her.

"Among other things." She winked at him.

Mark looked across the throng of people and shook his head. "Thank God Uncle Edward's health has improved, but I cannot believe I'm going to be a bloody duke one day."

"Oh, my darling, you may be a duke one day, but rest assured." She leaned her cheek against his strong shoulder and smiled. "You shall be a duke like no other."

Thank you for reading *A Duke Like No Other*.
I hope you enjoyed Mark and Nicole's tale. This has
been a particularly fun book to write because I
personally really love to read stories about feuding
couples who are reunited, so it's already become one
of my favorites.

I'd love to keep in touch.

- Visit my website for information about upcoming
  books, excerpts, and to sign up for my email news-
  letter: www.ValerieBowmanBooks.com or at www
  .ValerieBowmanBooks.com/subscribe.
- Join me on Facebook: http://Facebook.com
  /ValerieBowmanAuthor.
- Follow me on Twitter at @ValerieGBowman,
  https://twitter.com/ValerieGBowman
- Reviews help other readers find books. I appreciate
  all reviews whether positive or negative. Thank you
  so much for considering it!

Happy Reading!